D0582033

RUM WEEK

Novels by
NIGEL TRANTER

RUM WEEK

BY

NIGEL TRANTER

WARD, LOCK & CO., LIMITED
LONDON AND MELBOURNE

FIRST PUBLISHED 1954

MADE IN ENGLAND

PRINTED IN GREAT BRITAIN BY
NORTHUMBERLAND PRESS LIMITED
GATESHEAD ON TYNE

AUTHOR'S NOTE

No reader of this tale will require to be informed that the Rum and its community here depicted bears no remotest resemblance, save in mere geography, to the genuine Isle of Rhum in the Inner Hebrides, with its dozen or two of estate employees as population, and its English-domiciled sole proprietress, understood to be non-desirous of uninvited visitors. No delineation could be less applicable. Without a doubt the good occupants and owner of Rhum are as different as chalk from cheese, in character, aspect, and every other respect, from the scallywags here portrayed, just as conditions on the purely and perhaps thankfully fanciful island will bear no comparison with reality.

Every character is blissfully imaginary, including, of course, those from the more populous centres of Skye, London, and Detroit. Any resemblance to any living person is not only coincidental—it is extraordinary. The lustre of famed Skye Week ought to emerge undimmed from this peculiar competition, and the author wishes to take this opportunity to doff his bonnet to an excellent institution. Emulation as well as support, it deserves—not the following.

NIGEL TRANTER

Aberlady, 1953

I

ALISON MACLEAN, ARMS TIGHT TO HER SIDES, fingers outstretched down her thighs, stood stiffly to attention on the substantial timbers of Mallaig pier, heels close, shapely legs pressed together, skirt gripped fast between her knees, stood and stared stonily straight ahead of her at the *Lochgarve* —*through* it indeed, might have better described the quality of her regard, had the object been anything less material than the Hebridean mail-steamer. She did not allow her eyes to stray to the bridge, where the young First Officer was admiring her with frank appreciation, nor to the serried ranks of passengers that lined the rail—tourists, hikers, Skye-folk, and worse; she glared straight ahead, through number two porthole counting from the bows—and just the tip of the toe of her right brogue tapped the stout beam beneath her incessantly, though not sufficiently of course to loosen the grip of her knees. She ought to have known—to have thought of this. And she ought to have worn slacks, undoubtedly— even to a christening. Even if she hadn't had stockings on, it wouldn't have been so bad. . . .

It wasn't the National Anthem, or anything of that sort. It was just that Mallaig pier was like that, when the wind was skittish and a point or two north of west. Something to do with the wretched peninsula of Sleat, no doubt. Some part of Skye, anyway. It came wheechling under the kippering-sheds, and up through the gaps between the timbers—and whoosh! Up went skirts—even stout Harris tweed ones, if generously pleated, such as hers. She could move away, of course—make for the smoky shelter of one of the kippering-shed doorways; but not without a seventy per cent risk of disaster. Would that horrible ship never go, with its load of grinning apes?

In extenuation of the girl's somewhat unsportsmanlike attitude towards the good ship *Lochgarve* and its company, however, it should be made clear that she had more against it than its immediate situation *vis-à-vis* her own. As a vessel she found no particular fault with it; nor even with its crew—though she had had her usual altercation with the skipper on the way over that morning. She liked the Captain too, very well—but that did not alter the fact that he and his boat and his company and his British Transport Commission were failing her, failing all the inhabitants of the Island of Rum, deliberately, chronically, shamefully. He had brought her here to Mallaig, hadn't he? But he was not taking her back. Not he! He was sailing for Skye, of course—always Skye. Loch Scavaig round trip. Come and see the glamorous Cuillins, the terrible Loch Coruisk, Flora Macdonald's Favourite View—all in Glorious Technicolor! And Rum could go and distil itself! That was the way of it. Well might Alison Maclean of Kilmory glare, skirts or none.

It was a pity, just the same, that all this was necessary—for her mid-Thursday expression was no real enhancement to an otherwise comely, not to say winsome countenance. A black frown and stern glance came no more naturally to her pleasantly open yet delicate features than did the present stiffly military stance to her lissome but noticeably feminine figure. Moreover, she was on the small side for a Fury—and the ever so slightly upturned nose did not help the illusion either.

With real if not apparent relief, Alison saw out of the corner of her eye, the white cap of Captain MacAndrew appear up on the bridge beside his lieutenant. Bells tinkled in the bowels of the ship, deckhands pushed through the throng of the passengers to cast off ropes and pull in gangways, and amidst a great frothing of water and commotion of the place's myriads of herring-gulls, the *Lochgarve* began to edge out from the quayside. A single shattering blast from the siren, pulled by the First Officer—whose eyes undoubtedly should have been on his work—had a derisory, not to say vulgar, note, that drew a brood of mocking echoes equally deplorable, from the hill-

8

side that sloped straight up from the rocky shore, and up which the little town climbed and clung.

And down the very last of those slopes and on to the timbers of the pier, hurried footsteps came clattering, their tattoo becoming temporarily submerged in the siren's effects. Into sight around the great stack of fish-boxes a man came, running hard. He continued to run, round the dock-head and right along the quayside, despite the ever-growing gap between ship and pier. Right to the very edge he ran, almost as though he intended to essay one gigantic leap, trailing burberry, khaki grip, and all, on to the departing vessel, before coming to a spectacular halt beside the old man who had unhitched the ropes from the bollards and now sat upon one of the latter to light his clay pipe. Throwing up his free arm in something between a fist-shaking malediction, an imperious beckoning to the craft to return, and a direct appeal to his Maker, the would-be passenger groaned aloud. Obviously a strong-minded and dramatically inclined young man.

" Damnation! Goddam and blast it! " he gasped. And swallowing, necessarily, and all but choking, " Hell! " he added earnestly.

The old chap on the bollard struck a match within cupped gnarled hands. " Just that," he observed philosophically. " Och, aye. Man, you missed it, whatever."

The other thrust out head and neck at him—and he had rather a long neck, that young man, with a prominent and active adam's-apple. He had expressive features, too—at the moment working hard. He gulped audibly, lips moved, and he swallowed again. Then, as appropriate words seemed to be on the point of delivery, he became aware of the young woman standing so rigidly close by. Turning towards her, he drew a quivering breath, long as the rest of him, and threw down bag and coat on the fish-scaly timbering.

" Go on," she invited. " Don't mind me. I know just how you feel."

" I . . . I . . . that thrice-damned idiot! It . . . look, I guess . . ." He started again. " Say—you missed it, too? " Even in his indignant incoherences there was a distinct drawl noticeable in his breathless voice.

9

"Well—not exactly," Alison told him. "I was just waiting, sort of. But I can sympathize, just the same."

"Eh? Sympathize! Like hell!" the newcomer declared forcefully. "Say—that guy up in the bar told me this darned ship never sails before at least half an hour late." He jabbed an accusatory finger at his wrist-watch. "It's only ten to one, now! Blasted thing's started dead on time!"

"I'm afraid so," the girl nodded. "You see, this isn't one of the regular island sailings, with goods to land, and so on. It's just a sort of summertime trip they make on Thursdays, to Loch Scavaig in Skye."

"Eh?" Obviously the full significance of this escaped the young man, despite the fact that the elderly mariner removed his pipe, spat expertly, and nodded too, adding a just that in confirmation. "So what?"

If that was a question, Alison Maclean perceived no answer to it. Moreover, she did not see what *she* had done to be barked at. She raised her chin a degree or two, and held her peace.

The man did not seem to notice. "When is the next boat, huh?" he demanded.

"That depends on where you want to go," she pointed out, primly.

"Hell—to Skye. Where that one was going. What d'you think?"

"Then the next one's exactly a week to-day, at twelve-forty-five," she informed, sweetly now.

"Look," he said, "I asked a civil question, see. . . ."

"And isn't my answer civility itself? That's the next boat—to Skye." At his expression the girl relented a little. "From here, that is."

Appalled, he looked at her. The dropped jaw and prolonged intake of breath seemed to herald an explosion on truly Homeric scale. But instead, suddenly, the young man laughed, so generously as he produced his other reactions. "No kidding? Say—that a fact? So it's right enough—the genuine Highlands! The real M'Coy's back o' beyond! The country God forgot!"

Alison blinked, appalled in her turn. "How . . . how dare

you!" she gasped. "What a thing to say! You're quite wrong. We're not at the back of anywhere! It's just that Mallaig's not the place to come, for Skye. You should be up at Kyle of Lochalsh, twenty miles north."

"Eh? But say—what about that?" And he pointed after the departing steamship.

She sighed. "I told you. That's just a trip they run, on Thursdays. You were just lucky. . . ."

"Lucky!"

"I mean, any other day you wouldn't even have *seen* a boat going to Skye. Not direct, that is."

"Issat so! And how do I get to this other dump? This Kyle place, then?"

"Well—you can get to-morrow's boat, to Kyle. At twelve-forty-five . . . though it'll likely be a bittie late. . . ."

"To-morrow! Look—I don't want to go to-morrow. I don't want to go by your darned boat, either—I'm not all that keen on boats. I want to go to-day, see. Is there a train?"

"Well . . . no. Not unless you go away back to Fort William, up the Great Glen to Inverness, and right across Scotland again. But I doubt you wouldn't get there till the day after to-morrow, that way. . . ."

"Holy Smoke! I'll go by road, then."

The girl shook her dark head. "No road," she said.

"Suffering cats!" the other cried, and threw up eloquent appealing hands. "What a country! It's one helluva place to get to, this Skye! Say—don't they want anybody to get there?"

"Want!" Alison exclaimed, bitterly. "They want nothing else, at all! That's all they live for, those people—with their tours and their special trips, their Fairy Flags and Skye Weeks! My goodness—it's the easiest place in the world to get to, Skye. The difficulty is, not to get taken there!"

He stared at her. "Look—are you dizzy, or am I?" he requested, wonderingly.

But she was not looking. Not at him. She was watching a motor-boat that had just appeared round the pier-head.

The young man frowned. "And say—what are you standing there for, like a Christmas tree, anyway?"

He had his answer, if not by word. "Hughie!" she called, raising a hand, and took a step forward, nearer to the edge of the quay. And immediately, up went her skirts, in gallant style. "Damn!" she said, and promptly returned to the *status quo*.

The young man drew a hand down his long features—but did not succeed in wiping the grin therefrom. "Okay," he acknowledged. "I get you. Very nice, too!"

The motor-boat chuffered to a stop a little further along the pier, where a rusty iron ladder projected. Up this, presently, a man appeared, middle-aged, solidly built, red-faced and cheerful, wearing a much-darned fisherman's jersey. He laughed heartily at all in sight, out of some private store of mirth all his own.

It was inevitable that he received the frown which the younger man had earned. "You're late, Hughie," Alison accused. Which was more than a little ungracious, considering that he had come quite a distance out of his way to pick her up.

The newcomer, however, chuckled happily. "Later, I've been, Miss Ailie," he pointed out. And that was true, too.

"Well . . ." The girl glanced from him to the ladder-head and then over to the younger man, and bit her lip. She stretched her hands just as far down her flanks as they would go, without actually bending her knees. Then she nodded her head, almost defiantly. "Good-bye," she said, and started to stalk thus, stiff-legged, for the ladder, in a fashion distinctly reminiscent of a mechanical doll.

It was a remarkable and noteworthy performance, impaired only a little by the ultimate pigeon-stepped scurry with which she covered the final yard or so. The doubled-over backward caracole with which she negotiated the ladder-head, for speed and agility had to be seen to be believed. Hughie's bellow of joy, as she disappeared, out-voiced but did not altogether drown the frustrated traveller's appreciation.

Alison was sitting composedly, collectedly, in the stern-sheets of the one-time ship's lifeboat when the young man appeared above her, to call down:

"That was pretty good, y'know—reckon I could use that, sometime," he commented judiciously. "Say—you going out to the islands?"

She nodded, distantly, absorbed in far prospects.

"Will you give me a lift, then?"

Alison knitted her brows. "I don't see how. . . ."

But from above, Hughie's lung-power achieved its accustomed triumph. "Surely, man—surely. Och, yes, my Chove—plenties of room, there is." And a hand like a ham clapped down on the other's shoulder. "Down you get."

"But, Hughie. . . ! It's Skye he wants to go to!"

"Och, is that a fact?" Hughie looked disappointedly at his would-be passenger. "Mercy on us, where's the sense in that, at all?"

"I know. But he's an American, or something. . . ."

"Texan," she was corrected, strongly. "What's wrong with that? And what's wrong with this Skye?"

Hughie's laugh on this occasion was hollow, little better than a groan.

"Eh? Say—what's eating you folks? Look—how far is the nearest spot in Skye, from here?"

"Too near!" the girl volunteered.

"Och, to the Aird of Sleat—five or six miles, maybe," Hughie deplored.

"As near as that! My godfather—what's all the bellyaching about? I could darn near swim it! See—put me over there in your boat, and I'll pay you whatever you ask, in reason. A coupla pound notes. Three?"

"Tut-tut," Alison said.

"Och, my goodness me." Hughie examined the back of his great hand, shaking his head. "Mercy on us—no, no. Money!" He sighed. "Down you get, then, man. What are you waiting for?"

"Eh? How come? You mean . . . ?" Then, grinning, the Texan stepped over to pick up his bag and coat. "Catch!" he called, and slung the burberry down towards the boat. He kept the bag in his hand as he turned to negotiate the iron ladder. "I got a bottle of Scotch in here," he explained.

"That's what took all the time up in the bar. We'll be having a swig at it, any minute now, I reckon!"

"Then be careful, man—be careful!" the boatman boomed heartily, winking to the old man on the bollard, and set his wellington boots to the ladder in turn.

The burberry lay where it had fallen, one sleeve in the water. The young woman received them both in silence, with the preoccupied chill of well-born displeasure.

. . . . .

Out on the jabbly no-man's-water where the Sound of Sleat met the Sound of Rum, the little boat tittupped and slap-slapped its lively way into the cross seas, the end seas, and all the other seas of that fretted seaboard. The young woman in the stern had removed her beret, and her dark tresses streamed in the breeze. Beside her, Hughie Bain nursed his wheezy, bronchial engine in a benignant trance, while in the bows the younger man, longer and more ungainly-seeming than ever in the constriction of the boat, drew his coat round him against the keen air and the intermittent spray, and stared about him.

Well he might. Behind him, Mallaig, blurred by the blue haze from its kippering-sheds, was already dwarfed against the endless ramparts of the mainland hillsides, flanked on one side by the yawning mouth of dark Loch Nevis, and on the other by the startling white sands and green machars of Morar. To their left, the unmistakable Island of Eigg lay like a table set in the sea, with the old man of its tall Scuirr hunched over its head. On the right, the long heathery arm of the Sleat peninsula cut off all the northern vistas. And directly ahead, sheer out of the azure plain of the sea, a huddle of blue mountains soared, their bases ringed with foam-girt cliffs, their steep and riven sides towering up into the fleecy halo of cloud that wreathed their noble brows— almost the only clouds in all that breeze-blown summer sky.

It was on this latter prospect that the transatlantic character concentrated. That eloquent and dramatic arm swept out towards it, indeed, in a gesture only spoiled by the wet burberry sleeve. "That now," he declared, "is what I've come to see. Yessir. There it is—an eyeful. I sure have heard plenty about this place. I guess I sorta reckoned it would be a disappointment, when I got there. But no sirree—it's the goods, all right. Just take a look at those mountains."

His two companions took a look at him, instead, a shade doubtfully.

"They've got something. Line. Depth. Colour. But more than that. Atmosphere, see. The whole shooting-gallery. I get reaction, all right. Of course I got to be kinda careful. I'm a sorta special case. I got roots down there."

"Roots?" the girl echoed, vaguely. "I suppose *you* know what you're talking about. . . ?"

"Sure I do. Roots, I said, and roots I mean. I'm a Macdonald, see—Joel K. Macdonald!" And he gave a quick glance at both of his hearers to observe the effect.

Undoubtedly such reaction as his revelation produced, surprised him. "Well," Alison assured, with the next thing to a snort, "you won't find any Macdonalds there, I can promise you!"

"Eh? Say—what d'you mean? Isn't Skye where the Macdonalds spring from?"

"Skye, may be. But that isn't Skye. That's the Island of Rum. And we don't go in for Macdonalds, on Rum, believe you me!"

"My goodness—no!" Hughie confirmed, ravished of even the ghost of a smile.

"Rum. . . ? Hell—you mean that's the wrong place? But, say, I've seen pictures. Just like that."

"I'm sure you have. Who hasn't! Everybody's seen pictures . . . just like that. Or made to *look* just like that, anyway!" Sour, she sounded—and still did not look as though sourness suited her. "They're in every railway station, guidebook, glossy magazine, and picture postcard stand. The glorious Cuillins! Nevertheless—that's not Skye. That's Rum —a mighty different place." She turned to her right, and pointed. "That's Skye for you!"

The man swung round to stare at the long and admittedly

comparatively dull coastline of the peninsula of Sleat. "That?" he cried. "I don't believe it!"

"It's true, just the same," she assured. And then, her essential honesty prevailed. "Though admittedly you'll get a very different view once you can see round the Point, there." She turned. "But, Hughie—aren't you supposed to be putting Mr.—er—Macdonald ashore over there at the Aird?"

"Och, well, Miss Ailie—it's an ill sort of place to set a man down, there, and him with all them miles up yon Sleat to walk. I was thinking I'd just be dropping you at Kilmory, and then taking him over to Elgol on Loch Scavaig. . . ."

"That's mighty kind of you," the passenger acknowledged. "I sure won't say no to that. And you won't be the loser, see."

"Och, tut-tut. Never mention it, man. You're sure your bag is fine and safe, down there?"

"Eh . . . ? Oh, of course—the Scotch! I clean forgot it. . . ."

While this matter was being satisfactorily attended to, Alison Maclean gave her feminine curiosity a little rein. "So you've come all the way from Texas just to have a look at Skye, where the Macdonalds hail from?" she put to him.

"Gee—no." He wiped his mouth with the back of his hand in a professional manner. "Don't you believe it. Go on, Hughie—be your age. Have another swig. Hell—do I look like a tourist? It's a long while since I left Texas, Miss. I've come up here from London. And on business, see."

"Business? At Loch Scavaig . . . ?"

"Mercy on us—you're not a Government Inspector, man?"

"Say—do I look that way, either? No, no—I'm in motion pictures. Films. I told you—Joel K. Macdonald." He peered at them. But still, disappointingly, due recognition was denied him.

"Oh," the girl said, nodding. "I see. A film actor. That explains . . . well, a lot."

"Actor nothing!" the other disclaimed strongly. "Associate

16

Director, North Atlantic Picture Corporation—that's me. But just call me Joe."

"Oh . . . thanks."

Hughie had restored his spirits again, and handing back the bottle, laughed hugely.

"And . . . you're here on business, Mr. Macdonald? "

"Joe."

"Well . . . if you insist."

"Sure. We aim to make a picture up here, see. Highland stuff. The real M'Coy. Kilts. Bagpipes. Chiefs. The whole boiling. *You* know."

"Yes—I'm afraid I do! "

"Yep. Well, I've come up to have a look-see, first. Scout around. Having roots, see. Fix up a good location. Give the place the once-over."

"And this film's to be made in Skye, is it? " There was stiffness creeping in again.

Maybe the man did not notice it. "That's right. Obvious place. Lots of mountains. Lots of lakes—lochs. Lots of sea. Lots of folks. . . ."

"Folks . . . ? "

"Sure. This Skye Week holiday they hold in August. Brings them in, I hear, in a big way. We need lots of folks. Crowd scenes, see. This picture's going to be pretty good. About a reincarnation of Bonnie Prince Charlie. But bang up to date, of course."

"Oh. Is it? "

"What's wrong with that? "

"Oh—nothing. Nothing."

Hughie Bain took a comprehensive survey of the heavens. "Man—it's grand weather for the time of the year," he asserted, with jovial conviction.

"Oh, yeah? "

A silence descended upon the company—though not, of course, upon the *Kelpie*, which kept up the chug, slap, and gurgle of her altercation with the Western sea.

The young man eyed his companions thoughtfully. Then, shrugging, he turned to face the perhaps more rewarding panorama of the Hebrides. And presently he began to whistle. And most appropriately, he chose to whistle the Skye Boat Song:

> "Speed, bonny boat like a bird on the wing,
>   Over the sea to Skye."

His endeavour to keep time to both engine and waves was not entirely successful.

It took a little while for the melody to register—perhaps his hearers were not very musically inclined. Then the stamp of the girl's foot on the floorboards came clear above the beat of the motor. "Will you stop that!" she requested. A pause, as his whistling faltered and died. "Or, at least—will you whistle something else. Er . . . Joe."

"Ha, ha!" said Hughie earnestly.

The exiled Texan was turning to face them, brows wrinkled, when in the process his attention was distracted. Over to his right, beyond the long snout of Sleat, now little more than a mile off, the challenging saw-toothed skyline of the Cuillins of Skye, jagged, austere, uncompromising, was emerging, slashed with dark chasms that gloomed deeply even under the summer sun. The man's lips formed a different kind of whistle—one such as more frequently tends to be evoked by curvilinear feminine rather than scenic spectacle. And he glanced from thence to the Rum vista and back again, in patent comparison.

In the stern-sheets the girl threw up her dark head. "Well?" she demanded. "There it is. What's it got that Rum hasn't got—except publicity!"

Joel Macdonald judiciously took his time to answer that—having the elements of sanity in him. "I guess I wouldn't know—yet! Give me a little time, will you?" And then he rummaged in his grip for a pair of binoculars. It was noted that, when he got them out of their case, focused and trained, it was on the Cuillins of Skye rather than on the mountains of Rum that he concentrated them.

.   .   .   .   .

She gave him time—till they had covered the major part of the ninety-minute crossing. Then, as the young man was explaining how his old uncle in London had insisted that he must see Skye for the first time from this southward and sea approach, that the usual route by the ferry to the north was a dull business—hence his ill-starred dash for the Loch Scavaig steamer—Alison interrupted him ruthlessly.

"Mr. Macdonald—Joe," she said. "Why not come to Rum, instead of Skye? First, at any rate. This film—it doesn't *have* to be taken in Skye? I mean, the story doesn't relate to Skye, does it? Just somewhere in the Western Highlands? Well, then! Why do what everybody else does? Why show the same old scenes—Sgurr Alasdair, Sgurr Dearg, Loch Coruisk, and so on? Show some initiative, man. Come to Rum, and we'll show you scenery that'll make your cameras sit up! Won't we, Hughie?"

"My Chove, yes," the other chuckled. "If the rain keeps off!"

Their passenger eyed them wonderingly. "But, say—it's all set for Skye," he protested. "I can't just change it all round, that way. . . ."

"Why not? So long as you get the right scenery—mountains, and lochs, and sea. . . ."

"And folks," he reminded her.

"Yes—and folks, of course." If she faltered a little, it was barely perceptible, and might well have been put down to the lively motion of the *Kelpie* as she dipped to the quite substantial seas. "We're not an *uninhabited* island. We'll produce the people, too."

"Sure. But not the numbers Skye will produce in Skye Week. And we got to have the crowd scenes, see."

Alison took a deep breath. "Skye Week!" she said. "Have you ever heard of Rum Week?"

"Eh? No. Can't say I have."

Hughie Bain opened his large mouth—and all but choked as a small but vigorous elbow contacted his jersey-clad ribs. "Ho . . . ha!" he croaked.

"Well—you will!" the girl asserted. "If that's all that's worrying you." Her pleasantly soft and lilting West Highland voice quivered. "People! Crowds!" And then, she pointed. "Look! Can you beat that?"

Certainly Rum was co-operating. A single beam of yellow sunlight had managed to penetrate the curious cowl of cloud that presided over the island as though caught on the horns of its soaring peaks. Striking like a searchlight down between plunging fearsome slopes dark with naked rock and seamed with the white of falling water, it lit up in a golden glory the verdant floor of a central green and fertile valley that opened eastwards towards the sea, wherein small multi-shaped fields and a scattering of whitewashed houses were picked out amongst hanging birch woods and brackenny pastures. And on either side of the arm of the sea which opened into this sylvan haven, the great cliffs rose and stretched away unbroken, the white plumes of blown waterfalls smoking from their summits, the white spray of tortured seas foaming at their bases.

"M'mmm," the man commented. "Uh-huh. I see what you mean." And he raised his glasses.

"There's a lot more than that to see—that you won't see through any field-glasses," she persisted. "There's seventy square miles of Rum, Joe."

Sighing, and grinning at the same time, he turned to glance at her over his shoulder. "Okay," he said. "You win. I'll give you one day. Same as if I'd had to wait for the other boat. You get me to Skye to-morrow night, Hughie, and we'll call it quits."

She smiled in her turn. And when Alison Maclean smiled, it took a strong man indeed to concentrate on the scenery. Perhaps she should have smiled earlier in the proceedings.

That was Skye's, and British Transport's fault, of course. Normally, Alison was no miser with her smiling.

Joel Macdonald turned his back on Rum and the rest of the Hebrides, and settled himself comfortably, facing the stern-sheets. Men have been turning to face disaster thus brashly from time immemorial.

THE "KELPIE" DID NOT ENTER THE OPEN ARMS OF
the fiord that invited them into the green heart of Rum, but
swung away to starboard, around the northern perimeter of
the island, skirting at a respectful distance that tremendous
rampart of red-brown cliffs that jealously guarded its inviolacy.
The place was approximately diamond-shaped, with its facets
eight miles and more in length. Just past the thrusting
northernmost cape, another sudden breakdown in the cliff
barrier gave access to a pleasant shallow sandy bay, with
another long green valley behind it running directly deep
into the welter of the mountains.

"Home," the girl announced. "Kilmory."

And at the very echo of her words, the boat's engine
stuttered, coughed, faltered, and then chugged on into the bay
uncertainly.

"Och, mercy on us—isn't that grand!" Hughie Bain
burbled. "I was after thinking maybe the petrol would be
giving out on us. As well we hadn't to be rowing for it!"

"My godfather!" the passenger exclaimed, staring.

Alison looked from the engine to the boatman thoughtfully,
calculatingly, for a moment, and said nothing.

They landed at a small stone jetty, somewhat dilapidated,
under the enthralled regard of two or three big-eyed children
and a shaggy black calf, just as the rain began to fall. The
visitor turned up his burberry collar, though neither his
escort nor the lookers-on appeared to notice it. Hughie,
whose turf-roofed cottage crouched nearby amongst a confusion of upturned and disintegrating boats, peat-stacks,
tumbledown outhouses and festooned nets, was abandoned,
with firm instructions to be ready to take him over the sea
to Skye in approximately twenty-four hours.

Moving up the sandy shingle-laid track that crossed the green levels of the machar and lifted and coiled alongside a well-doing splashing stream, up past odd-shaped strips of cultivation amongst outcropping rocks, patches of emerald bog, and clumps of alder, they went, the young woman, the young man, the children, and the calf, to the crunch of gravel, the chuckle of the burn, and the hiss of the slanting spears of rain. Alison was altogether a different character now, lively, laughing, eager—presumably the effect of her native heath beneath her feet—and the raindrops made a diadem for her most evidently naturally curling hair. She positively chattered, naming the urchins and calf, pointing out Old Beathag's cabin, Ewan the Road's cottage, the crofts of Angus This, Donald That, and sundry others, and declaring that the hill behind that cloud was Monadh Dubh, or the Dark Moss, and the one on the left, if only they could see it through the shower, was Mullach Mor, or the Great Ridge. The really big fellows, of course, were at the other end of the island. . . .

Her companion peered along the track which mounted slowly but steadily onwards, threading the foothills, to disappear behind the grey curtain of the rain. "Say—don't you reckon we'd better shelter, some place?" he suggested. "You're going to get wet." He seemed altogether absurdly and unsuitably preoccupied with a little rain, the man.

She laughed, and shook her head—in fact, she shook her entire self, much as a dog would, and a cascade of glistening drops flew from her Harris suit as from her tresses, the which seemed equally impervious. "It's just a bit of a shower," she asserted. "And we've no distance to go, at all." She pointed towards a long low whitewashed house partly hidden behind trees, that occupied a terrace above the valley floor, backed by climbing birch woods. "That's my home. Kilmory House. I'd have you there—at least, Daddy would—with the greatest of pleasure. But it wouldn't be fair to Morag Ross. She keeps a sort of hotel, and you'll be a godsend to her."

"Oh, yeah?"

"Yes. But you must come and have dinner with us, of

course." Alison paused. "Er . . . dinner will be late to-night, I'm afraid. With me being over to Mallaig, and all that. A lot to do. . . ."

"Sure. But don't you go to a lot of trouble over me, see."

It is doubtful if she heard him. Her knitted brows seemed to indicate an intense concentration on domestic timetables. Almost, her lips moved in involved calculation. "At least . . . no. Dinner will be *early*. Yes, early. Make it—let me see—say six-thirty."

He blinked. "Anything you say." A runnel of water coursing down his long neck caused him to hunch his shoulders and draw his coat closer. "Hell—those kids are going to be soaked!"

"Nonsense. They're all right—aren't you, my trouties? Look—that's Morag Ross's house, beside the waterfall. You'll be fine and comfortable, there."

Where a tributary burn joined the Kilmory River from the high ground, they crossed a plank bridge and pushed their way through a group of entirely immobile milch-cows a-steam in the rain, towards a two-storeyed slated house that peered out modestly from behind a semi-tropical riot of creeper, rambler rose, and tropaeolum. A large cattle beast was wedged within the porch, rubbing its flanks with evident satisfaction on the rustic uprights, which shook alarmingly to the impact. Domestic poultry sheltered two deep on the window-ledges on either side.

"This an hotel?" the man demanded.

"Well—sort of. But Morag Ross has other interests beside hotel-keeping, of course."

"So I see."

Not seeking to enter into competition with the stirk in the porch, Alison led the way round to the back door. This stood open, and from within came a curious moaning sound, that rose and fell.

"Whassat?" Joel wanted to know, suspiciously.

His companion, frowning a little herself, did not answer. "Morag!" she called.

"Is that yourself, Miss Ailie? Here I am," a soft and gentle voice answered from nearby.

23

They turned. Sitting on one of the perches within a decrepit henhouse, set against the braeside, was a little old woman, knitting.

"Snakes!" the Texan whispered, "say—is she nuts, or something?"

Alison, though looking a little surprised, shushed at him below her breath. "Of course not," she murmured. "A little eccentric, perhaps. . . ." She spoke up. "Are you all right, Morag?"

"Och, never better, my dear. I'm just keeping my knitting dry." She was a tiny dainty pink-and-white creature, fragile-seeming as any Dresden china, and on her snowy hair a black cobweb from the henhouse roof sat rakishly. Her smile was kindness itself. "Is that a gentleman you've got with you?"

"Well, he's a kind of American from London. I thought you'd like him for a guest. . . ."

"Of course, of course. My goodness me—that'll be splendid." Beaming, the small person jumped out into the rain with extraordinary agility. "You are entirely welcome, sir. Well, you are, I hope?"

"Eh . . . ? Oh, sure, sure. Look, you're going to get wet, ma'am."

She ignored that. "You are going to be very comfortable, sir," she assured. "Just make yourself at home, what-ever."

The guest looked towards the younger woman.

He got no help there. "This is Mr. Joel K. Macdonald, Morag."

"Never mind," the old lady said, sympathetically, "he can't help that, I'm sure. And he's a real comfort, coming just now. You see that ladder, Mr. Macdonald—leaning against the peat-stack? Och, it's just too heavy for me to move, at all."

"You want it moved, some place?"

"Yes, please. If you will bring it over here, and put it up to that attic window, we'll climb up and get in that way."

The man passed a hand over his bare head, found it very

wet, and shook both hand and head. "You . . . reckon that's best?" he wondered, warily.

"Oh, yes. You see, the front door's locked from the inside, the windows don't open nowadays, and the bees have swarmed in the back passage again. We'll get in by the attic, though—and then we'll have a cup of tea. I'm sure you could do with a cup, after that Mallaig."

Joel swallowed. "Sure. Though I reckon a drop of Scotch would go down, right now. I got some left in my bag. . . ."

"Good. Just the thing. We'll have that, too," the old lady agreed. "And maybe an egg to our tea."

"Well—you two seem to have everything under control," Alison Maclean declared, brightly. "I'll get over to the House."

"Say—you going?" the man demanded, a shade anxiously.

His unspoken plea gained no response. "Of course. Daddy will be fuming for *his* tea. Be over . . . let's see—it's turned three now. Be over at six-thirty, for dinner. We . . . we go to bed pretty early, on Rum. Now—I think you should go and get Morag's ladder for her."

With an expressive glance that slid comprehensively from the speaker, to the back door, to the attic window peeping from amongst the luxuriating ramblers, to the critical children and the faithful calf, the little old lady and the spouting rain puddles, Joel K. Macdonald set down his bag, and stalked heavily for the ladder. It shouldn't be all that heavy; half of its rungs were missing.

The young woman had a quick, urgent, all but furtive word with the elder, who beamed and nodded with warm understanding, before she hurried off.

.   .   .   .   .

Despite her parent's proclaimed need for his tea, Alison Maclean did not hasten straight across to the large white-washed house on the opposite hillside. She hurried, but it was to a cottage nearby, notable for the number of aged vehicle bodies and rusty bicycle frames that adorned its vicinity. The door stood open, and she went straight in, turning unhesitatingly to the right and into a dark room where a sandy-haired young man slept outstretched before a smouldering peat-fire. Him she shook by the shoulder.

"Dougie," she said. "Wake up. You'll have to go round the island."

The sleeper opened his eyes, yawned cavernously, and lifted to his feet, all concurrently, as out of established custom. "Och, well—if you say so, Miss Ailie," he acceded, handsomely for a man disturbed in perhaps the best sleep of the day.

"Yes. Go to all the Committee. Tell them to come to Kilmory House to-night. At ten-thirty."

"The Committee. To-night. At ten-thirty. Aye, then. A bittie late, that." Reasonably, he said it.

"I know. But it's important. I've got an American here, and we haven't long. He talks about going away again to-morrow. To Skye."

"Skye, is it!" The messenger made no further quibbling. "I'll tell them. Will he be a millionaire, the American?"

"I don't think so. But better than that. He's a film-man. He has infinite possibilities. And look, Dougie—tell them all not to arrive *before* ten-thirty. I don't want any of them getting mixed up with this American before I've had a word with them. Better tell them not to get into conversation with him beforehand, if by any chance any of them happened to meet him. Not that that's likely, for the man seems worried about a drop of rain."

"Rain?"

"Yes. He goes about dodging drops. I expect Texas will be one of these desert range places that you see on the films. Anyway, Morag will keep him busy till dinner-time, and then I'll have him over at the House till ten. So he shouldn't be straying about. Now—you'd better be off, Dougie. The bike's going all right?"

"Och, Miss Ailie!" the other protested, reproachfully. He reached for his postman's peaked cap from the mantel, and led the way out, with commendable absence of fussy preparation.

Selecting one tall antler-handled contrivance of rusty metal from amongst the derelicts, he bent down and alternately sucked and blew into a little hole in an intricately-placed carburettor, till, spitting out a mouthful of petrol, he nodded triumphantly and threw a leg across the tied sacking of the saddle. "Push," he directed, with authority.

Alison, stooping, grasped the carrier at the rear, and pushed, the driver aiding the process by using his thigh-booted legs hobby-horse fashion, and at the same time work-ing convulsively a tine-like lever on the nobly-branching handlebars. Pursuing an involved but unerring course through miscellaneous ironwork and outcropping stone, they reached the sandy track, engine and girl breathing hard. Then a series of shattering explosions caused the venerable motor-cycle to buck right out of Alison's hands straight into onward and violent action, and she was left standing amidst a hail of gravel and a dense cloud of blue smoke. Standing upright on the foot-rests in a fashion that a good Texan of bronco-busting ancestry would have appreciated, the driver gave the thing its spirited head to negotiate at remarkable speed the undulations of that coiling track.

The girl, panting, nodded approvingly after him. Dougie the Post was one of the major assets of Rum. Besides his official duties—which left him a certain amount of leisure, as the mail-boat called only three times in the week—he was the island's mechanic, plumber, and engineer. Secure on his Civil Service emoluments, he was one of the few young men in an ageing community, and made an excellent Treasurer to the Rum Community Association, as lieutenant to Alison Maclean the Secretary.

The latter, shaking gravel and rain from her person with the satisfaction of a job well done, turned and hastened home-wards.

Kilmory House on its shelf amongst the green birch-glades, though it seemed to take up a lot of space, was not very large, additions having been stuck on to a simple four-square struc-ture where and when required by many Maclean generations. The result was picturesque rather than convenient. Currently, Alison and her father, Major-General Hector Maclean, were occupying the northern extremity.

The General, like the postman, was sensibly asleep, in what was known as the library, though it served other purposes, a large and comfortably untidy room bristling with stags' heads, stuffed fauna, weapons, targes, and varnished fish. A number of dogs slept with him, a golden and a black retriever, a couple of spaniels, and a West Highland terrier at least, and tended to neutralize the aromatic fragrance of the dying birch-log fire.

Into this scene of peace Alison bustled, and soon had dogs and sire up and doing. The General was like the room—large, comfortable, and untidy, a florid bull-like man and an unlikely parent for his trim, dark, and sprightly daughter. Without being actually a lazy man, he found her energy a constant source of astonishment and admiration. Before he had managed to get all the sleep out of his surprisingly blue eyes, he was peeling the potatoes for dinner, and having to gulp down his tea and scones in the bygoing.

"But, Alie. This chap, this American . . . ?" he wondered. "How can you expect to make the fellow change all his plans, and this film company's plans? How can you hold him here?"

"Pressure," she revealed. "Sheer inexorable pressure."

Her father grinned all over his red face. "Dammit—I know you pack a good load of pressure in small bulk, my girl. D'you think you'll be able to dazzle him to that extent? He'll be used to pretty high-powered pieces in the film world, remember!"

She had the grace to flush. "Of *course* I don't mean that!" she cried. "Not that sort of pressure. You should be ashamed of yourself!"

"You've got other sorts available, then?"

"Naturally. And not only me. The whole island. We'll all have to do our bit. You, too. I've sent for the Committee."

"Committee? You mean, the Community Association Committee?"

"Is there any other? It's the only organization we have on this island. And this is going to have to be organized. They'll be here at ten-thirty."

"Oh, I say—that's a bit late, Ailie."

"I know. But we've no time to lose. And I don't suppose I'll be able to get rid of our Joe much before ten."

"Lord—we're in for a night of it, then!" the General grumbled. "Look—is this enough of these dam' potatoes. . . ?"

.   .   .   .   .

The dinner-guest arrived somewhat late, and though not normally oppressed by any slavish notion of punctuality, Alison, with a time-schedule on her hands, had been beginning to fret.

"I was thinking I'd have to come for you," she mentioned.

"Maybe you should've done. The old dame had me so almighty busy. Say—I been milking the cows, and fishing a nest outa the chimney, and getting these goddam bees back into their hive! Look—I'm stung. . . ."

"Never mind," the girl sympathized, perfunctorily. "Come and meet my father. He's moaning about life, too. You and he will get on famously, I'm sure."

She was right in that, too. They did. From the first, for no apparent reason, they seemed to consider themselves to be some sort of allies. The girl found her task both eased and complicated. She had asked her father to co-operate, but this was going a bit far. . . .

The visitor perhaps did less than justice to an excellent meal of soup, cold salmon, curds and cream—and, of course, potatoes. He had a certain preoccupation with old Morag Ross—obviously she had made a deep impression. Also, she seemed to have fed, as well as worked, him steadily since acquiring him.

All this created something of a barrier to effective—though, of course, courteously indirect—questioning. But long before the evening was out, the hostess at least had gleaned that Joel was thirty years of age, had graduated to motion pictures via the U.S. Air Force Photographic Section, came from a place called Dallas, a good Scots name where apparently men were men, that the "K" stood for Kruger, which sounded Dutch, and that his father was in oil and not steers and dogies and suchlike as might have been expected. Also, that he was un-

29

married—though the way this latter item was conceded gave Alison grave suspicions as to his future.

The revelations, of course, were not entirely one-sided. The visitor learned, for instance, that Rum was no less than an untapped gold-mine, from the filmic point of view. That its people could be described only as born actors. That the Macleans had been there for a long time—infinitely longer than the MacNeills, who were fifteenth-century incomers from Barra—despite all the efforts of Skye and its Macdonalds and Macleods to dislodge them. Direct enquiry revealed that this latter was not the sole reason for the apparent lack of warmth displayed towards the neighbouring island, with the latest dislodging attempt some two hundred and ten years back; it was rather the insufferable self-complacency of Skye, with its deplorable flair for publicity and consequent revolting prosperity, that was responsible. The guest would have gone rather deeper into this had he not got involved in Gaelic place-names, on which the General was something of a missionary.

As an evening, there was hardly a dull moment. At least, the younger man seemed very loth to bring it to a close. From nine-twenty onwards, his hostess had to struggle, politely of course, but with increasing urgency, against his seeming reluctance to return to Morag Ross's hospitable roof—a task in which her father utterly failed to support her. It was not until ten past ten, indeed, that she finally got him out into the rain—and even then the General insisted in convoying him home. Joe mightn't find his way, he asserted; the half-dark could be highly confusing—especially to a man whose stomach was unused to their Rum whisky. They would sing a little song about the Isles, and maybe even Texas, as they went. . . .

Alison got the door closed on them in some relief. Fortunately the Committee members weren't likely to be very punctual, either.

Nevertheless, from the candle-lit privacy of his attic room, into which Mrs. Ross had hustled him with charming firmness, at the same time as she sent the General about his business, her bedtime evidently grievously delayed, the traveller was surprised presently to hear considerable activity. Peering through the creeper-screened window, he could make out little or nothing, through the soft curtain of night and rain—but it sounded like a motor-cycle gymkhana, with a shooting-range thrown in.

He was in two minds as to whether to go and ask the old dame what it was all about; but apart from his candle the house seemed to be in complete darkness, and the thought of disturbing her at her bed-going daunted him.

Philosophically getting into his own bed, he leapt out again with a curse as a long pole-affair thrust up his pyjama leg and his foot contacted seemingly red-hot metal. Muttering, he dragged out what appeared to be an outsize in frying-pans, which he deposited in the fireplace from which he had already extricated the bird's nest.

This for an hotel . . . ! Shaking his head, he explored the bed thoroughly before climbing back in. The sheets were clean at any rate—though the lace around the pillows was sure going to emboss him. What a set-up! Though, that whisky of the General's was mighty good . . . better than the stuff he'd gotten at Mallaig. And the girl had nice legs. . . .

.   .   .   .   .

The Committee made quite a muster in the library, its damp personnel steaming gently in the mellow lamplight. There were fourteen present—only two short of a full house, with the Nurse and Tina Gillies mutually involved in the delivery of what was hoped would be a fine boy. Which was pretty good for such short notice, such a late hour, and when certain members had had to travel as much as ten miles around cliffs and headlands on the backs of motor-cycles. There were one or two cars on the island, but their usefulness was restricted by lack of roads, and two-wheeled and four-footed transport had the preference. Morag Ross sat between the Minister and the Reverend Father Joseph on the couch, her knitting needles busy; Dougie the Post took up an official position near the door in case a collection had to be taken; and Hughie Bain laughed amongst the ladies at the back.

As chairman, General Maclean presided, sitting on the table and swinging substantial plus-foured legs; but after having welcomed them all individually, mentioned that it was a fine night, and automatically called upon the secretary to read the minutes, allowed his daughter, probably wisely, to take over.

"No minutes required," she declared. "This is a special meeting. I'm sorry to bring you all out so late, but I expect you'd prefer that to being fetched away from your work to-morrow. Hughie Bain and I have managed to collect an American. He's staying with Morag for the night. He missed his boat for Skye—the Scavaig trip—and we prevailed on him to come here. But he intends to stay only the one day, and wants Hughie to take him on to Skye to-morrow."

Something like a corporate groan rose from the company.

"He's not just an ordinary tourist," Alison went on. "He's quite young—not the millionaire type, at all, I don't think. But he's more important. He's a film-man. A director of some sort."

"Mercy on us!"

"Is that a fact? The Pictures!"

"Yes. But he's on his way to Skye to look for a place to make a film. Skye! That's all he can think of. Well, now—it seems to me that it's up to us to make him think differently!"

"Hear, hear!"

"My Chove, yes!"

"We've got scenery here that will beat the Cuillins into a cocked hat. We want that film company to come here—not to Skye. They don't need it—we do. This is our chance—think of the publicity it would bring us."

"Publicity, Alison, can have its dangers," the Minister mentioned, gravely.

"I'm not so keen on publicity, myself," the General agreed. "Dammit—we don't want everybody talking about us. . . ."

"But we do!" his daughter cried. "That's what's wrong with Rum. We're backward. We don't advertise ourselves. Nobody ever comes here—nobody knows about us. And what's the consequence? The population goes down every year. Young folk won't stay on the island. We'll soon be deserted, like Soay, if we don't do something about it."

The mention of Soay sounded like a death-knell to all present. A neighbouring island, its few remaining inhabitants had petitioned to be evacuated only the previous year.

"Quite right," Morag Ross agreed. "Miss Ailie's right. I always say, you've got to move with the times, whatever." And she smiled on them all.

"You know what I've been saying for ages," Alison continued. "The only way we can survive is by making people come here—bring money to the island. Tourists and visitors. The only advantage we have is our scenery. But that's the only advantage Skye has, too—and look what *they've* done."

"Dear me," the Minister protested, "you're not after holding up Skye as an example now, are you?"

"In a kind of way, I am. Look what they've done, with their Skye Week, and their 'Come to Skye' publicity. The place is just rolling in money—mostly dollars!"

"Tsst-tsst!" the Minister deplored. "And corruption stalks the unfortunate island!"

"Och, man, man—it's not so bad as all that," Father Joseph asserted, jovially. "The best half of the folk are Catholics!"

"Anyway," Alison hastened to revert to the major theme, "if we can get this film company to come here, we'll get not only a lot of trade and custom and so on, but publicity in the papers that we'd spend thousands of pounds to get in the advertisement columns. Pounds we haven't got!"

"Hear, hear."

"You're dead right, Alison my girl," Father Joseph substantiated. "She's right, you know, General. It's what we're needing, my goodness."

And the Catholic section of the Committee weighed in solidly and relievedly.

"I agree, b'Jove," Major Rory MacNeill exploded. He never talked much, finding speech evidently something of a trial. But when he did achieve words, his delivery was apt to be forceful. "We'll have these film-chappies, hey."

"Thanks, Rory." Alison smiled her sweetest. And Major

MacNeill of Dibidil grew as ruddy as his name, with pleasure. He owned the south-western half of the island—that part nearest to Barra—and had always a hope that he might one day unite the whole place by a match suitable in every way.

"But it's not going to be just as easy as that," the young woman warned. "There'll be a lot of opposition to overcome. Like all the rest of them, he's bung full of prejudices in favour of Skye. We won't convince *him* too easily—and then there's his company, who are all set for Skye. And there are two main snags, that we can't overlook. Crowds and clouds. We haven't enough of the one, and we've too much of the other. He needs lots of people, for crowd scenes, and lots of sun for his cameras. He's not much of a one for rain!"

There was a reflective silence.

Then Dougie spoke up. "It rains in Skye, too, mind. What's it the posters call it—the Misty Isle?"

"Yes. And we'll have to play that up for all we're worth. But still, they haven't got our cloud, our *parasitical* cloud."

The emphasis on the adjective was not derogatory. Quite the reverse. They were all rather proud of their island's unique parasitical cloud—even though it had its disadvantages. While the mountains of Rum and Skye vied with each other as the first lofty land masses to puncture the great rainclouds coming in from the Atlantic, Rum alone boasted a home-made, indigenous, and highly faithful cloud of its own. Meteorologists waxed lyrical about it. Encyclopædias described it. Surely they weren't going to have to disown it, now?

Alison did not overlook this. "There's not much we can do about the cloud," she went on. "But people are a different thing. We can, and must, get people here, lots of people, for his crowd scenes. Or . . . or, at least, we must convince him that they'll *be* here, by the time the crowd scenes come along. . . ."

"Alison Maclean!" the Minister warned, as in duty bound.

"The second might be easier than the first, I'm thinking," Father Joseph pointed out, judiciously.

"We must try to achieve both," the girl asserted. "After all, it's people that we want to come here, anyway. The film thing's only a means towards an end. But it will take work, and organization—by us all. However, Hughie and I have struck the first blow. We've instituted Rum Week. Haven't we, Hughie?"

"Eh . . . ?"

"Mercy to goodness!"

"My Chove—what's that?"

"It's a week—a sort of rival to Skye Week, you see. A week when we do everything we can to get people to visit Rum."

"Good show!" Major Rory blurted.

"But how, Miss Ailie?"

"Dammit—how are we to get them here, girl?"

"I haven't worked out all the details yet," Alison admitted, and achieved the necessary helpless-little-girl smile that could be guaranteed to carry the day. "We'll decide that sort of thing later, won't we? At least, all you clever men will!"

"Every time," the Major supported that appeal. "Hear, hear."

"But have we got the capacity, the facilities, for this sort of thing . . . ?" the Minister doubted.

"Of course we have. We've got everything Skye's got, except the . . . the machinery. I was just coming to that." She sounded satisfactorily business-like again. "I propose herewith that this Association changes its name to the Rum Development Association."

"Seconded," said Dougie.

"Passed unanimously," old Morag agreed.

"Hang it—wait a minute!" the chairman objected. "I don't think you can do that—at least, not just like that. It's not in the constitution, I shouldn't think. What d'you say, Padre?"

"We'll need an Annual General Meeting," the Minister thought.

"Then we'll just turn this Committee, *en bloc*, into the Committee of the Rum Development Association. A new organization. That all right?"

"Proposed, seconded, and passed," Dougie averred loyally.

"Exactly," Father Joseph nodded.

"Well . . ." the General said, "I suppose we can do that, if we want to. But I must say, I don't see what we're going to develop."

"Rum, Daddy—Rum," Alison declared earnestly. "We're going to sell Rum to the world, through the North Atlantic Picture Corporation. But first we have to sell it to our Joe."

"How?"

"Well, I've *got* some ideas about that. But you'll all have to co-operate. Really get down to it. But it'll only be for a day or so, in the first instance. We'll have to make a big impression on him. Under a number of headings. There's Population. We'll have to give him the impression that there's a lot more of us than there is, I'm afraid." And she shot a sidelong glance at the Minister, an excellent man but over-finicky about some things. "And there's Industry. And the Weather. There's Folklore. And History. . . ."

"But we haven't *got* any history," Colin the School objected. One of the old school of educationists, he was very sound on basic principles, but perhaps lacked the elastic mind that Glasgow University might have given him. "Nothing historical ever happened on Rum."

"Rubbish!" the girl asserted, though kindly. "Look what a history Skye's given itself! If a collection of Macdonalds and Macleods can produce that, what couldn't Rum's Macleans and MacNeills do! We can have the finest history in the Isles!"

"By George!" Major Rory exclaimed, impressed.

"A little initiative's all we need," Alison cried, uplifted herself, as vision gestated within her. "We'll start with Population—how to impress him on that score. Well—listen to this. . . ."

It was one o'clock before the Rum Development Association's inaugural meeting broke up, and adjourned to the kitchen for fried potatoes and herring, suitably washed down.

Morag Ross, tending to find her hotel-keeping responsibilities weighing upon her, led the homeward cavalcade.

3

IF THE NOISE OF PETROL ENGINES HAD BEEN JOEL
Macdonald's lullaby that night, it was the noise of petrol
engines that awakened him next morning. Up and down, up
and down, outside the house, motors roared and spluttered and
throbbed. When he could stand it no longer, the man got out
of bed and staggered to the small window. It was barely
eight o'clock, and it was raining. Staring out, with jaundiced
eye, he perceived a motor-cyclist in oilskins and sou'wester go
bouncing up the track in a splatter of spray and gravel. A
minute or so later, just as he was climbing back into bed, a
further uproar sent him back to the window, in time to see
another traveller, sandy-haired and in fisherman's jersey and
sea-boots this time, hurtling *down* the track at equal speed.
The staccato echo had barely died away before the beat of
engines began to wax again, and a third jehu came lurching
up from the direction that the other had gone, clad this time
in a postman's coat and cap. A peculiarly antiquated type of
machine seemed to be highly popular in Rum. Also long
rubber boots.

The hotel-guest was shaking his head—though heedfully,
out of respect for a hint of headache—and deciding that despite
the rain he might as well get dressed as lie listening to this
hullabaloo, when a knock at the door heralded the tiny
proprietress with a breakfast-tray, all smiles, solicitude and
enthusiasm for the fine day it was going to be.

"It's as wet as ever," the man pointed out, a trifle un-
graciously. "I reckon it hasn't stopped since I landed on this
island."

"Och, you don't want it too bright first thing in the
morning, whatever," Morag assured. "It'll be a grand day

when the sun gets out—just grand. You'd sleep well, Mr. Macdonald? Nothing disturb you, at all?"

"Sure. Except for the speedway outside there. What's going on?"

"Och, that's just the traffic, see you. Fair incessant, it is. An active place, Rum. But you'll get used to it, Mr. Macdonald."

As he took the tray from her, he caught a glimpse of still another motor-cyclist on that busy road. He must have combined belief in better weather with a healthy caution, for he affected shirt-sleeves and a sou'wester. And of course, thigh-boots.

By the time that Alison Maclean arrived, a picture of morning freshness in jodhpurs and high-necked jumper, with a couple of shaggy Highland garrons in tow, the traffic had thinned down a bit. "Hiyah, Joe!" she said.

The man was unaffectedly glad to see her. He dropped the handle of the butter-churn, with his somewhat dramatic gesture, and wiped the sweat from his brow. "Uh-huh," he panted. "Fine day—or so I'm told."

"Yes, isn't it? It'll be hot, I shouldn't wonder. Good morning, Morag. How's the butter coming? Can I take Mr. Macdonald away, meantime? I'm going to show him round the island."

"Surely, surely. The roads will be a bittie quieter, now. Mr. Macdonald was by way of being a bittie disturbed by the noise of the motors, I'm afraid."

"A pity. But the worst of it will be over now—everybody will be at their work. We're an industrious people on Rum, Joe."

"Oh, yeah!" Joe flexed his arm and finger muscles, without further comment. "You going riding?"

"*We* are. I've got the ponies here. It's the best way to get round the place. That way, we don't have to bother about busy roads and so on. I've got sandwiches. Coming?"

"But . . . say—don't you reckon we'd better wait till the rain goes off?"

"Oh, no. No point in that. We might wait . . . I mean, that would be just a waste of time. Anyway, it's nothing—

38

just a smirr." She changed the subject. "You'll be an expert horseman, I expect, Joe—coming from Texas?"

"Well . . . I guess I'm sorta more at home in a convertible. But I reckon I'll stay on . . . if I'm not washed off. . . !"

The broad-backed, short-legged garrons took them up Kilmory Glen at a stolid trot. On either hand the hillsides rose, to disappear into a solid ceiling of cloud. The rain fell with a soft persistency, and the only colour to the entire landscape was provided by the young woman's yellow jumper. Joe sat hunched in the saddle, his burberry collar up, and regularly blew the drips from the end of his nose.

After passing a croft or two, they were into empty country where a few long-horned cattle grazed and sundry shaggy sheep were discernible amongst the outcropping stone. The track rose steadily, as the glen narrowed in, the river and a host of lesser streams shouted, the ponies' hooves clop-clipped, and Alison Maclean discoursed on history. The Celtic civilization, clan warfare, the Forty-five, the Clearances—she dealt with them vigorously, graphically, and Rum in the vortex of it all. There was plenty of mute evidence of the Clearances, at any rate, around them, in the broken gables and tumbled stones of deserted cot-houses amongst the heather; but in the circumstances the girl forbore to point them out.

Joe noted that traffic had indeed died down, as prophesied. No living soul enhanced the admittedly somewhat limited landscape.

Presently they came to an open amphitheatre in the hills, where four glens seemed to join. And right in the midst, a solitary cottage stood, noticeably small and lonely-seeming under the towering hills and the lowering clouds. But that was only the first impression of an uninformed visitor. As they drew near, people were seen to literally swarm about the place. Here were living souls in plenty. Half a dozen men and women were grubbing and delving in the tiny field alongside, men and dogs were chivvying bewildered sheep hither and thither with much outcry, old ladies were applying themselves urgently to spinning-wheels in various corners about the place, and in the nearby peat-bog peats were being cut

39

by the score. There seemed to be a lack of children, but no doubt they would all be at school.

Alison contented herself with pulling up a little way off, and demonstrating with her hand. "Bobadil," she said simply. "Macleans."

The man watched, wondering. "By hokey! " he exclaimed. "They sure got skids under them."

"Just the unassuming and essential industry of a small rural community," she mentioned.

"Is that so? But say—where do they all roost? You won't get half of them into that shanty."

"Oh, these cottages are roomier than they look," she assured. "And, of course, there are other houses not so far away."

He failed to identify these, but Alison was already moving on—not down to the cottage, but right-handed, westwards. "We'll need all our time," she announced. She waved an arm southwards. "That's the best part for scenery. All the high mountains there. Askival and Allival and Ashval and so on. But we'll come to that later. Come along."

Joe waved farewell to the industrious Macleans, but they were all too fully occupied to notice, or at least, to respond.

They clattered down this right-hand valley in great style. Glen Shellesder it was, the young woman informed, over her shoulder, and it ran straight down to the north-west coast, at Guirdil. If they had gone the other way, to the east, they'd have come to Kinloch, where the island's largest community was settled, and Loch Screscort where the ship came in—when it came.

The visitor found the geography less rewarding than the history.

This was a comparatively short straight glen, and soon the grey sea, dotted with the foaming fangs of skerries and reefs, was opening before them. The valley widened to a grassy wedge that ran down to a shingly beach. Here were three or four crofts, and a small building down at the shore, out of which belched and billowed vast clouds of smoke.

"Gee—there's a fire!" Joe cried, urging his beast onwards.

"No, no. That's the smoking-shed. Where the fish are cured. Guirdil is a centre of trade and commerce. It's . . . it's a sort of fishing port."

Admittedly, the little bay, flanked by the swiftly rising cliffs, was full of boats. Some seemed to be on the small side, and others were very low in the water, but there was almost enough of all shapes and sizes for a regatta.

"The fishing fleet's in," it was pointed out.

Stirring activity patently was going on. Folk were hurrying in and out of the smoking-hut like bees at a hive. People were carrying fish boxes up and down between the water's edge and the shed. Boats were plying back and forth across the little bay in vigorous fashion. Neither was the crofting being neglected. It was all most heartening—especially in the downpouring rain.

"I must say, you're real go-getters on this island!" the traveller marvelled. "You've got that Mallaig dump licked. Some special rush on?"

"No. Nothing like that. We're just a—a progressive people, that's all."

"Well, you sure got me guessing. I heard you Highland folks were kinda different. Took things easy. But maybe that's Skye? Maybe Rum's not typical . . . ?"

Doubtfully she shot a sidelong glance at him. "No. I mean, yes—Rum's entirely typical, of course. Couldn't be more so. This is the real Highlands—without any of the ballyhoo they put on in Skye. . . ."

They had come to a point, perhaps quarter of a mile from the scene of activity, where the track forked. The man was for proceeding down the right-hand fork, to the shore, but his guide turned her garron into the other, that headed up towards the cliffs and the south.

"Say, aren't we going down there?" Joe protested. "I'd like a word with these busy guys. I've never seen fish smoked. . . ."

Alison was quite definite. "We mustn't disturb them at their work," she declared. "Anyway, we haven't time. It's a big island to get round, you know." The girl seemed to divide her attention between her wrist-watch and the lowering heavens. "And there's a school round here, that you ought to see."

"Okay. Anything you say."

She led the way along the upper path at a brisk trot. "At least, I hope they're in," she threw back at him. "They *ought* to be there—but they might be out. On a demonstration or something, you know. Nature study."

"In weather like this?"

She was shaking her head almost irritably at this constant harping on the weather, when, rounding a small shoulder of hillside, they were reassured, at least, about the presence of the scholars. In front of them an ordinary low-browed thatched cottage crouched into the heather, and from it waves and billows of sound surged and throbbed. Lusty young lungs were being exercised to the full, in the interests of nature study or otherwise. At sight of the riders a small character whipped like a weasel indoors from a vantage point amongst the overgrown berry bushes of a tangled garden. A sudden and uncanny quiet followed, broken only by the snorting and whinnying of welcome of a bunch of garrons tethered at the back.

In silence the visitors rode up. A flushed, breathless, and harassed-seeming female met them in the doorway, taking off an apron. "Goodness me—yourself it is, and me thankful to be seeing you!" she gasped. "We're after doing the History of Rum, and that was the Battle of Papadil!"

"Indeed, Jessie—how interesting," Alison exclaimed. "This is Mr. Macdonald, from Texas. We thought we'd just drop in . . . when we were passing, you know."

Dismounting, they went inside. It seemed to be only a two-roomed cottage, with the kitchen at one end and the room at the other. This latter was crammed as full of children as an egg is of meat. They sat, stood, squatted, and roosted, not at desks but on the floor, on whatever furniture the place boasted, fully a score of wide-eyed infants, frozen thus into improbable immobility.

"Good morning, children," Alison greeted. "I hope you are enjoying your history lesson."

A certain exchange of round glances left the matter open to doubt.

"A lotta kids. Sorta crowded, eh?" Joe suggested.

"Well, yes. This is only a sort of temporary school. Auxiliary, you might call it. Overcrowding's a terrible problem, isn't it?"

"I guess so. Seems like it. But they don't look unhappy." He stooped down. "Say—you like it here, young fella?"

The diminutive individual addressed went almost as red as his hair, but found that he had misplaced his tongue. Not so the pert miss next to him. "Fine it is, yes," she assured, brightly. "Better than school."

"Eh . . . ?"

"She means, better than an ordinary schoolroom," Alison interpreted, quickly.

"We came all the way on the ponies," the younger lady added, not desirous of yielding the initiative. "There was three on my pony. Brown, it was, with a black tail."

"Ours was grey, and Father Joseph led it . . ." a neighbour put in.

"We've got pieces, for our dinner—like a picnic. The teacher said . . ."

Alison interrupted peremptorily, lest this flood of information should weary the visitor. "Time we were off," she decided. "We've got a lot to do. Good morning, children. And pay good attention to what you're told. Remember? Good morning, Jessie." And she was out of there in less time than it takes to tell. The man actually found his arm taken, in the process.

"Cute kids," he suggested, outside in the rain.

"You think so?" she said. And, strangely, she sounded less enthusiastic than she might have done. But as she mounted, her tone changed briskly. "Now for some scenery."

Sceptically, the guest upturned his gaze to the level canopy of cloud above, and said nothing.

.   .   .   .   .

The girl was right again. Scenery she did show him, clouds and rain notwithstanding. Their path led them up to the level of the cliff-tops, and thereafter took them, turning and twisting, southwards along that lofty terrace above mile after mile of the most tremendous crags and precipices of that iron-bound seaboard. On their left hand the braesides continued to lift up into nearby cloud, but on the right the land was cut away sheerly, to drop dizzily to the wrinkled rocktorn heaving sea, five hundred, six hundred, eight hundred feet below, in a breath-taking succession of promontories and cauldrons and headlands that daunted the eye and the pit of the stomach, and challenged the imagination. Black and sepia and red, unbroken, unscalable, the cliffs reared themselves as might the dire walls of the pit itself, to the endless sob and sigh of the waves beneath and the screaming plaint of the wheeling sea-birds above. And all was seen only through chill screens of fine spray where the myriad burns that rushed headlong from the hills plunged over the edge and were lost in smoke.

The man did not withhold acknowledgment, and as they went on, despite the grimness of the scene, the girl shed some of the slightly brittle assurance of her manner, and relaxed. Presently, indeed, with miles of this sort of thing ahead of them, she was behaving so naturally, and had become in consequence such excellent company for any young man, that Joel K. Macdonald was tending to concentrate unsuitably on herself rather than on the scenery. Which is just typical of the contrariness of human nature and the agley-going propensities of the best-laid schemes. Though it is to be doubted if either of them perceived this at the time.

Their sure-footed mounts followed the dizzy cliff-tops track with entire placidity.

They were well past the thrusting cape of A'Bhrideanach, the most westerly point of Rum, when the man's bemused glance, sweeping the far-flung plain of the sea, perceived what should have been apparent long before; namely, that out there the sun was shining. There was no doubt about it. Beyond the curtain of rain and spray and the shadow of cloud, a golden glow spread far and wide. Colour could be sensed.

Visibility seemed to be excellent. The Outer Hebrides, from Barra to North Uist, were strung like a necklace on the bosom of the sparkling sea. Near at hand Canna and Sanday were green leviathans basking in the sun. And backwards, to the north, the Cuillins of Syke soared into the cerulean heavens.

"Say—that's fine," he said. "Looks like it's going to clear."

"So it does," the girl admitted briefly. "Tell me about this university you were at. Cornell. It sounds amusing. . . ."

At a break in the cliff rampart, presently—the first that they had come to—Alison led the way down a steep side-path towards a brief grassy terrace, Joe following with his eyes firmly clamped between his horse's ears, and his heart half-way to his mouth. He reckoned that he had seldom seen a more slippery-looking and uninviting track.

Alison saw the boats below them, suddenly—but did not draw attention to their presence. They were very close in, considering the nature of that savage coastline. Indeed, hugging the shore, they would not have been visible to all beneath the towering cliffs had it not been for the riders' descent of this little gap and the outward swing of the path. The safe reaching of the grassy shelf released Joe's locked gaze some-what—just in time to glimpse the three heavily-laden cobles as they worked southwards round the next thrusting head-land and out of sight, rising and falling alarmingly on the regular surge of the tide.

"Look at that!" he cried. "Boats. What are they up to —creeping round there?"

"Nothing. Or at least, fishing. Just fishing," the girl explained.

"So near in as that? And full of folks?"

"It takes a lot of hands to deal with salmon nets . . ."

"But, say—looked like they had no room for a net, not to mention a salmon! And weren't there women amongst them . . . ?"

"The women on this island work as hard as the men—harder!" That was almost prim. "Now—here we are."

At the end of the little terrace a cave yawned, and in its wide mouth they dismounted.

"Quite a hideaway."

"Yes. I thought we'd eat our sandwiches here," the young woman said. "It's a favourite spot of mine. Sort of suspended midway between sea and sky. . . ."

"Yeah. And outa the rain," her companion pointed out.

So there, after the girl had shaken herself, and the man had stripped off his sodden burberry—and seemed infinitely the wetter of the two—they sat above the heaving tide and ate their lunch. And Joe was led to talk of films and film-making and film people—especially female ones—and necessarily therefore of himself, his achievements and ambitions. In which, being a subject that a man can really get his teeth into, he did not fail her—nor got involved in any searching and unprofitable questioning of his own; nor into the meteorological observations to which he seemed so prone. The only modest words which his hearer felt called upon to insert here and there were of admiration, encouragement, and a gentle underlining of the obvious and marked suitability of this island of Rum for each of the filmic requirements that he had happened to touch upon.

They concluded their lunch—and quite a post-prandial interval thereafter—in mutual esteem and satisfaction. Indeed, they were a good way up the path to the cliff-top again before the man realized that it was still raining as persistently as ever, despite, apparently, glorious sunshine everywhere else.

"Hell—does it never stop raining on Rum?" he demanded, tactlessly to say the least of it. And thereby spoiled everything. Thereafter, they rode along the summit path in what was little better than thinly interrupted silence.

. . . . . .

Where at long last the cliffs began to break down to the trough of another glen with its widening access to the sea, Alison paused, and bit her lip, staring, frowning, not downwards into the hollow, but rather upwards. Obviously, beyond the glen, great land masses loomed and towered—so much was evident behind the sombre screen of rain and cloud. But of shape and outline, of colour or detail, nothing was to be seen.

"A pity." For the first time that day, the girl permitted disappointment to appear. "I had hoped . . . You get the best view in Rum here—in all the Isles, in all Scotland, probably. The big hills are there, going up over two thousand five hundred feet, straight from sea level—Askival, Allival, and the rest. However . . ." She shrugged. "This is Glen Harris. There is a thriving community down here. Come along."

"Tough." Was there just a hint of sympathy in Joel K. Macdonald's monosyllable?

As they came down to lower ground the familiar pattern of an industrious peasantry was repeated. And again there was billowing smoke, this time coming from several spots along the slender sickle of sandy bay—on which were drawn up a trio of fishing cobles. This smoke, drifting over to them, had a peculiar smell.

"More fish-curing?" the man wondered, eyeing those boats.

"No. That's kelp-burning. Sea-weed. For fertilizer, for the fields. We do a lot of that."

"Fertilizer, huh? No kidding? But . . . where's the fields . . . ?"

His pertinent query was interrupted by an explosion that shook the ground beneath their garrons' hooves, and rudely woke the echoes of a score of hidden hills.

"Gee—what's . . . ?" he was beginning, when a second eruption added to the din. They swung round, to see a cloud of smoke and dust rising from the cliff-side to their right.

"Just blasting. Stone-quarrying," his informant mentioned. She sounded just a trifle smug now. "One of our heavier industries."

"Ye gods—what an island! D'you never slacken off? Take a rest . . . ?"

"You—an American—ask that?" she reproved. "I thought you people were the hustlers?"

"So did I—until I came to this Rum! I reckon—Listen! That a bell?"

Sure enough, the mellow ding-dong, ding-dong of a bell

came drifting up from the noticeably thin scatter of cottages below.

"A church-bell," she nodded. "That's a church—beside the pens where they're clipping the sheep." Casually she said it. "A wedding or something, it'll be."

"By . . . hokey!" Joe shook his head. "Never a dull moment—barring the weather! I must say, I hand it to you folks. . . ." A third explosion completed his remark for him, adequately.

But when it became apparent, by the girl's direction, that they were not actually going down to this centre of activity either, the man protested. They ought to go and look in at the wedding. A Hebridean wedding should be quite something. To which she countered that that wouldn't do at all. It was a Catholic church and they wouldn't want droppers-in. Moreover, they hadn't time. This was a lightning tour of the island itself they were making. They still had to see Papadil, Dibidil, and Kinloch. They were only half-way . . .

"Half-way!" Joe cried, looking at his watch. "Say—it's two o'clock now. I got a date with that Hughie guy in just about an hour. To take me to Skye. You've not forgotten that, have you?"

Alison blinked. "Er . . . no. No, of course not. But an hour or so is neither here nor there, surely . . . ?"

"Would you have me break my word to the guy?"

"No. But . . . well, Hughie's not likely to be so very punctual himself perhaps."

"Then I guess he needs a lesson in punctuality. Say—can you get back to your end of the island through this valley?"

"Yes. But if we went over to Papadil, and then round by Glen Dibidil, it wouldn't take so very much longer. And the mist might clear. . . ."

"Mist? What mist?"

"Well, cloud, then. The rain. . . ."

"Could we do it in an hour?"

"Not just an hour, no."

"Two?"

"Well, perhaps . . ."

The man shook a decided head. "Nope," he said. "We

48

go this way. I'm for Skye this afternoon, see." And he turned his garron's head northwards.

His companion grimaced at his back. " Major MacNeill will be disappointed," she said.

" Who's he? "

" The Laird of Dibidil. The man who owns this part of the island. He's sort of expecting us, for tea."

" But how come he knows anything about me? I haven't seen a telephone-wire on the island! "

" Oh, there is one. We've had it for quite a while. But . . . well, he happened to drop in last night. After you'd left."

" Oh, yeah? With a bodyguard of motor-cyclists? "

" Eh . . . ? "

" Skip it. And didn't you tell him I was fixed up to cross to Skye at three o'clock? "

" I . . . I thought perhaps you'd have changed your mind when you'd seen a bit of Rum! "

" You did, huh? " He made no further comment than that. And the silence descended upon them once more as they rode up Glen Harris into the crouching hills, the man this time leading the way.

And behind them, the rain muffled the joy-bells. The blasters seemed to have run out of high-explosive.

．　　　．　　　．　　　．　　　．

Their valley climbed more rapidly on this side and soon they were in a long high pass that cradled a long-lost loch, austere, brooding, beneath black beetling crags. They went in the skirts of the clouds here. Red deer drifted off into hidden corries on every hand like silent spectres. Herons stood in sombre reflection at the steely water's edge. Grouse flew off on down-bent wings, kabek-kabeking scoldingly. And over all, the curlews yittered their inconsolable refrain. As well that these latter had something to say, at any rate—for the wayfarers seemed to have exhausted their conversation.

Beyond the loch in the pass, when they began to lose height again, the girl suddenly found her tongue and came

RW—D

pushing up alongside to urge that they leave the valley floor here and slant off up the heathery hillside to the right. To save time, she asserted—to avoid wet and boggy ground. Her companion looked a little bit surprised—perhaps because of the wheel-tracks and hoof-marks on the path that seemed to go straight on—but he followed her lead like a good guest should.

Soon it was apparent that they had come to that wide central amphitheatre that had been their first call of the day —were indeed skirting it, to the east. It struck the man that the main path that they had left would have taken them straight on to that place—Bobadil, or whatever ridiculous name it was called. He looked down now, to try to pick it out. It was not very clear, in the distance and with the rain in between. But as they progressed and began to dip down into the transverse glen of the Kinloch River, he had a moment or two's fairly uninterrupted view of the place—despite the speed to which his guide had abruptly whipped up their pace. And not a soul was to be seen in its formerly so busy vicinity.

He mentioned the fact as soon as his garron could come up with hers, down near the river. "They've all gone," he reported. "Not a doggone soul to be seen at that what's-it place."

"They'll all be indoors—having their teas. They deserve a small break, surely, in a hard day?" And the heat with which she hurled that at him left the man more surprised than ever, and wisely wary too.

He did not say anything about his wondering as to where the saving of time came in as they worked back to the north-south axis of Kilmory Glen again. Nor did he mention, as they clattered down its deserted reaches, that for all the traffic of the early morning, they had not met a soul on one of the island's tracks all day.

It was well after three before Alison left her charge at Morag Ross's path-end to collect his baggage. She herself moved down to Dougie the Post's cottage, where, after a brief and less than cheerful account of progress, she dispatched her lieutenant off post-haste on his bicycle to Kinloch and points south. Joe, emerging with his grip, was just in time to see him disappearing up the road in spray and smoke.

"Traffic begun again?" he commented. "Say—no sign of the old dame about the place. Will you settle up with her for me? What'll she charge? A coupla pounds?"

"Oh, that would be much too much. I don't suppose she'd ask more than ten shillings. . . ."

"Well, give her the two pounds, will you? Tell her to treat herself to a new ladder for next time her bees swarm. . . ." Joe mounted, his bag in front of him, and they rode down the remaining quarter-mile to the shore.

Hughie Bain, habitually punctual or not, was present. So was his *Kelpie*. It was drawn up on the shingle, and alongside it was spread a somewhat tattered tarpaulin. And on the tarpaulin, neatly laid out, were the major portions of the *Kelpie*'s vitals. Beside them all the owner sat under the gentle caress of the rain, picked them up seriatim, tapped them with a spanner, and laughed to himself with essential philosophy.

"Hell!" the American said.

"Nothing wrong, I hope, Hughie?"

"Wrong?" The boatman glanced up, to notice them for the first time. "Good afternoon. A fine day it is for the growth. No, no—there is nothing wrong at all. Och, it's just some small thing that does be stopping the engine from going, see you."

"But . . . but—say, what about taking me over to Skye?"

"Yes, yes. I wouldn't be forgetting a thing like that. Skye! Och, mercy me—no. We'll be away just as soon as I'm finding this small thing I was after telling you about. Och, it'll be nothing at all—just something in the petrol, maybe." He chuckled. "Man—the things that do be getting into the petrol!" And he waved a corkscrew petrol pipe genially.

The girl held her peace.

Joe moistened his lips. "How long d'you reckon you'll take to find this . . . thing?"

Hughie scratched his head with the petrol pipe. "Not that long, likely—no, no. It's just a question of time . . ."

"Perhaps you'd better come back to the House with me and wait, Mr. Macdonald? Er . . . Joe," Alison suggested.

"Nope," the younger man decided. "I wait here. Maybe I could even give our friend here some advice. Speed things up!"

"And welcome you'd be, sir. . . ."

"In the rain? You'd be more comfortable under cover. Having a meal, while you're waiting. . . ."

"Thanks—no. I aim to get to Skye this afternoon, see." He glanced around the little bay. Only two or three small rowing-boats offered alternative transport. "I reckon I better stick around right here. In case Hughie sorta gets tired and lonely!" And he dismounted.

Taking his garron's reins, the girl shrugged, and held out her hand. "Well—good-bye, Joe. Or rather, *au revoir*—for I hope that you won't forget Rum, and that it won't be so very long before you're back."

"I sure won't forget Rum!" he agreed. "It's been a—a memorable visit! You've been mighty kind. Shown me a lot of attention. . . ."

"It was no trouble. Don't say any more." Undoubtedly the young woman seemed eager to be gone. "Remember— You haven't seen half of Rum yet. 'Bye, Joe. And good luck, Hughie!"

"Look—I . . . Okay, Miss Alison. And, thanks." That last followed the substantial rumps of the two ponies as they trotted off inland. And the visitor scratched his wet head as he watched them go.

At one of the library windows of Kilmory House almost two hours later, Alison Maclean set down her tea-cup. "You know, Daddy," she said, "I think it would be a humane act if you were to go down to the beach and put that young man out of his misery. He must be getting tired of pacing back and forwards there—though even he, you would think, would be beginning to perceive that it's unlikely that Hughie will get to Skye this night! I should say, what he needs is a drink and a little sympathetic company."

"Why not give him both, yourself?" the General asked. "After all, it's you that . . ."

"No. It's masculine company that he needs, I feel sure. Anyway, I'm going upstairs to my room for an hour or two. I . . . I've got a headache."

"M'mm. Do I sympathize? Or don't I?" her father wondered.

"You just go and be a thoughtful kindly host," she directed. "And, look—don't make any cosy arrangements for me this evening. I'm sure I won't be readily available!"

4

BRILLIANT BLINDING SUNLIGHT FORCED OPEN Alison's eyes in her east-facing bedroom next morning. For a moment she blinked in the level flood—and then leapt out of bed and over to the window, half closing sleepy eyes against the dazzle. Out there, all Rum reared its clear-etched, shadow-slashed and colourful splendour, with its parasitical cloud reduced to a golden-laced pocket-handkerchief, caught by the merest corner to no more than the topmost spur of thrusting Askival. It was ten minutes to six on her wrist-watch.

As has been hinted, that girl was no sluggard when the need for action arose. Though early, this seemed to be the hour. Ten minutes after that first reluctant parting of eyelids she was trotting out of the Kilmory House gates on her garron, munching a somewhat stale scone from a haversackful hastily collected—or not quite full; an auspicious-looking silver flask and a bottle of milk shared the accommodation.

Straight down to the glen track, over the plank bridges and up to Morag Ross's house she rode. Dismounting, she looked for the ladder, found it helping to hold the cowshed roof in place, and, struggling drunkenly under its unhandy weight, brought it to lay against the house wall. In no time at all she was up its precarious length, panting admittedly but very effectively, and knocking at the open attic window of the hotel-guest's room.

Joel K. Macdonald slept admirably sound, so that a modest young woman, sufficiently respectful of convention to hesitate to invade a man's bedroom while he was still recumbent, was forced to throw bits of twig and creeper at the sleeper. She was a fair shot, however, and after two or three casts the tousled head jerked up.

"Hell!'" he mumbled.

"Not at all," the apparition at the window maintained cheerfully. "It's heaven. A perfectly heavenly morning. Up you get. Time we were on our way."

"Eh? What . . . ? Where to . . . ?"

"We're going to have a look at Rum. Properly."

"But, gee—we did that yesterday!" The man rubbed his eyes. "Look—I've seen Rum, see. I'm going . . ."

"Nonsense. Not properly. Not what I brought you here to see. Do come along. I've got the ponies here."

"But, say—what about my breakfast . . . ?"

"I've got that too."

"Look—I'm going to Skye. If this Hughie's blasted boat isn't ready to-day I'll get one of these other boats to take me, see. A fishing-boat."

"Yes, yes. Of course. That was bad luck about Hughie's boat. But there's lots and lots of time for that. . . ."

"Yeah? And what's more, your dad tells me the steamer calls to-day. If none of these doggone boats can take me, some way or another, I'll take the steamer back to Mallaig, and hire from there!"

"M'mmm. Daddy told you that . . . ? Well, I suppose you *could* do that. But, my goodness—the ship doesn't sail till the early evening. You've got loads of time. Just come to the window here and look out."

"With *you* there! Say—doesn't a guy get some privacy around here?" That was plaintive.

"All right. I'll go down. But only if you promise to come down after me. Right away—just as soon as you're dressed."

54

"Okay, okay. . . ."

"And, look—there's no need to start shaving or any nonsense like that!" She did not wait for his further grumbles, but backed and all but fell down that ladder in double-quick time. She had plenty of time at the foot to ruminate on the widely propagated fallacy that women take longer about their toilet than does the opposite sex.

Consequently, when eventually, less than sparkling and still complaining, Joe did get down, there was no time to be wasted. The girl was mounted and handing him his reins before he had stepped off the ladder.

"What's all the hurry?" he wanted to know, querulously.

With an eye on the pocket-handkerchief of cloud on noble Askival, she shook her head. "No *hurry*. It's just that the light and shadow effect of the morning sun oughtn't to be missed."

"Oh, no? And maybe you're scared of the rain coming on again?" Which was little short of churlish in the circumstances.

"Don't be silly," she requested briefly, and digging jodhpured knees into her garron's broad flanks, sent it off at a clatter.

Perforce, he had to clatter after.

But even the sour humours of grossly interrupted slumber were not proof against Rum and Alison Maclean that early morning. Ahead of them reared such a breath-taking array of jagged peaks and thrusting buttresses, hanging corries and yawning chasms, riven precipices and plunging screes, all washed in yellow light or stained deep in blue and violet shadow, as to mock man's every mood and temper. Nearer at hand the lower hills lay glowing, bold-etched and colourful, their birch-clad skirts a chequer-work of lemon and black, and behind, the Sound of Rum was a plain of molten gold.

The showman, if nothing else, in Joel Macdonald, responded inevitably.

Alison rode in silence, and let the scene speak for her. Some assistance she gave it, indeed, with her offer of the scones and the flask—but their acceptance did not promote chatter. And the concurrent munching was a companionable thing. It was not until they were in sight of the lonely croft of Bobadil that conversation advanced beyond monosyllables.

"Having a vacation to-day? " the man wondered, eyeing the placid scene.

"Let them have their sleep out, surely. It's early yet."

He glanced at his watch, apparently for the first time that morning, stared, shook it, and put it to his ear. "Snakes! " he exclaimed. "It's not seven o'clock yet! " And he transferred his gaze to his companion.

She in turn passed it on elsewhere. "That's Barkeval just in front. Just under the two-thousand mark. We can get the ponies to the top of that quite easily. From there, we can get on to Allival—though not by pony. We might even make Askival. . . ."

The man all but choked over the crumbs of his scone. "I can see them pretty well from here . . ." he spluttered.

"Have a drink of milk," she suggested. "This is nothing to what you'll see from up there." And, touching up her mount, she was off into a fast trot, into a canter.

There was nothing to do but follow her, of course; it is always the man who must observe the scruples.

.   .   .   .   .

They climbed Barkeval—or at least their garrons did—in just over the hour, and from its long summit ridge gazed down on most of the Hebrides and much of Highland Scotland, spread out for them in gleaming sea and dreaming island and serried range to all infinity. The giants Allival, Askival and Ashval towered close now—or seeming close—overpowering in their barren grandeur, and obviously no pony was going to scale those rugged and brooding heights. A fleecy airy-nothing of cloud now hovered above the horned head of Askival—but Alison kept a wary eye on it, just the same.

Joe absorbed all that he saw—and was not unresponsive either to the picture that the young woman herself made,
56

small but lively, vital, against all that tremendous background.

They would climb Allival, the girl decided, leaving the horses in a hollow that she knew of, part-way up. To her companion's suggestion that the view could not be any better than it was from right here she turned a deaf ear.

As they climbed, Alison explained to him the meaning of Rum's curiously named mountains. The suffix val was only a corruption of the Gaelic *meall*, meaning a lumpish hill, and the prefixes were equally descriptive. Allival was an anglicization of *Ailbe-meall*, the barren hill; Askival was *Aisgemeall*, the rocky massive hill, and Ashval from *Ais* or backset, as its position demonstrated. All of which helped a long climb to a conclusion.

From the narrow top of Allival, the feeling of its great neighbours bearing in on it was almost overwhelming, stifling. Joe was impressed, sure enough—but he reckoned that he had seen enough. How about getting down . . . ?

But Alison would not hear of it. They hadn't come all this way to fail at Askival, the highest point of Rum—and it only three hundred feet above them? Perish the thought! And she was watching that cloud as she said it. The thing was lower, undoubtedly, tipping the ultimate pinnacle of rock.

The man made a compact with her. After that, they'd go down? He had to see about this boat. . . .

Of course they would. That was the top, wasn't it?

There was a dip, a mile-long ridge, and then a sharp ascent, and that would be Askival. The dip and the ridge were easy, but the climb beyond was steep and rough going, entailing a certain amount of hands-and-knees work. But Alison gave lightsome lead—and it would have been a poor man who would have called a halt, assuming that he had the breath to call anything. Even when, three-quarters of the way up, suddenly they were enveloped in cloud.

The girl did not slacken her pace. "Only a hundred more feet or so to go," she called back. "This won't stop us." And admittedly, this was not the usual unpleasant cold and clammy mist of the high tops, but a glowing iridescent cotton-woolly billow, shot through with gold, and no displeasure to anyone. After all, it was Rum's own familiar domestic cloud.

Though it did reduce visibility to a matter of a foot or two.

"No view in this," was the man's only comment.

"It may lift," she said. "And anyway, you'll be able to say you've conquered the highest point in Rum."

Theoretically, he was able to say that in a few breathless minutes—though it might have been a jumble of stones and naked rock anywhere. Wiping a wet brow with his sleeve, Joe left the huzzas to his companion. He was glad to follow her lead and sit down, while the fleecy blanket heaved and boiled around them, its dazzle a trial to the eyes.

"I'll tell you the story of Hector Mor Maclean, and Mac-Neill of Barra—on this very hill," she said.

And she did. It was a good story, too, if a trifle blood-thirsty and with wide ramifications.

The cloud had not cleared by the time that they moved on again—in fact, it seemed thicker. Alison guided her guest in the right direction.

And then, suddenly, she grabbed his arm and pulled him back. In front all seemed as heretofore—except that there was no ground at their feet. Nothing but a yawning pit in which the cloud seethed and coiled.

"Snakes!" Joe ejaculated. "That was a near thing. . . ."

"Just one of the corries," she explained. "There are quite a few of them. Perhaps we'd better move this way."

But a few steps in the advised and amended direction brought the man to an equally abrupt halt. "My godfather—look at that!"

"M'mmm. A pity. Obviously we must be careful. . . ."

"I'll say!"

Careful they were, edging over on a third tack that seemed more hopeful—until it precipitated them on to what was little better than a springboard into space, from which they retired still more carefully.

"Gee—I guess we better sit down and wait a while," Joe decided, at length. "There's precious little future in this."

Reluctantly the girl allowed herself to be persuaded. "Perhaps you're right," she conceded. "Just till it lifts a bit. Have another scone. No? Then a drink—your flask

58

won't be empty yet? Have you heard how Macdonald of Sleat was pushed off Kilmory Head?"

"No," the other admitted, heavily. "Should I?"

"Oh, definitely. We'll just sit here, shall we . . . ?"

.   .   .   .   .   .

It was amazing where all the cloud came from out of that formerly cloudless sky. Endlessly it flowed and eddied past, silent, unbroken, inexhaustible as time. And time itself slid past, so as even to exhaust the saga of the Macleans of Rum versus the Rest. And the alternative subject of Joel K. Macdonald, his life and works, was not so readily switched to as it had been yesterday. Time, in fact, lagged as compared with the hurrying cloud.

At last the man got to his feet, a little stiffly. They had climbed up; surely they could get down the same way, even if they had to crawl on their knees? And despite a lack of enthusiasm from his now cautious companion, he set off to creep around the perimeter of that shrouded mountain top. He found a way down, too, presently—though whether it was the route by which they had ascended, he knew not. Anyway, it did not take them out of the cloud with any speed—though perhaps the cloud was now lower on the hill. Nevertheless, the man's spirits rose as they descended—especially when, after a few hundred feet of difficult going, he thought that he sensed a thinning of the cloud below them.

But Alison shook her head. No use going down there, she claimed. Had he forgotten the ponies? She thought that she knew roughly where they were, and she didn't advise going any lower down, or they'd miss that ridge between Askival and Allival.

And so the cloud retained them.

It was a long time before they reached Allival, and longer before they eventually found their garrons, tethered in their hollow. They were still in cloud, but now the young woman declared that she knew the way—and certainly she set off at a good round pace. And Joe was thankful enough to be getting somewhere at last, and off his own feet, not to question her. Anyway, they had got rather out of the way of talk during the last hour or two.

When at length they trotted out of the opaque constriction of the cloud, it was into an eye-widening immensity. All the world save Askival, Allival, and Ashval lay bathed in blinding sunshine. There was no limit to view, and colour and line and detail smote the perception.

The impact of it all was so great that it was some time before something else percolated to Joe's perception. And that was the position of the sun. It was on their right front, flooding only a little aslant up the deep valley which opened before them right down to the burnished sea. And though his geography was sketchy, under no circumstances could he conceive of it in that position if they were heading north for Kilmory.

"Say—we're going in the wrong direction!" he cried. "We're going south."

Alison looked about her. "So we are," she said. "Isn't that ridiculous. This must be Glen Dibidil. A confusing thing, that cloud. Still—never mind. We'll be able to have tea with Major MacNeill. I'm peckish, too. . . ."

"No," the man jerked. "I'm taking no tea. . . ." He paused. "Say—this Major. Will he have a boat?"

"Well . . . perhaps, yes. But . . . I don't think he'd take you to Skye in it. It's the wrong end of the island for Skye, you see."

"Then how about getting back to the right end, pronto?" he suggested crisply. "Just the shortest way we can."

"Certainly. Just as you wish," she agreed, suddenly amenable, almost meek. "We'll go over that way, to the left, through the gap between Askival and Beinn nan Stac, and work round. Unless you'd rather go back over Barkeval? Through the cloud . . . ?"

"No. Not on your life!"

They worked round, then, assuredly, towards the right end for Skye—but under no stretch of the imagination could the process be described as pronto. By what seemed endless leagues of trackless heather, bog, and peat-hag, they circled the great cloud-cowled hills, with the cliff-bound east coast on

60

their right. It is astonishing how much sheer land an island eight miles by eight can embrace. Joe Macdonald reckoned that *they* had embraced every clutching, cloying and water-logged acre of it before Kilmory Glen opened once more before them, smiling in the mid-afternoon sun. Hollow-stomached, saddle-sore, and tired, he gave thanks for the sight—but not vocally.

Out of her own reverie, his companion reacted with true Highland hospitality. "You must come to the House for a meal," she said. "You'll have an appetite, I dare say?"

He opened his mouth to speak, and then shut it again. "Before I do anything else, I'm going down to that beach to see about that boat!" he asserted.

To the beach they went—and no *Kelpie* and no Hughie Bain graced its sun-soaked shores. Only old Morag Ross sat knitting beside the jetty, a pleasing picture in the Victorian tradition.

"Och, is that yourselves?" she greeted them. "You'll have been having a picnic? And a fine day for it, too."

"No picnic," the man said, a trifle hoarsely. "Where's the boat? Where's that Hughie?"

"Hughie Bain? Och, he's just away on a bit of a sail."

"A sail . . . ?"

"To test it, just. The motor, you know. It was going fine . . ."

"When'll he be back?"

"Och, any time. He'll not be that long, likely."

Joe let out a long breath. But Alison spoke first.

"Obviously, the thing to do is to come up to the House and eat. You can see this jetty from there, and you'll know when Hughie comes in."

Heavily, wearily, the man nodded, and allowed himself to be conducted back to Kilmory House.

There, varied refreshments worked wonders, both with Joe's spirits and his determination. He sat at the window, his eyes glued on the little jetty, a picture of a man with a purpose. But look as he would, the *Kelpie*, test passed or otherwise, failed to put in an appearance. General Maclean, even with

61

the entire Malayan Campaign to explain, found the conversation heavy going.

As five o'clock struck on the mantelpiece clock, Joe could stand it no longer, and jumped to his feet. "I'm going over to that Girdle place, where they cure the fish, to get one of the fishing-boats to take me," he declared.

"Guirdil?" the girl said earnestly. "Oh, I wouldn't, Joe. The—er—fishing-fleet won't be in just now, I'm afraid."

"No?"

"No."

"Then I'm going to this other dump, Kinloch, for the steamer to Mallaig. It calls at six-thirty, you said, General?"

"Yes. About then. . . ."

Alison's glance at her parent was less than dutiful.

"I'm not waiting for that guy Hughie any longer, see. He's had it. I'll say good-bye now, sir. . . ."

"How are you going to Kinloch, Joe?" the young woman wondered.

"On one of these ponies, I reckon. . . ."

"They'll be tired. And it's six or seven miles each way. . . ." She looked up. "Dougie the Post might give you a lift on his motor-bike."

"Sure. Suits me."

So Alison accompanied her guest down to the road, and once again, while he went for his bag, she looked in on Dougie.

Postman and vehicle had been waiting ready for ten minutes by the time that the island-bound visitor reappeared. It transpired that he had actually had a quick shave, which seemed an astonishing thing to trouble over at this time of day. Dougie, introduced, assured that och it was no trouble at all, and him with the mail to take anyway. To the passenger's concern as to whether there would be room on the motor-cycle with the postal packages, Dougie produced three somewhat crumpled letters from the top of his sea-boots. Mr. Macdonald would find plenty of room on the carrier, with his bit bag across his knees. But first, would he be giving a bit push . . . ?

The push took them fifty yards up the road, with Alison running alongside with Joe's grip. Consequently both were in need of breath when the vehicle burst into life and fare-wells fell to be renewed. Anyway, the noise was deafening. The girl nodded and sighed, Joe shook his head and shrugged, and Dougie bellowed and pointed authoritatively.

The passenger mounted the iron carrier somewhat gingerly —and anything but gingerly was hurtled away towards Kin-loch, Mallaig, and eventually, it was to be hoped, Skye.

.   .   .   .   .

It was approximately three-quarters of an hour later, with Alison and Morag Ross strolling up from the shore, accompanied by Hughie Bain who had put in an unexpected and unheralded appearance overland—that a walking figure was seen to be approaching down the glen-track, preceded by a cheerful whistling. It turned out to be none other than Dougie the Post, with the dire news that he had gone and run out of petrol on the very highest point of the track to Kinloch, and here was him having to walk back for a tin to fill up from. The pity of it, and the mail undelivered for the first time this month—and the poor American man left sitting beside the bike in the mist. Yes, the mist was after coming down there, now—likely it would be a wet night.

The others were nothing if not sympathetic and helpful. Hughie could produce petrol. Morag bethought her of a poke of scones for the unfortunate traveller. Alison would provide garrons on which to ride back to the breakdown. None allowed themselves to be cast down by this latest misfortune. But there was a fair amount of concerned consultation of the girl's wrist-watch.

By the time that petrol had been brought up from the shore, the ponies from the House, and the scones from Morag's kitchen, the watch said ten-past-six. And the steamer was scheduled to leave Kinloch at six-thirty. Amid sombre head-shakings, Alison and Dougie mounted the garrons and rode southwards.

After a mile or two, as the glen floor rose, the sun was blotted out under the ever-increasing and descending pall of cloud. Soon they were into its familiar toils.

"The bike's just over the head of the pass," Dougie informed.

It was, too. But Joel K. Macdonald was not. Only a scrap of paper, torn from a diary, and tucked into the empty petrol-tank, on which was scrawled, GONE ON. J.K.M.

"Well, my goodness—can you beat that?" Dougie demanded. "Gone. And him with my letters, too!"

The girl knitted her brows. "Gone on . . . ? Eh—what's that about letters?"

"Och, I was after telling the man that it was a terrible thing me missing the mail-steamer. I was telling him just to be waiting there, and maybe some—some traffic, see you, would be picking him up!" Dougie produced a weakly smile. "So he said, leave the mail with himself, in case he was getting this lift. . . ."

"But who would give him a lift?"

"Never a one, at all. Och, it's no more than a trick the man's played on us . . . with Her Majesty's mail, whatever! Slippery they are, these Americans. . . ."

"Be quiet, Dougie! If 'gone on' means anything, it means he's gone on towards Kinloch. Towards the boat. Presumably on foot. Could he possibly do it? I mean, in time? When did you leave him, exactly?"

"Och, well—I couldn't just tell you the likes of that. It wouldn't take that long to get here on the bike. And I'd take a whilie walking back. Say just after five-thirty, I left him. And over four miles to go!"

"But only three, if he cut across, over the corner of Mullach Mor."

"Och, but he wouldn't know to do a thing like that. And in the mist . . ."

"He might. He's passed this way twice, now, and may have used his eyes. Three miles. And if the steamer was a few minutes late . . . he *could* have done it. Come on!"

Though it certainly was too late for the riders to reach Kinloch in time for any boat, they rode hard. As the land level dropped, they drew out of the cloud, and were able to cut off a sizeable corner, dodging the peat-hags, over sloping moorland, amidst flying turf and the pound of hooves.

The *Lochgarve* was still in sight, but half-way to Eigg, as they came down towards the scatter of crofts and the little church that made up Kinloch. The small boat that was used to meet the steamer out in mid-loch—for the landfall was too shallow for the mail-vessel's draught—was tied at the jetty again, and Jamie MacVarish working at her.

They clattered down to him. "Jamie—did he make it?" the girl cried. "The American gentleman?"

The old man in the boat looked up, surprised. "Och, he made it fine, yes, Miss Ailie. I was just after casting off when I saw him, running sort of. So I waited."

"You did!" That was heavily said.

"Just that. I took the letters, Dougie."

"Oh, aye. I'ph'mmm. That was right, Jamie." The postman sighed. "Uh-huh."

Dismounting, they stared out across the Sound of Eigg to the diminishing ship under its black plume of smoke, while the frothing horses snorted and trembled.

Old MacVarish scratched his grizzled head. "Would there be anything wrong, at all?" he wondered. "And you in a great hurry? The letters, would it be . . . ?"

"Confound the letters!" Alison said petulantly.

"Just as you say, Miss Ailie. Not that worth making the bit sail for, either—three letters just."

"Surely you didn't forget to charge your passenger a fare?"

"Passenger? But there was no passenger in it. The last passenger I had was your own self on Thursday morning. . . ."

"But . . . Mr. Macdonald? The American . . . ?"

"Och, him. He just gave me the letters, and said he'd been sort of entrusted with them, and mentioned that it wasn't raining at all, and away with him again."

"Wha-a-at! You mean . . . he didn't sail . . . ?"

"Was he for sailing, then? Mercy on us, he didn't say anything about sailing. Not him. He just walked up to the church there and sat on a bit gravestone and watched me out to the *Lochgarve*, and it sail away." The old man raised gnarled hand to brow. "Seems to me like he's there still."

Swallowing, Alison turned to stare. Sure enough, a grey-suited figure sat on one of the recumbent stones of that ancient God's-acre, apparently smoking a pipe. "Well,

RW—E   65

I'm . . . ! " Her voice tailed away, as slowly, almost reluctantly, she began to walk in that direction.

Dougie the Post took busy charge of her pony as well as his own. "It is a very fine night, Jamie," he asserted with conviction. "Very fine indeed."

.   .   .   .   .

Joel Macdonald did not give her any help at all. He just sat there on the mossy stone, smoking and at ease, preoccupied apparently with the glittering waters of the Sound. The little plain church stood on a rocky mound, its graves scratched in around it wherever a pocket of soil permitted, and Alison had to walk up to him, the westering sun in her face, and feeling herself to be at various sorts of disadvantages.

"I . . . I didn't know you were a pipe-smoker, Mr. Macdonald," she said, therefore, next to accusingly and a little breathlessly, as she came up.

He took his time to reply. "I don't do a lot of it," he admitted. "But I found it in my bag. Reckon I find it an aid to contemplation."

"And you needed an aid to contemplation?"

"Sure." He waved his pipe-stem at the evening scene. "It's a motion-picture set for contemplation."

"I see."

"You were in an almighty hurry on those ponies of yours?" he mentioned. "Not a lot of contemplation there! "

"No. We . . . we were worried about the letters."

"Ah, yes—the letters." He nodded. "They got through! "

Her eyes flickered over his face. She turned away to gaze seawards. "So you didn't go after all! " she said.

"That's right," he agreed. "I didn't go."

"Why, I wonder? "

"I guess I got to contemplating."

"A sudden change of tune, surely? For two days you've been trying to get off this island by any means you could. Then you come here—and you must have hurried to make it—and deliberately let the ship that you came to catch sail away without you. It just doesn't make sense."

"Maybe Rum and sense don't go together?" he suggested. "Would you say this act you've been putting on was all that sensible?"

"Act? Me . . . ?"

"Sure, Innocent. The biggest community act I've ever seen put on—and I'm in the way of seeing a lot of acting, sister!"

Alison bit her lower lip. "I . . . I don't know what you mean," she said.

"You are a better actress than you are a liar," he told her mildly. "I reckon about everything I've sampled on this island to date has been phoney—except your liquor!"

"Oh!" she exclaimed. "How dare you?"

"Say—you're not going to deny it? You're not dumb—and I'm not dumb, either! This Rum may be a great little island—but it's not the island you've been trying to put over to me. All of you. I reckon you held some sorta get-together the night I arrived so as to haze me. . . ."

"How can you say such a thing?"

"Easy. Look—you're telling me all that motor-cycle traffic was genuine? I guess your buddy Dougie burned up a lotta gas yesterday morning—maybe that's how came he ran out of it to-night! And that croft place—Bobadil, is it? All those guys working fit to bust, and the old dames popping outa plumb near every corner with spinning-wheels! They couldn't all get *into* that house! I guess you brought them from far and near. Same like you rounded up all those boats for the fish-curing act, and the kids for that sham school?"

"You have a terribly suspicious mind . . ." the girl faltered.

"Oh, yeah? A guy wouldn't have to be all that suspicious to question fishing-boats, filled to the cork with men, women and children, and creeping under the cliffs close in to *that* doggone shore! I reckon they were ferrying the folks round from the fish-curing act to the seaweed-burning act? Hell— I don't believe there was even a wedding either, for all the bells! Was there?"

Alison almost had her back to him now. "I don't know, since you disbelieve everything you've seen and heard on Rum, why you didn't take the opportunity to get away from

67

it all on that steamer," she said. "Obviously, you came here intending to sail."

"A guy can change his mind, can't he? "

"Why didn't you go, Mr. Macdonald? " That was a demand.

He half-shrugged. "Well, I guess you just had me beat in the end. That last performance, when Hughie's boat made itself scarce, and the motor-cycle ran outa gas back there on the top of the trail—it sorta got me down. At first, mind you, I was mad, and was plumb well going to catch this mail-ship, come hell or high water. But walking it here I got to thinking some." The man cocked an eye at her back. "I reckon walking by yourself sorta stimulates thinking, see. Maybe you'd have been better just to let me walk around Rum on my lone from the start! Anyhow, it came to me that any folks that could work so doggone hard to keep me on this island, and put up such a hundred per cent act, must be kinda folks motion-pictures could use, see. Folks with what it takes. Actors. So—well, I reckoned I'd stay."

Alison no longer had her back to him. Excitedly she cried: "You mean—not just for a day or two? You'll bring your film company here—make the film in Rum . . . ? "

"I'll try, anyhow," he nodded. "Though it won't be all that easy, maybe, with Skye set for the location. Of course, I guess we'll still have to go to Skye for the crowd scenes. . . ."

"No! Never! " the girl declared. "Rum will find the crowds, somehow."

"Say—how many folk are there on this island, anyway—honest-to-God, and no kidding? "

Her pink tongue ran round red lips. "Well . . . there's one hundred and twenty-nine—no, one hundred and thirty, now that Tina Gillies has had her new baby."

"Holy Mike! One-thirty—including the kids! " Joe stared at her for a moment. "Sister—I sure take off my hat to you! " And he tipped a finger to his bare head. "It was a better act than I reckoned. . . ."

"But, look—we'll get the people for you, even if, if . . . well, we'll get them. This Rum Week. We'll get it organized. You'll see."

"Maybe I will. If it can be organized, I guess you'll organize it! And maybe I'll take a hand myself, come to that."

"You . . . ?"

"Sure. I'm in the show business too, you'll recollect! And maybe you've given me some ideas."

The girl shook her head. "You know, Joe—I think pipe-smoking agrees with you!" And she laughed, light-heartedly, gaily, naturally, and infectiously, in a fashion that he had not heard from her previously. "I say," she said, "I think we're going to have some fun now!"

"Now . . . !" he repeated, eyebrows up.

"Yes, of course. We haven't started yet." She glanced round. The cloud had settled between them and the sinking sun, and a chill breeze came down from the hills. "Don't you think we'd better get home to Kilmory before, before . . ."

"Before the rain starts?" he finished for her. "Sure. Hell—what an island!"

5

IF RUM HAD PREVIOUSLY MADE A CONSIDERABLE impact on Joel K. Macdonald, now the tables were turned. In the days that followed, days mainly of rain and cloud and wind, but with intervals and flashes of an ethereal, indescribable, and unsurpassable loveliness, Joe created an impression on Rum, if not deeper at any rate wider—for from the beginning his sights were raised the higher.

He started with all the advantages, of course. He was The Man Who Turned Back. And he was an American, from the land of action and hustle—moreover, a film man, a professional showman, used to the almost daily working of miracles. Rum having made its modest gesture, was now prepared, determined, to be impressed by the expert. Apart from all that, a new face about the place was a lightsome thing, especially when young men were scarce. Most people considered his presence amongst them to be an example of one of the more kindly dispensations of an inscrutable Providence —the more so in that Skye was obviously the loser. And none more so than old Morag Ross, who not only saw the hotel trade booming, but perceived a hundred and one other excellent possibilities as well.

He was co-opted as an interim member, at a specially called meeting of the Rum Development Association Committee, two nights later, which was the earliest possible opportunity, the intervening day being the Sabbath, when no such activity was possible in the godly north of the island—though what went on in the Catholic southern half a no-doubt seething Creator alone knew. And haste in the matter undoubtedly was urgent, for with Skye Week only a fortnight hence, and the North Atlantic Motion-Picture Corporation expecting to be on location before that, expedition was the first essential. Sunday was not altogether lost to the cause, however, for while attending the kirk at Kinloch with General Maclean and his daughter that wet forenoon, Joe conceived and developed an entire scene for the new film epic, based on the strong meat and damnatory fervour of such a service as this, wherein beetling brows and beetling cliffs, billowing black robes and billowing storm clouds and a parallel assault on highest heaven by stern peaks and sterner prayer, formed a pattern that would set the cinema patrons wriggling on their tip-up seats.

The Committee was not long in recognizing that it had acquired a go-ahead reinforcement, Father Joseph particularly approving of a man after his own heart and not foolishly trammelled by any slavish regard for conventions or orthodoxy, who saw essentials for what they were, and went for them. On the problem of getting the rest of the film company to change their plans and come to Rum instead of Skye, for instance, Father Joe and his namesake saw eye to eye. There was no sense in troubling them with difficult and involved arguments and explanations which they could not possibly comprehend when none of them knew Skye from the Garden of Eden anyway. Let them come *here*, thinking it *was* Skye, and let Rum itself do the rest—and save packets of trouble. After all, Joel himself had mistaken the place for its more highly publicized neighbour—others might well do the same. This simple and uncomplicated solution took a little accepting by the less elastically minded, perhaps, the Minister going so far as to suggest that it verged on the deceitful. But the short-sightedness of this view was pressed home vigorously by the more realistic, and the sensible decision won the day by Dougie the Post announcing that it was moved, seconded and carried unanimously. Thereafter, just to avoid unnecessary delay in future, Alison, on the whispered advice of the newly co-opted member, proposed that a small Executive Committee should be appointed to go into such details of procedure, to save the time and trouble of the main Committee. She suggested that it should consist of the Secretary (herself), Dougie the Treasurer, Father Joseph, and Mr. Joel K. Macdonald. And as an afterthought, Major MacNeill of Dibidil. This was seconded and passed unanimously with the usual expedition by Dougie, and the meeting was enabled thankfully to break up for refreshments with a minimum of delay, only the Minister murmurous about the Constitution, and General Maclean scratching his chairmanly head.

After that, of course, everything went without a hitch. The Executive Committee looked upon itself as more or less in continuous session, owing to shortage of time and the exigencies of the situation, and few were the proposals put before it that it did not adopt unanimously and forthwith. The development of Rum, on paper at least, proceeded apace. News items were drafted and dispatched to all Chief Reporters of the National Press—for the cost of advertisements would have been prohibitive—informing them that the Island of Rum would be At Home to all comers for the first week in August, and urging all who would sample the genuine High-land way of life, and see genuine Highland scenery (as distinct from picture-postcard and railway-poster stuff) to take the Road to Rum. Special events would be staged—a Pageant of Rum, Highland Gathering and Games, ceilidhs, pony-trekking, regatta, fishing competition, etcetera. All enquiries as to accommodation and transport and the like could be obtained from the Secretary, Rum Development Association. As a theme song, "Yo-Ho-Ho and a Week on Rum", had been adopted, and it was hoped that the B.B.C. might co-operate by playing, for instance, the opening bars of that immortal air before each Scottish News Bulletin throughout the week. And so on.

They chose the same week as Skye Week for more reasons than mere malice, and the fact that if Rum's crowds failed to materialize, alternative multitudes would be available for the film cameras not too far off. Quite a number of other matters they considered tentatively, also. As committees go, that one went to some purpose. And it went very largely on things called skedules. It was a term which became increasingly familiar to all concerned as time went on.

Joe caught Thursday morning's steamer for Mallaig, the railway, and the South, with the greatest of ease—no mishaps, no breakdowns, no delays; in fact, he had to wait for the *Lochgarve* which was twenty minutes late on its run-in from South Uist and Canna. On Alison's suggestion, he was going to break his journey to London at Glasgow, where a cousin of her father's in the coastal shipping business might be able to help him.

Though it was only seven o'clock, half the island was present at Kinloch jetty to see him off. Indeed a deputation accompanied him out in Jamie MacVarnish's boat to the steamer, and Jamie would not hear of a charge for the trip.

"Haste ye back," they told him. "And bring you the film-stars with you."

"Sure. All this is going to give the outfit a kick," he agreed. "Specially Mariota Marr."

Despite the fine excitement of the leap from the heaving open boat into the yawning aperture in the ship's side, Joe left Alison Maclean at least in a somewhat subdued mood.

.   .   .   .   .

There was little time or occasion, however, for moodiness or pensivity during the next few days on the Island of Rum, for Alison or for anyone else. The task before the community was Homeric. Nothing less than the transformation of the island was envisaged. There were forty-eight occupied houses on Rum, the majority of them croft-houses, many with turf roofs. But almost every one was scheduled to be turned into a show-house, a folk-museum, or a catering establishment. Since other materials and appliances were hard to come by at short notice in the Hebrides, this would have to be done largely by means of brightly painted notice-boards. Scarcely a house was to go without one, and some would rise to two. Hotels were the first priority, of course, and every house with a slate roof and some with corrugated-iron were set aside for this very necessary purpose, and their occupants instructed on the preparation of notice-boards. Kilmory House itself was to become The Rum Palace; Dibidil Lodge, The Grand Hebridean; the Catholic Presbytery, The Harris Central; and the Manse, very reluctantly, The Kinloch Temperance. Lesser establishments selected suitable characters, such as Seaview Family Hotel, Bayside Board Residence, and The Sunset Isle Guest House. Paint was no problem; during the war a ship, presumably heading for the naval base at Scapa Flow, had conveniently struck a skerry off the south-west coast of the island, and Rum had been almost overstocked with great drums of battleship-grey paint ever since. And pitch, such as was used for boat repairs, served perfectly well for black. Any lack of variety in the colour scheme was amply compensated for by striking individuality in nomenclature, spelling, design, and workmanship. The difficulty of finding suitable wood for the boards was overcome when somebody realized that the stern-pieces of old boats made admirable signs, hung up one way or another; whereafter sign-writing and decoration went on unabated—to such an extent as to seriously endanger the projected regatta.

Morag Ross was prevailed upon to give a course on hotel-keeping on alternate evenings at Kinloch and Harris, and undoubtedly made a considerable impression on the new entrants to the profession. Fortunately Catering Licences, like

73

many another mainland folly, were not to be considered.

The folk-museums, ceilidh-houses, and show-pieces generally were less urgent. There was time enough for these. The repair of the various jetties warranted a higher priority. It would be a pity if they were to have any accidents with folk not in the habit of using the faculties a merciful Creator had given them.

Alison, then, was busy—busy as she seldom had been in her life before. For besides superintending everywhere else, she had practically single-handed to convert Kilmory House, temporarily at least, into The Rum Palace Hotel—and she got no help from her grumbling father. And more than notice-boards were needed, for it was intended to quarter the hier-archy of the film-makers here. Considerable reorganization was required, then, with much putting up of beds, washing, polishing, and dusting. The General withdrew, disgruntled, to the extreme northern corner of the building, deciding that it was worse, far worse, than spring-cleaning—and as un-necessary.

Time by no means hung heavily.

Saturday's boat brought three days' newspapers. On the whole, the Press had reacted disappointingly to their spirited announcement of Rum Week. Only three papers had men-tioned the matter at all, and of these only one had given it any space or prominence. But this journal, *The Sentinel*, had risen to the occasion. Thus it dealt with the situation:

RUM CHALLENGE TO SKYE
SCANDAL, SAY MISTY ISLE SPOKESMEN

The Inner Hebridean Island of Rum, mountainy, off-the-beaten-track, announces the launching of Rum Week, in an attempt to capture some of the tourist trade that its larger neighbour Skye has so successfully built up by its Skye Weeks. Sponsors of this project, advisedly or otherwise, have chosen the first week in August, the same time as Skye Week, for their enterprise, a choice which has given rise to considerable comment on the larger island.

Said Colonel Lomax-Lincoln of Tornadamh, one of the

Skye Week Committee, by telephone to *The Sentinel*: "This is nothing short of a scandal. It is a deliberate attempt not only to cash-in on the success of Skye Week, but to sabotage our beneficial activities. Skye Week has done great things for the Western Highlands, and this impudent and provocative gesture from a backward and undeveloped island that is little better than a tract of barren and scowling rock, would be insufferable were it not so utterly laughable. Since coming to Skye from Bournemouth six years ago, I have heard nothing so ill-mannered and ridiculous."

Mr. Charlie Macdonald, Postmaster at Stravaig, and Deputy Convener, said: "This is a bad thing. But I do not think that Skye has much to be fearing. Skye has Bonnie Prince Charlie and Flora Macdonald. Never have I heard that either of them ever set foot on Rum."

The Sentinel understands that the matter will be brought up vigorously at the forthcoming meeting of Inverness-shire County Council.

There was no instruction as to enquiries to be directed at the Secretary, Rum Development Association. Only *The Courier* featured this, under three-line mention in District News.

Rum, needless to say, took no very grateful view of this journalistic reaction. The name of Colonel Lomax-Lincoln was noted and etched deep on long memories. Charlie Macdonald, whose Bonnie Prince Tea Rooms were well known, could be ignored. If there was some disappointment with the Press, there was no despondency, however. They would make the newspapers say more than this before they were finished.

On the following Thursday, by the peculiar means which telegrams took to reach Rum, by steamer via Mallaig and most of the Outer and Inner Hebrides, a wire arrived from London. It said:

HOPE ARRIVE FIRST INSTALMENT MONDAY OR TUESDAY S.S. AILSA STOP PRAY NOT RAINING JOE.

This fired the enthusiasm of all concerned—an enthusiasm scarcely a whit damped by the poor four letters that came by the same boat, and were all the response produced by their Press appeal for enquiries. One explained that an airfield was a prerequisite for any successful modern development and popularization scheme, and offered to build the necessary airfield for Rum quickly and at a thoroughly competitive figure. A second came from the R.L.S. Club of Market Harborough, protesting against the shameful mutilation and prostitution of Stevenson's glorious epic *Yo-Ho-Ho*, and threatening unspecified action should this disgraceful vandalism be proceeded with. The third came from the Catering Wages Board, North British Sub-Section, requiring full details, in triplicate, of all catering industry operators and/or employees, maximum working hours and Trade Union affiliations. The last was from the United Kingdom Temperance Alliance, suggesting that owing to its unfortunate connotation, the Rum Development Association should change its name, and preferably the name of the island, in deference to the overwhelming weight of public opinion against the trade in intoxicating liquors.

The Executive Committee of the Association considered this correspondence with due care and attention, and unanimously remitted all four questions to next year's Annual General Meeting.

In the meantime, there was work to be done.

6

LOOK-OUTS POSTED ON VANTAGE-POINTS AROUND the south coast of the island from first thing Monday morning watched eagerly for the s.s. *Ailsa*. Unfortunately their range of vision was limited to something like two hundred yards by a fine misty rain which caressed the place unremittingly throughout the day. Whether or not the ship was in the vicinity, or possibly had passed Rum in the mist, was any-body's guess. The fear that she might have gone past and wound up at Skye after all, by mistake, began to haunt Alison Maclean.

But during the night a gusty wind grew up, and Tuesday morning dawned to scudding clouds, hail showers, and visibility cold and clear. The watchers repaired to their eyries in better heart.

There were one or two false alarms, of course—a trawler or two working up from Oban, and a fishery-cruiser poking its grey nose into other folk's business. But Alison at least was not put off by such. These craft all proceeded northwards well out to sea, whereas Joel Macdonald, if he had any sense to him, would surely bring his vessel up closer in to the mainland, so as to ensure that the bulk of Rum blocked out of view the outline of Skye to the north. Otherwise those wretched Cuillins might well upset their plans. That was elementary.

It was early afternoon when Dougie the Post came bouncing down to Kinloch on his bicycle from high ground. Most of the island's population was gathered here. He brought word that smoke from a ship's funnel had been espied away south and a little west of Eigg, closer-in than usual, and coming up fairly fast. Sure enough, before long what appeared to be a smallish coasting steamer came into view between Muck and Eigg. Breathlessly the assembled Rumaich watched its course. Would it steam on northwards, or turn in towards them? A shout of triumph arose when clearly the high smoke-stack in the stern was seen to be swinging westwards—which meant that the bows were turning in directly towards Rum.

A considerable commotion followed, as last-minute preparations and finishing touches were made. Alison, Dougie, and Father Joseph hurried down to the jetty, where Hughie Bain had brought the *Kelpie* to reinforce Jamie MacVarish's craft, and Major Rory MacNeill sat in his Dibidil launch. Hughie and Jamie, each from his own boat, were having a lot of bother unrolling a double-poled banner made out of old tarpaulins, the gusty wind frustrating whatever they were trying to do with it. Alison, getting into the Major's launch, advised them to leave the thing furled in one boat until they got into position out in the loch. Father Joseph, who had a fine rich voice, relayed final instructions to all and sundry from MacVarish's boat, while Dougie jumped in beside Hughie. And amidst a notable heartening clamour of stuttering engines, shouted precepts, practising bagpipes, and screaming seagulls, the Reception Committee sailed out into the sea-loch.

Loch Scresort stretches inland for a mile and a half, with Kinloch at its head, and by the time that the motor-boats were half-way out, the ship was turning in at the mile-wide cliff-girt mouth. A succession of high sharp blasts on the siren proclaimed recognition and greeting. Hughie's and Jamie's boat throttled down and drew close together, to re-commence the tussle with the banner. The Dibidil launch shot ahead at gallant speed to meet the visitors.

The s.s. *Ailsa*, a long narrow coaster of mature years and rust-patched sides, feeling its way cautiously into these narrow waters, dropped speed to dead-slow to await pilotage. Major Rory swung in a wide arc round her, slapping up spray from the jabbly sea. Alison, standing up with one hand on the Major's shoulder, waved with the other—though she quite failed to pick out Joel Macdonald amongst the motley and highly colourful throng that lined the rails. A tribute of whistles, cat-calls, and pleasantries followed the motor-boat round on its circuit, till it took up its position a hundred yards ahead of the coaster, to lead her in to the anchorage.

And now, in their path, the other two boats were stationed, stern on, each supporting a pole, between which, heaving, dipping, and waving to the motion of the waters, was slung the improvised banner. Painted upon it in large letters in pitch was the legend "MILE FAILTE". WELCOME TO THE MISTY ISLE. And standing up in each boat, a piper blew lustily and in approximate harmony—Father Joseph and Dougie the Post.

The wording on that banner was the result of a compromise. The more forthright had wanted to word it WELCOME TO SKYE. But there were those who felt that this was too much—and moreover, that the Minister would never stand for it. It was one thing, they suggested, to give the general impression that

78

this was Skye, and quite another to say so in writing. The idea of using the phrase Misty Isle instead had been Father Joseph's; after all, Skye couldn't claim to have a copyright of the words, and their isle was quite as misty as Skye ever was. This had been accepted with acclaim—and so far the Minister had not made vocal protest.

As the launch and the *Ailsa* drew near, the two waiting boats revved up their engines and started forwards, landwards, side by side more or less, the banner reeling and lurching precariously between them, and the pipers, maintaining their stances by a sustained and magnificent effort, changed whatever they were rendering into the presently recognizable "Over the Sea to Skye". What it cost good Rumaichs to play this hated anthem of their rivals, can only be conjectured; undoubtedly here was the measure of their single-minded adherence to a worthy cause.

Actually, however, not a great deal of the deplorable and hackneyed tune survived to defile the Rum air, owing to the still more potent noise emanating from the s.s. *Ailsa*. This was occasioned by Joel Macdonald, now easily recognizable up on the ship's bridge beside the expressionless skipper, tugging with enthusiasm and unfailing regularity at the siren-cord. Yip-yip-yippee! Yip-yip-yippee! the siren ululated, blasting an incessant drumfire of echoes from all the enclosing hillsides.

In such fashion the North Atlantic Motion-Picture Corporation came to the Hebrides.

Some four hundred yards off-shore, no doubt to the very real relief of the *Ailsa's* captain if to the consternation of most of her passengers, Major MacNeill waved the ship to a stop, and with a rusty shriek and a splash the anchor ran out. Joe gave a final flourish on the siren, and then came running down the bridge-ladder. The pipers in the two motor-boats relinquished their task to other instrumentalists on the shore, and their craft, along with the Dibidil launch, moved in alongside the coaster. Sundry other rowing-boats and small fry put out from the beach. A tentative raindrop or two fell.

Alison, from the launch, looked up. "Hullo, Joe!" she said. "Good work."

From the rail, the Texan grinned down at her. "Hiyah, Toots. How's Skye?"

"Oh, fine. Splendid. Been having a bit of a drought, but . . ." Her voice tailed away. On either side of Joe had appeared the head and shoulders of a spectacular companion. On the right, the large parchment-hued, curiously flat, almost dead-seeming face of a big man dressed in what at first sight looked like a double suit of pyjamas but which resolved itself into a tussore yellow jacket over a lavender silk shirt with an open tartan collar. He had hooded, heavy-lidded, expressionless eyes and a thin-lipped slit of a mouth. But a strikingly mobile and active slit; it was never still, twisting, writhing, contorting, as though made of rubber, what time it transferred the stump of a cigar from one side to the other and back again with fascinating expertness. And on the left, a vision of assured and flawless loveliness, virginal in white sharkskin with crimson trimmings, a tawny-haired, green-eyed, honey-complexioned, scarlet-mouthed and ivory-toothed twentieth-century goddess, chewing gum.

Unutterably silent, indeed with her mouth slightly open, Alison Maclean stared.

"Say—how d'we get outa this?" the big man jerked, from out of the unoccupied corner of his mouth. The cigar leapt, apparently of its own volition, to this side. "Breeches-buoy, or sump'n?"

"Just over the side and down the ladder into the boats," Joe explained. "Nothing to it. Too shallow to take the ship closer in—same like all these islands."

"My God!" the goddess cried, "Not down *there*! A *ladder*! I'll die, first."

"No, you won't, sister. No such luck!" the cigar-man snapped. "Anyway—the best bits of you are insured, ain't they? And your neck's unbreakable!"

"Shurrup!" the lady said, but conversationally. "Look—stunt men get a hundred bucks a day for doing less than this!"

"And how many bucks do you get, for sitting on your fat fanny and doing goddam-all?" And the cigar thrust forward at her aggressively on an outflung lower lip.

Alison withdrew her all-but-hypnotized gaze, and her eyes met Father Joseph's in the next boat.

"Och, the man's nothing but an ogre!" the priest said, low-voiced and shaking his bare head.

"By Jove, yes," Major Rory agreed fervently.

Unreasonably, Alison frowned at both of them.

The big man had now swung on Joel Macdonald. "See here, Joe," he rasped, "I ain't kicking about the darn personnel. They can swim for it if they like. It's the gear—the props and the apparatus and the cars. We got tons of it. They got no better landings than this, on this Skye?"

"It's the best on the whole island," the younger man assured. "But don't you worry, Hank—the skipper and the locals'll fix that, with derricks and a sorta raft they've got. Like they get their own heavy stuff ashore from the mail-steamer. It's okay. And don't you worry either, Sweetheart —I'm taking you down in my own two arms, see. You'll love it!"

"Well, that's different, I guess, Joey," the goddess acknowledged. "Do I disrobe for this act, or do we just go down like we are?"

"I say—are you people coming down, or do you want us to come back to-morrow?" That was Alison Maclean, and surprisingly frosty.

"Okay, okay—here we go," Joe called down, and threw a leg over the rail on to the first rung of the ladder. "Come on, Beautiful."

The lady, lifting her sheath-like white skirt high and hand-somely out of harm's way, gracefully slung one long and shapely limb up on to the rail, and there let it rest awhile, in practically all its sheer and arresting excellence.

Down below, Father Joseph, the Major and Dougie hastily looked away and away—though with varying degree of haste. On board, there was little discernible reaction, save from the man Hank.

"Wrap it up, willya?" he requested heavily. "The cameras ain't unpacked yet!"

Joel Macdonald leaned over and put an arm around the statuesque lady's waist, and with a thoroughly efficient if notably artistic composite movement, she was over that rail and clinging snugly to him, her arms wound round his neck, her legs arranged to best advantage—and not a hair out of place. Here was no beautiful doll, but a cool, agile, and highly competent performer, fully as expert with her person as the Hank character was with his cigar. Cheek by jowl and with great effect, they descended to the waiting launch.

"Meet Mariota Marr," Joe announced, and there was not enough breathlessness to hide a certain pride in his voice. He guided his charge to the best seat in the boat—and almost bumped his head against Major MacNeill's as they both dusted the thwart for her to sit down.

"It's a fine afternoon for the time of the year, ma'am," Father Joseph's voice boomed from the next boat. "The pity we haven't got a proper pier for you."

Alison turned her back on the lot of them.

The big man came down next, with a minimum of fuss once he came to the bit, and after him half a dozen others, all male but exotically clad. Certainly that launch had never carried so colourful a cargo. When she was full, the Major swung her away, making room for other ferries. Alison found the man Hank beside her.

"So this is Skye?" he accused.

"Well . . . not exactly," she faltered. "I mean—this is Loch Scresort, and that's Kinloch. . . ."

"Sure, sure. Look—is it gonna rain?"

"Oh, I shouldn't think so. Though, of course, we *need* rain. . . ."

"Hell—you nuts?" the man almost snarled, and after a ferocious glare, turned a tussore shoulder on her. "Joe—this dame says we need rain!"

"Eh . . . ? Oh, I guess she means it's been sorta dry—for the crops, y'know, Hank. Say—I reckon I should have introduced you two. Miss Alison Maclean. Pronounced Lane not Lean, see—they're kinda hot about that. Her dad, the General, owns half this island. That's the General at the jetty there—with the bottle. And this, Toots, is Hank Delmonte . . . with the accent on the monte, see!" Joe's introduction finished on that slightly heightened note of anticipation that is heard after the identification of the truly great.

Perhaps Alison rather failed him. The fact was, she was just a little bit preoccupied with the honey-pot sitting in the stern-sheets and being buzzed around by every man in the crowded launch—except this Hank individual. Again, Rum not being on any cinema circuit, she was not as fully conversant with film notabilities as undoubtedly she ought to have been. She merely said "Oh", and with no sort of exclamation-mark behind it.

Mr. Delmonte, however, noting her lapse, did not let anybody down. "Delmonte," he enunciated sharply, unmistakably. "Number One Director, motion-picture industry." And he nodded the head under his wide-brimmed Stetson crisply.

There was a murmur of approval and substantiation from his company.

"Oh!" Alison said again—but the exclamation-mark was suitably in place this time.

The launch came alongside the jetty, and a surge of islanders moved down to assist the visitors to land. Hank Delmonte turned to Major MacNeill. "How much?" he demanded.

"Eh? Oh . . . ah . . . ummm." Rory's pink face turned a rosy red. "Nothing. Of course. A pleasure, sir."

"Say—be your age, man!" the other growled. "Here's a coupla bucks. Buy yourself a coke, some place." And he thrust a pound-note at the alarmed Major.

"Oh, I say—no. Not at all. I couldn't . . ."

"Rory—take it!" Alison muttered, *sotto voce*. "Remember the dollar drain."

And miserably the Laird of Dibidil accepted the Treasury-note, between finger and thumb as though it might bite him, the first martyr in the cause of Rum.

The General, especially arrayed in his kilt, and with a tray on which stood a bottle and sundry glasses, was the first to greet them—a reception obviously to the taste of the travellers, the lady in white not excepted—even though the suitable things said in Gaelic and English were lost to them through the enthusiastic efforts of the half-dozen pipers who blew at their ears. The Minister thereafter stepped forward and intoned a speech of welcome, but this also was inaudible—no doubt fortuitously but possibly fortunately, since he could not be trusted altogether to give the right impression as to the island's identity.

By this time the other boats were landing their loads—and Alison at least was astonished to see the numbers of people disembarking. Between thirty and forty she assessed them at, and there appeared to be one or two more to come. They seemed to form distinct groups, that did not mingle—and some looked considerably more formal than others.

Her father, Rory MacNeill, and Father Joseph now making the usual pathetic fuss over Mariota Marr, Alison was able to get a word with Joe Macdonald, a yard or two away from the musicians—and a frigid word it was.

"If you can spare a *moment's* attention from your heavy responsibilities?" she said. "How many of your friends have we to accommodate altogether? Have any of them any suspicions about Skye? And what about the ship's company—*they'll* know where they are?"

"Sure—but I got that fixed before we left Glasgow. They're keeping their mouths shut. And the others reckon Skye's the only island on this coast, anyhow!"

"Indeed!"

"Yeah. And there's forty-four of an outfit. But, say, Allie—anything eating you? You not feeling so good, or something?"

"I'm feeling perfectly well, thank you. My preoccupations are just a little different from yours! And my name is Alison . . . or Ailie, to my *friends*!" Her serenity of expression was not all that she meant it to be. "Now—if you will collect the dozen of your—er—associates whom you consider most important, we'll make a start for Kilmory. Father Joseph will look after the others, and Jamie MacVarish will see to the luggage."

"Yes, ma'am," Joe said, and tipped his brow with chastened finger.

.   .   .   .   .

Two of the island's few cars, the General's and the Nurse's, were detailed for the Kilmory party, with Dougie and another motor-cyclist as reinforcement. Amid a certain amount of comment, Miss Marr, Mr. Delmonte, and some of their closer associates were prevailed upon to wedge themselves into the vehicles, a brisk shower of rain assisting. Firmly Alison transferred Joel from his ravishing fellow-traveller's side to the back of Dougie's motor-bike. Herself riding pillion on the other, the procession started off.

It was not the sort of run for sight-seeing, seat-retaining demanding priority. For all that, intriguing indications were discernible for the observant in the frequent sign-posts and notice-boards. At one point where a winding cattle track moved off into the bog-myrtle, a boldly lettered legend proclaimed, LOCH CORUISK VIA ELGOL, 15 MILES. It was, too—mainly by boat, of course. Another read: TO FLORA MACDONALD'S VIEW, THE BLOODY STONE, and MACLEOD'S DOOM—imaginative admittedly, but who could assert imaginary? Rum was full of bloody stones, views on which Flora must have rested her eyes, even at a distance, and spots where wretched invading Macleods must have met their well-merited ends. A third said simply: TO THE CUILLIN MOUNTAINS—and the direction was dead right.

Joe Macdonald perceived that he was not the only one who had been busy.

Lurching and rattling down Kilmory Glen past finger-posts and placards intimating the perhaps surprising existence of craft-centres, guest-houses, and folk-museums amongst the heather and outcropping rock, the cavalcade was brought to a temporary halt at the Kilmory House road-end, where a galaxy of signs pointed out the Palace Hotel on the left— the Rum having been carefully deleted meantime—various enticingly named establishments down by the shore in front, and The Beehive Inn to the right. Towards this latter hostelry —proprietor, Morag Ross—Alison pointed authoritatively.

"This is where we drop *you*, Mr. Macdonald," she announced. "You'll find your old room awaiting you."

"But, say . . . !" The rest of Joe's protest was lost in the suddenly accelerated roaring of Dougie's engine.

A lull permitted the girl to continue. "It's all arranged—for maximum convenience." She was not going to have Joe and this Mariota Marr living under the same roof if she could help it. "And Morag would be most disappointed if you went anywhere else."

"But, look—I got to be near Hank. We got to discuss things, see. . . ." More internal combustion from the engine.

"You're within three minutes . . . I say you're within three minutes' walk of him. Besides, Morag's got the ladder repaired for you! " She gestured to Dougie, and the bicycle bucked forward into Morag's pathway. After it, she flung a minor concession. "We'll be eating in about an hour. You'd better come over then—I don't suppose Morag's at home."

And she led her two car loads on to the House, making a hasty reallocation of rooms, so that Miss Marr might not be enervated by any sybaritic luxury. She also took a mental note to be particularly nice to this Hank Delmonte, who, not only obviously was the boss, but who, despite a certain hardness of exterior, no doubt was lonely on his throne.

Kilmory House took its metamorphosis into the Palace Hotel in its stride and with quite remarkable equilibrium—and surprisingly, General Hector Maclean blossomed out as an even better host than did his daughter. The guests were prepared to find Skye cute; no one on Rum allowed them to be disappointed.

.   .   .   .   .

It took a little while for Rum to grasp all the ramifications and departments of the film-makers' entourage, their significance and intricacies. For the first day or two all the visitors were treated as stars, or at least name-part actors. But it transpired in time that, in fact, only nine out of the forty-four were players of any sort and, of these, eight were treated with studied disrespect by the rest of the company—though amongst themselves certainly they spoke knowledgeably and continually of their close relations with Larry Olivier and Ty Power and other immortals. It seemed that the hero, who was to play the part of the reincarnated Prince Charlie—an

86

Englishman, in deference to national sentiment—had not yet arrived from the Riviera where he was completing the lead in an epic of the South Seas; Joe was to meet him at Mallaig with a motor-boat in a week's time. It was revealed also that Mariota Marr, who was Flora Macdonald's modern counterpart, was Cockney-born herself—though she had made the most of her years in Hollywood. Nathan Greenbaum, the Casting Director of North Atlantic Pictures, always made a point of having his nationalities right, where possible.

The thirty-five other members of the company were a strangely assorted and curiously entitled throng, laterally divided very distinctly in importance as in country of origin; an American hierarchy and a London technocracy. Over all was Hank Delmonte, as Director, with Joel as his Associate. His other lieutenants were the Directors of Casting and Photography, the Production-secretary and the Continuity-girl. There was a shadowy figure called the Associate Producer, and a depressed Script-writer who, it seemed, was also the author— though he barely qualified as one of the hierarchy. These all spoke with the accents of authority and the States. Below this rigid line, the accents of Shepherd's Bush, Mile End, and Tottenham Court predominated—though the nomenclature might as easily have derived from Timbuctoo. There was Clapper-boy and Master Prop, Camera-grip, Operator, and Focus-puller, Wardrobe, Make-up, and Drapes, each with his assistant. There were the less inspiredly designated Electricians, Carpenters, Painters, Plasterers, Riggers and Hairdressers. Each apparently had a specific task to perform, which no one else could or would do. The Unions saw to that. Patently, film-making was an exacting and expensive business.

This became more clear to the ignorant inhabitants of Rum as time went on—even if the full departmentalization did not. It was not conducted on any of the usual hackneyed commercial principles. Everybody seemed to be extremely busy, not to say preoccupied, and seldom moved at anything less than a run—yet for the great proportion of the time the great proportion of the company did absolutely nothing at all. There was something delightfully akin to the Highland character in this, though it took a little while for the Hebrideans to perceive it. Time seemed to be assessed on an entirely different basis from that of most business undertakings. Hours, even days, were unimportant—but seconds were vital. Sequence was no more relevant than chronology. The film was half made before they began; indeed, it was finished before any foot was set in Scotland—all the indoor scenes having been shot in Hollywood. All that remained to be done here were such out-of-door sequences as required a background such as Messrs. Master Prop, Plasterer, Painter, and Drapes could not conveniently fabricate. That, and certain actual encounters between the hero and heroine, who had not actually met as yet. And the title, of course, which was still the subject of argument. It appeared that though the entire action of the saga was supposed to take place somewhere in the Scottish Highlands, something less than ten minutes' actual running time required to be shot here. The uses of the Continuity-girl became evident—also, why she earned in the region of £50 per week.

The very ordinary, dull, not to say humdrum folk of Rum could only marvel and make respectful noises.

Curiously enough, though it would be a mistake to suggest that everything went like clockwork and according to plan, nevertheless much that Alison Maclean and her colleagues had feared faded away harmlessly like snow in summer. Wednesday morning, for instance, dawned bright and sunny, with a chill breeze and white-capped waves, but ideal weather for film-making—even though no film-making was attempted. It was raining again by mid-afternoon, admittedly, but that was neither here nor there. Again, none of the cinematographers seemed in the least suspicious on the subject of Skye, or indeed interested. In fact, when in the clear atmosphere the challenging serrated outline of the Black Cuillins of Skye reared into view for the first time across the twelve miles of the Sound, no questions were asked, no comments made. Perhaps not all having roots in the place, like Joel Macdonald, the company as a whole was not greatly exercised about Skye as such. A really Scotch and cutely Hebridean location was what they were concerned with, and here they had it, without stint. Rum was Hebridean enough for anybody—and actually considerably more Scotch than usual, in their honour. There were no complaints on that score.

Except for the kilts, that is. This was an alternative and unexpected, if lesser, trouble that materialized. Hank Delmonte was disappointed about the lack of kilts to be seen— and when Hank was disappointed, people knew about it. Hank had expected to find kilts worn by the inhabitants, the picture called for kilts, and kilts there must be. Since naturally enough, the only kilts on Rum were the two lairds', a first-class crisis developed straight away. Alison's own tartan skirt, though something, was too long for Hank; he ordered three inches off the bottom forthwith, and the girl, sighing, acceded as a placatory gesture. But this was a mere drop in the bucket. There were numerous old plaids on the island, of course, used as shawls for elderly ladies and extra blanketing, and these were collected, cut down the middle, and wrapped around the shrinking persons of various unhappy crofters and fishermen—none of whom had known bare knees since childhood. But Hank declared that these were inadequate, both in style and numbers. Something further had to be done. The Executive Committee devolved the problem on Major MacNeill, who was given *carte blanche*—but no funds—to deal with it, promptly.

Another unforeseen complication was the shortage of castles. Apparently since Joe had left London on his northern scouting-tour, a castle had been introduced to bulk largely in the screen-play. This was a refinement of the Director's own—and he was not going to be baulked of it. It was a well-known fact that Scotland was literally strewn with castles—and yet here was this island without a single specimen. Hadn't there been some place where there was a dame that had a fairy flag or something? Dangevan, or something . . . ?

Headed hurriedly off this dangerous ground by the assurance that that was on another island altogether, far away, Mr. Delmonte gave orders that a castle must be built, right away. The Properties Department accordingly got busy, and with quite surprising virtuosity as well as industry produced out of aluminium scaffolding, canvas, plaster and paint, an imposing fortified pile that would have gladdened the heart of any desert-bound Legionnaire who would have sworn it no mirage but the real thing. Only a couple of date-palms were lacking.

But despite all this exhilarating overcoming of difficulties, Alison Maclean at least found the first few days of the cinematic invasion a trial and a harassment—and not wholly on account of the endowments of Mariota Marr. It was the weather that did it—wonderful, phenomenal weather, with the sun shining sometimes for as much as three hours in the day. And yet, no film whirred through the cameras. No shots were taken. The Camera-grip and the Focus-puller went idle. Endless conferences were held—largely in monologue—people were sent scurrying hither and thither, apparatus was moved with much labour over the island's difficult tracks. The castle rose apace. The sun shone. But no pictures resulted. It was enough to send anyone distracted.

The fact that the longer the delay, the longer the film-makers might be expected to stay on Rum, the more money they would spend on the island, and consequently the better were the Rum Development Association's objectives achieved, did not register as strongly as might have been expected. As a development promoter any inadequacy Alison had was probably in commercial acumen.

7

THERE WAS NO DOUBT THAT THERE HAD DEVELOPED a certain coolness, not to call it an estrangement, between the Associate Director of North Atlantic Pictures and the Hon. Secretary of the Rum Development Association, out of causes unknown. The Executive Committee of the latter body, especially, were aware of it, and shook foreboding heads over the situation—except for Major Rory MacNeill, that is, who

bore up with true military fortitude; besides, he was somewhat preoccupied with kilts. What to do about it was not
readily discernible, but obviously something was required, or
much that they were working for might be prejudiced.
Father Joseph, a man of initiative and vigour, had thought
over two or three tentative schemes that at least were bound
to have a rousing effect on all concerned, when the matter
providentially was taken right out of his hands. A visitor
was responsible.

The word came to the Rum Palace post-haste by Dougie
from Saturday's mail-steamer. A passenger had disembarked
from the *Lochgarve*, wearing plus-fours and a deer-stalker
hat, giving the name of Smith, and making enquiries about
Rum Week.

In the initial flush of enthusiasm over this, the first-fruits
of their propaganda campaign, Dougie's further tidings tended
to go unheeded. But presently it was revealed that the
traveller had a cold eye—which possibly accounted for his
monocle—and moreover had been overheard by Jamie Mac-
Varish tell the *Lochgarve's* mate that he would be picked up
by the boat again on its Monday afternoon's call. So he
wasn't going to stay long. Altogether, Jamie didn't like the
looks of him.

This being the way of it, there was nothing for it but for
Alison Maclean to go pillion over to Kinloch forthwith to
investigate.

They ran the visitor to earth eventually upon open hillside above the loch, where they found him sitting on an outcrop systematically quartering the entire area through a
pair of field-glasses. So intent was he on this exercise that
he quite failed to note their approach until they were almost
upon him, whereupon he dropped his glasses hastily, coughed,
half-rose and then sat down again, and finally fishing out his
monocle, eyed them through it with a distinctly challenging
stare. "Ha!" he said.

"Good evening," Alison greeted pleasantly. "Are you
enjoying your visit to Rum?"

"Ah. Mmm. I'm afraid it is too early to say much,"
the other returned. He was a thin elderly rat-trap-jawed man

in the indubitable leather-bound gun-club checks of the gentry. Rum had landed no minnow at its first cast.

"Are you interested in scenery?"

"Scenery . . . ? No, young woman—I'm not. Why?"

"Oh . . . nothing. But something must have brought you here. . . ."

"Am I being cross-examined, pray?"

"Oh, no. No—I'm sorry."

"Och, Jamie MacVarish was right enough, just," Dougie observed.

"See here." The gentleman cleared a peremptory throat. "This Rum Week affair, that I read about in the Press. Is there anything in it? Eh?"

"In it? Why, yes—of course. Naturally." It was Alison's turn to clear her throat. "That week, Rum is At Home to the world! We open our doors and our hearts . . ."

"Yes, yes—I read all that. But, your programme? Are you really arranging any special—er—attractions, for instance?"

"Oh, definitely. Highland Games, ceilidhs, a regatta, shinty-matches. . . ."

"And where is the—ah—personnel coming from, pray?"

"The personnel is—is entirely adequate," the girl asserted, a trifle shortly.

"Indeed. This regatta, now—how many boats are you able to muster, on Rum? Are there any yachts . . . ?"

Alison looked from Dougie to the cloud gracing Askival's noble brow. "Was that a drop of rain, Dougie?" she asked, earnestly. "It would be a pity to get caught in the wet."

"It's right you are, Miss Ailie—my Chove," her escort agreed. "We'll away down just, before it comes on. It's a terrible nuisance, the rain."

"And accommodation," the visitor persisted. "I fail to see how you can possibly set out to accommodate any number of sightseers—at least, in quarters acceptable to even third-class tourists . . . ?"

"You are quite wrong, sir. We have no fewer than eleven hotels, seventeen guest—and boarding—houses, and . . ."

"Humph! I've seen some of 'em! Even the place I've

put up in myself, calling itself the Kinloch Temperance Hotel, turns out to be only the Manse. It hasn't even got proper sanitation, much less electric light. I can't . . ."

"My goodness—there's another drop of that rain! We'll be soaked," Dougie cried, grasping Alison's arm. "Come you."

"Yes. That's right. Good-bye," the girl said, over her shoulder. "Sorry we must hurry away."

"Damn it—it's not raining! I've not felt a drop. Hardly a cloud in the sky. . . ." The visitor still was protesting as they hurried downhill.

"Mercy on us all—a Government Inspector if ever I saw one!" Dougie gasped. "He'll be from the Income Tax, likely. Did you ever hear the like of that? A right busy-body—my Chove, we'll have to get rid of *him*!"

"A perfect horror," the young woman agreed. "But I don't think it would be the Income Tax somehow. He might be something to do with this Catering Wages Act. . . ."

"Och, it's the Income Tax—I could see it in his eye," Dougie asseverated. "Lucky we were to get away before he had the shirts off us . . . if you know what I mean, Miss Ailie. Goodness—the questions he was after asking!"

"Yes. And if he asks them of us, he'll ask everybody. And he's staying at the Manse! You know what the Minister is —goodness knows what he'll let out!"

"Och, the Minister's a fine man, just fine," Dougie averred loyally, as the youngest elder. "Just a wee thing soft maybe —nothing more. And him from the mainland. Maybe we should be having a bit word with him?"

"I think that would be wise, yes."

So, recovering the motor-bike, they hurtled down to Kinloch again, and up to the Manse door. They found the Minister laying the substantial foundations of Sunday's sermon, and not over-anxious for social chit-chat. He was not over-happy about his guest, either. Not that he had anything against the man himself, he hastened to point out—but he wasn't all that keen on having guests at all. He had hoped that the Temperance in his hotel's title might have kept them away. . . .

Dougie's revelations as to the true character of his visitor shocked him, naturally, but he was unable to give them any further information on his own. He had been busy with his sermon—hadn't had time for talking with the man. . . .

Just as well pleased at that, Alison proceeded to give him some good advice, while Dougie excused himself to go and have a word with Tina the housekeeper, who was his own mother's sister.

He was back inside five minutes, almost dancing with excitement. "My goodness me—listen to this!" he cried. "That's not the Income Tax, my Chove, at all! It's a boy from Skye—Colonel Somebody-Lincoln, from Tornadamh!"

"Lincoln? From Skye? Colonel Lomax-Lincoln? Heavens—that's the man who said those disgraceful things in the papers!" Alison exclaimed. "He's a scoundrel!"

"He is so. He's here to spy out the land, just. A snake in the grass, nothing more."

"Of course. That's what all the questions were for. Good gracious—it's that Skye trying to put a spoke in our wheel, that's what it is! You're sure that's who it is, Dougie?"

"Sure I am indeed. Aren't there three opened letters addressed to himself in the pocket of his raincoat in his room upstairs there!"

"Dear, dear—you shouldn't have done that, Dougal," the Minister said, grey head ashake. "Not into his pockets. Reading letters."

The younger man drew himself up. "Amn't I the Post?" he asked, with simple dignity. "Her Majesty's mail could be getting into wrong hands, whatever. Here's this one calling himself Smith. . . ."

"Dearie me—it's all most deplorable."

"It's worse than that. It could be serious," the girl declared. "If he finds out about these cinema-people. The film-company was expected to go to Skye. He'd go straight to Hank Delmonte and tell him, if I know the style of him."

"There you are!" the Minister sighed. "The result of deception. I said no good would come of it. . . ."

"He couldn't know already, could he?" Alison interrupted. "And that's why he's come? There's nothing in these letters, Dougie?"

94

"Not a thing. One's nothing but a bill just. And the other's from his brother, who seems to be some sort of a bishop in England, and is for coming up for Skye Week. . . ."

"A bishop, is it!" the Minister cried, transformed. "That settles it. We'll have no bishops' kin poking their long noses into Rum business! We will not. The insolence of these people!"

"Quite," Alison acceded. "Well—the main thing is that he mustn't be given any information, especially about the film-company. It's nearly nine-thirty now, so he should be in soon. I'd go to bed, if I were you—then he won't be able to question you. You can finish your sermon there. And we'll tell Tina not to say a word."

"But, to-morrow . . . ?"

"We'll see about to-morrow when to-morrow comes," the young woman said oracularly. "Come along, Dougie—we've work to do."

"Just what I was thinking my own self, my goodness."

.   .   .   .   .

The Executive met in urgent session, and wasted no time on preliminaries—nor even on the story-telling. That action was required was self-evident; the only question was how drastic was to be the action.

"He must be circumvented," Father Joseph declared, positively.

"Hear, hear!" Rory MacNeill agreed.

"Och, more than that—he must be stopped," Dougie amended.

"Yes. But how?" That was Alison.

There was a moment's silence.

"We could sort of be sending him to, to Coventry . . . isn't that the place?" Dougie suggested. "Nobody be speaking to him, at all."

"An un-Christian thing that," the priest objected. "I'd sooner see him knocked on the head."

"Anyway, that wouldn't stop him using his eyes, Dougie," Alison pointed out. "He still could see the film-makers."

"I wonder if the man drinks, at all?" Father Joseph said.

"You mean . . . ? Oh, that would be a doubtful business, wouldn't it? A bit of a hit or a miss."

"Could lock him up. At Dibidil. Got some pretty fair cellars," the Major jerked, almost apologetically. "Be a pleasure, Alse."

"That's nice of you, Rory . . . but we couldn't keep him there indefinitely," the girl put to them. "We don't know how long the film people will be with us." And she looked at Joe Macdonald for the first time that evening.

Thus appealed to, the Texan shrugged. "Can't rightly say. Depends on a lot of things. But I thought you were sorta keen for us to stay a while? I kinda reckoned that was the idea. . . ."

"Quite. So it is, of course. Have I said anything to the contrary, Mr. Macdonald?"

"Well . . . maybe not. Just a notion I got."

"This Colonel Lincoln . . ." Father Joseph reverted tactfully to the subject under discussion.

"Yes. What will we do?"

Joe examined his finger-nails. "Where I come from," he mentioned, "if a guy gets into the country that we don't want, we deport him."

"Deport! Ah!"

"My Chove!"

"You mean . . . send him back to Skye?"

"Sure. If you got no use for this guy, wrap him up and return him."

"But if he won't go . . . ?"

"Don't ask him. Pick him up at night, put him into a motor-boat, and run him back home to Skye. Nothing to it."

Neither there was, when they came to think of it. Only, what about repercussions?

The chances were there wouldn't be any, Joe claimed. The guy wouldn't be likely to make a fuss, afterwards—he'd look too big a fool back home in Skye. He was here under a false name, wasn't he? What could he do? And if he did squeal, think of the publicity for Rum Week! It was a cinch!

Enthralled by the simplicity of it all, the Executive members looked at each other. It was only a question now of who was to do it, and when.

"To-morrow is the Sabbath," Dougie pointed out, thoughtfully.

"Give me a boat—a boat that goes, see—and I'll do it. To-night," Joe assured.

And that was an offer that no Development Association could afford to refuse. The meeting broke up, Alison to rout Hughie Bain out of his bed and get his *Kelpie* sailed round to Loch Scresort, Dougie and Joel Macdonald to motor-cycle to Kinloch with a call at the film unit's Props store *en route*.

.   .   .   .   .

At the dark back of the Manse, the conspirators paused. It was after eleven, and raining slightly—a satisfactorily dark night for deportations. Both young men wore hats pulled well down and had scarves tied over the lower portions of their faces. Joe knew the entire procedure through having directed a similar operation in his second last film.

"Wait you here a wee, till I have a bit word with my Auntie Tina," Dougie advised. "We wouldn't want her skirling on us."

"The door? Won't it be locked?"

"Och, what would there be to lock up in a manse, at all?"

In a few minutes Dougie was back, hissing between his teeth from the black pit of the doorway. Joe followed him into a passage and along a dark corridor, holding the other's coat-tails and putting down careful feet.

Dougie stopped. "We're at the foot of the stairs, just," he breathed. "Tina says the fourth and seventh steps creak —so watch you."

Climbing the treads right against the wall, one at a time, they crept up, counting. One step that was neither fourth nor seventh creaked wickedly—and immediately thereafter Joe's long person brushed against a picture hanging on the stair-wali, that slithered but fortunately did not fall. Frozen still they stood for a little, and then moved on.

Before they reached the landing a high-powered snoring was delighting their ears. But when Dougie passed the door from which it emanated, it was to shake his head and whisper, "The Minister." They edged on past two more doors, and then halted, listening, beside a third. No sound issued to compete with that from the other room.

Dougie sighed. "Och, mercy—who's to know if the man's asleep or not? "

"Where's the bed? " Joe murmured, through his scarf.

"To the right."

"Nobody else in the house? "

"Not a one."

"Okay. Come in right behind me, and shut the door. Got your rope handy? "

"Yes."

Joe stepped in front, tested the handle carefully, and then pressing it down, turned and pushed open the door in one swift movement. In four strides he was at the bed, seen dimly against the blue glimmer from the window. Whether the figure thereon stirred or not, he did not know. Throwing himself bodily across the pillows, he clamped himself down— and the unfortunate occupant's head and shoulders with him. A muffled gasping and groaning came from beneath his middle and a certain convulsive threshing of legs under the blankets —but nothing to disturb even the lightest sleeper in another room. Dougie, with the door shut behind him, came up burbling.

"You got him? Man, man—isn't this just great! " he observed. "As good as the films, whatever."

"Get your rope round his legs," Joe directed, heaving about a little on top of subterranean struggles. "Wrap him up, pronto."

A certain general entanglement followed, as tossing bed-clothes, waving legs, coiling rope and Dougie enmeshed themselves in the darkness. But there was plenty of time, with both respiration and gravity on the side of the upper layer, and presently with the undulation reduced to a mere spas-

98

modic jerking, the Texan was able to insert a pillow under him where he felt the hard bump of a head, and thereafter, keeping it well pressed down, to resume the upright, with everything under control.

Dougie replacing him at this stance, Joe delved into his pocket and produced a wide roll of surgeon's plaster. Muttering imprecations over the inadequacy of finger-nails—though he had carefully turned a flap over beforehand—he got a strip unstuck eventually, and advanced on the bed again. "Get your hand under the pillow and over his mouth," he ordered. "And, say—don't let him bite you."

"My goodness—and how am I to be stopping him, then?" the accomplice demanded, in alarm. "Och, mercy—this is as bad as at the lobsters. . . ." Gingerly he inserted a groping hand under the pillow.

"Make it snappy!" he was urged. And then, "Damnation!" That was the surgeon's plaster at its accustomed tricks.

Then a crow of real gratification came from Dougie. "Man—it's fine and grand!" he reported. "There's devil the tooth in it! False ones they must go in for, in Skye."

"Okay. Turn him over. Now, where's that mouth . . . and your hand?"

More by intuition than by either sight or feel Joe managed to slap at least some proportion of the adhesive tape across a thin-lipped protesting mouth and clipped military moustache—though Dougie objected that his hand was partially included. Only a muted moan or two escaped from the hotel-guest—who, no doubt, was missing his dentures.

"Then get your great paw outa the way and let me get a second piece on," his colleague requested. "If only this stuff wasn't so goldurned sticky . . . ! Now—up with him."

Grabbing the pillow, Joe removed the slip and proceeded to draw this over the head and shoulders of their victim, Dougie's extremities once again tending to get in the road. Pulled well down, this had an excellent effect on the prisoner, and the rope which Joe went on to transfer from his own middle to pinion the other's arms, scarcely was necessary.

99

Letting the object of their attentions flop over on the bed, the two young men stood back a little, to admire their handiwork by the light of Joe's little electric torch.

"Is that not just a treat?" Dougie demanded. "Och, you could send him Registered Post that way, and no trouble at all. We'll away, then."

"Just a minute. There's his clothes—yeah, and his teeth. We got to collect them. Where's his bag . . . ?"

Their packing perhaps was less efficient than their captive's, for by dint of no pushing and prodding could they get all his belongings encased. But fortunately there was a second pillow on the bed, whose case made an admirable kit-bag. After a hasty inspection of the room, there remained only the setting up of a somewhat crumpled note on the dressing-table, which read: "Forced to return to Skye on urgent business. Regret any inconvenience caused. J. SMITH." Pinned thereto was one of Joel Macdonald's useful pound-notes.

All completed, the Texan slung the trussed martyr across his shoulder—fortunately, though knobbly, there was little real weight to him—while Dougie took charge of the baggage, and led the way.

Going downstairs, every step creaked—but the snoring from the Minister's room remained constant. Dougie had a reassuring word with his auntie, and they were out into the night. The rain was heavier now, so the raincoat was fished out of the pillow-case and draped approximately over their grunting burden, who turned out to be a devotee of the old-fashioned nightshirt.

Getting balanced on the carrier of Dougie's bike, with their appendage, was quite a feat, but with the body wedged between them they were able to coast downhill from the Manse to the shore without a spill at any rate—and, what perhaps was more important, without waking up the neighbourhood by having to engage the engine. Down at the jetty they disposed themselves to wait—for, of course, the *Kelpie* couldn't possibly be there yet, with a ten-mile voyage round the north of the island to negotiate. A smoke seemed to be indicated, with contemplation. Humane men both, they regretted that they could not offer a like solace to their guest—but that would have entailed a general unsealing, and unpredictable complications. Better to let him lie in peace.

They had almost half an hour to wait before they heard the throb of the motor-boat coming up the loch, and Joe flashed his torch once or twice to guide it in. Throttled back, so that the engine was no more than ticking over, Hughie brought his craft quietly alongside the jetty.

"Everything in order?" a girl's voice queried anxiously, out of the darkness.

"*You* came?" Joe exclaimed. "No need."

"Did you think I'd pack up and go home to bed?" Alison demanded. "What d'you take me for?"

"Guess I could tell you—but I won't right now," the man declared, grimly. "Too much talking."

"Oh! Oh, yes—I'd forgotten." It had been arranged that operational silence should prevail in the quarry's presence, to offer him minimum opportunity for identification. And the presence of a woman on such an affair would be noteworthy.

"Dougie's got our friend back there—I'll go fetch him. You coming ashore?'

"No."

Joe went back for the Colonel, and Dougie helped him to the boat. At such sight as she was vouchsafed of the curious mummified-looking creature, all long bare legs and muffled white superstructure, the girl emitted a single stifled gasp, and then maintained the requisite silence. The vibrations of great but soundless laughter came from Hughie Bain. But both gave a hand as the unfortunate deportee was lowered into the boat, and Alison did her best with the raincoat and some old sail to make the man as comfortable as might be.

Joe jumped in after him, but Dougie stayed on shore. There was no need for his further services, and he had his bike to get back to Kilmory.

A wave, a gentle acceleration of the engine, and they were off.

It was a strange sensation, sitting there silent, watchful, in the open boat under the damp canopy of the night, chugging over dark seas—with always the trussed figure on the floor-boards turning and twisting, the picture of restless impotence.

The sea was calm save for the great swell that was the heart-beat of the wide Atlantic. Once out of the narrow waters of the loch, the *Kelpie* lifted and fell slowly, regularly, endlessly, as she swung north-eastwards on the long following seas. It was a thirteen-mile sail to Elgol, the nearest landing-place, on Loch Scavaig of Skye.

The girl was aware of her companions in that boat, as she did not recollect ever having been before—Joel Macdonald, who might be looking at her and might not, of whomsoever he was thinking; the unchancy pillow-cased figure at her feet, a ghostly white blur; even the motionless person of Hughie Bain outlined in the stern against the pale phosphorescence of their wake, and the occasional red glow of his pipe, the warmest thing to that strange journey.

It was one-thirty when they drew in to the landing-place below the crofting township of Elgol. There was no jetty, only a shelving beach of pebbles, but the mouth of a small stream allowed Hughie to bring his boat in to a dry landing. Their cargo was bundled out, Joe taking him over his shoulder once more, while Hughie, with the baggage, led the way across the pebbles. Alison remained in the boat.

It was difficult unsteady going—especially when an upheaval and snorting from under their very noses all but capsized them, as a couple of shaggy shadowy cattle rose, to blunder off into the gloom, their hooves clicking like castanets on the stones. But in no more than fifty yards, a building material-ized before them, in the side of the hill—the little school and schoolhouse of Elgol. In the doorway of the former Joe set down his burden. Taking the precaution to replace his own scarf across his face, he untied the rope that bound the prisoner's arms to his sides, and drew off the pillow-case. Even in the dark he could feel the malevolence of the eyes that glared at him. Stooping, he patted the night-shirted shoulder reassuringly. Hughie dumped the bag alongside, and emptied out the second pillow-slip. And without a word spoken, they turned and left him there. He could unwind the rest, himself.

Two-thirds of the way back to the *Kelpie*, they heard a single angry cry—and then silence again. Colonel Lomax-Lincoln, like a good soldier, was engaged in appreciating the situation.

At the boat, Joel Macdonald stretched his arms. "Well—that's it, I guess." He yawned. "So I finally made it! I made Skye—where my roots go down! Yessir—I made it."

"You did—in more ways than one!" Alison agreed. "Come aboard, hero!"

On the journey back to Rum they made up for the silence of the outward trip. Congratulations led to wit, and wit gave place to music. And when the rain came on in earnest, with a thin hissing on all the flattened surface of the sea, the girl moved in under the old sail-cloth with Joe—at the latter's insistence, of course, and in the cause of harmony. As a voyage, it was a distinct improvement.

Alison's eyes closed presently—as well they might, at after two in the morning. She slumped a little to one side, too, as time went on. It happened to be the side at which Joe sat. And in due course he slid a protecting arm around her —which was no more than a gentleman's duty in the circumstances. She did not stir—unless it was to nestle in just a little more snugly, with subconscious but touching trust— or so the man conceived it. Thus, nursed on the broad bosom of the night-bound ocean they crossed the Cuillin Sound.

It seemed a long voyage—or timeless might better describe it—though there were no complaints on that score. Perhaps Hughie's navigation was at fault, and he took them the long way home—round by Canna, or the Land of Nod itself? Sitting there, wordless, motionless, but laughing to himself every now and then, who was to know by what unseen star he steered? And it was a very dark night.

But at length Kilmory Bay received them, and its jetty bumped gently at their bows, and voyagers must disembark, however snug. In another hour it would be dawn of a Sabbath morn. Joe helped Alison out of the boat heedfully, and retained a grip of her arm along the upward track, just in case she should stumble. Almost they forgot to say good night to Hughie Bain, who was much amused.

In silence they walked up the road between the outcrops and the sleeping cattle, though now and then the man hummed a snatch of some melody, without beginning or end, under his breath. Alison would have paused at Morag Ross's path-end, but Joe turned her firmly into her own opposite road, and they continued with their quiet pacing.

At the door of Kilmory House, under the proud sign of the Rum Palace, they halted.

"Will you come in, Joe?" the girl found her voice in a whisper. "A drink?"

He shook his head. "Another night, maybe. Time respectable young women were in their beds."

"M'mmm. And you feel that I am—am essentially respectable!"

"Yeah. Every time."

She sighed a little. "It's . . . it's an awful handicap, isn't it!"

Joe grinned. "I guess it cuts both ways," he suggested.

"You think so?"

"Yeah."

There was a pause.

Then Alison touched his wet jacket lightly. "I want to say thank you," she said. "For everything. For to-night. For all you've done. . . ."

"Say—what *is* this?" he interrupted. "This sure don't sound like Alison Maclean!"

"Yes, it does. I mean . . . I'm serious, Joe. You have been good—kindness itself. I'm grateful, really."

"Yeah? That so?" He looked down at her, for a moment, as if in thought, and then stooping, kissed her full on the mouth, firmly, efficiently.

"Oh!" she said, as soon as she could.

"Uh-huh. That's right," he agreed. "Now, *I'm* sorta

grateful. So we're quits. Good night, Allie." And nodding, he strolled off into the night.

Wordless, she watched him go. Words had been of only minor import that night, anyhow.

8

HANK DELMONTE, LIKE GENERAL BERNARD MONT-gomery, liked to have everything lined up and in order, everything to hand and no ends loose, before he started shooting. Which was often trying and exasperating for those who had to wait. But once ready to move, like his fellow-tactician, there was no holding him.

Monday morning, six days after his arrival on Rum, he was ready—not satisfied, of course, but prepared jaundicedly to give the signal to start. The castle was built; the island surveyed and mapped; the generators set up and tested; the props all in order; even the players knew their pieces after a fashion. Hank said shoot, and they shot.

And now no one could complain of dilatoriness; indeed, the complaints all were the other way—but were not expressed aloud in the Director's hearing, except by Mariota Marr, and that warily. Over and across and up that island he drove them, all forces mobilized—cars, motor-bikes, ponies, the entire entourage, with half the manpower of Rum enrolled as bearers, and the other half tailing along as gallery. Alison, constituting herself liaison-officer between the home and allied forces, withdrew all her censure and disparagement on the score of lassitude and time-wasting. Without being exhausted, she was indubitably tired before that first day was out. They took shots and stills and rushes of a large proportion of Rum— of the castle, from every angle, of the cliffs and headlands, the lochs and bays, the mountains, individually and collectively, of men at the nets and the peats, women washing clothes in burns, children singing. Even, they climbed most of the way up Allival, to get a shot of Askival trailing its faithful pennant of cloud. All this was going to provide wonderful publicity for Rum—so long as the world didn't receive it as a graphic picture of Skye! Throughout the entire day Hank Delmonte's megaphonic shouts of " Cameras! " and " Shoot! " and " Cut! " and " Wrap! " resounded on the Hebridean air, liberally interspersed with pungent comment and blistering invective. No one escaped the edge of his tongue. The motion-picture industry's Number One Director was a perfectionist—and he had very individual ideas as to perfection.

Alison found it hard to sustain any suitable air of constraint between herself and Joel Macdonald, the latter being far too busy to co-operate. As Associate Director, his primary task seemed to be to act as a buffer between Delmonte and the rest of the company—and particularly, of course, to ensure that Mariota Marr was approximately where Hank reckoned that she ought to be at any moment of the day. This was in the nature of a full-time job in itself, the lady being as demanding, indeed compelling, in her own way as was the Director in his.

Temperament was not the only difficulty with which the film-makers had to contend, of course. The weather made an able second—though for Rum it behaved extraordinarily well. It rained, naturally, frequently, and the cloud was much in evidence. But the sun shone too, intermittently, brilliantly, and with a fine impartiality. The trouble was, apparently, that the position of the sun was not constant, and therefore the shadows cast were differently placed and shaped. It would not do, it seemed, for a scene to be shot with the sun in one position, and then another dealing with the same incident with the sun and shadow differently placed. Alison would have thought that this was a mere detail to anyone prepared to swallow that castle. But no—Hank was a perfectionist, and details made a picture. So the comings and goings of the sun did not pass without comment, the climate, the island, indeed the entire country.

Throughout it all, Alison sought diligently to discover some inkling of the theme of the story being filmed—but without success. Presumably somebody knew—beyond the mere generality that it was about a reincarnation of Charles Edward Stewart. The script-writer-author denied all knowledge; the thing had been so altered, amended and improved so as to become quite unrecognizable to him. The Continuity-girl might have been expected to have some ideas on the subject, but her remit was confined to the brief section that was to be shot in Scotland; besides, she was quite the busiest person on location, and found stories a bore at the best of times. Nobody else was able to proffer any coherent account of the epic as a whole. Inquisitive folk would have to await the finished article, without a doubt.

After a late and somewhat silent meal in Kilmory House that evening, Chip O'Hare, the Director of Photography, gave them a run-over on his projector of some of the day's rushes and stills. Alison thought that they were wonderful, pointing out this and that recognizable feature and character. But Hank Delmonte's reaction was otherwise; with picturesque pithiness he consigned practically the entire showing to the flames. Lousy, he said. It stank. His cigar positively stabbed the air. They would be lucky, apparently, if they got a minute's running-time out of the whole day's toil, sweat and invective.

The lay understanding of the film business remained hazy.

It was a somewhat dull and lethargic company which watched the Hebridean sunset at its technicolor extravaganza that night. Seemingly no sunset scene was as yet incorporated in the saga.

The dullness and gloom were enhanced, as far as Alison was concerned, by the fact that Monday's mail-steamer had come and gone without delivering one single notification of a Rum Week visitor—or even an enquiry after accommodation. And twice or thrice that day, Delmonte had made some ominous reference to crowd-scenes. Rum Week was due to start in five days' time, and so far, apart from the film company itself, they were without a solitary patron. The position was becoming serious. Something would have to be done. The Executive would have to meet. To-morrow, Tuesday night.

Tuesday was the day appointed for Joe to collect the male lead, Victor Dufour, at Mallaig. Hughie Bain took him, in the *Kelpie*, on a still grey morning. He was to be at the station at four minutes to noon prompt—not out of any particular respect for the star, but in order to obviate any unnecessary geographical complications on the Skye-Rum axis, such as might arise if Mr. Dufour began making idle local enquiries. Joe also was commissioned to buy a selection of the daily papers; if Colonel Lomax-Lincoln had made any public pronouncement on his Rum adventure, it could hardly have appeared before that morning's editions.

The rest of the company were on the job early. One of Hank Delmonte's Roneo-ed operation-orders had been circulated last thing on Monday night, declaring tersely that a much higher degree of activity and co-operation was expected from all hands, giving detailed instructions as to transport equipment and personnel, and stating that all would be on location at Number 3 Cliff at 9 a.m. sharp. Alison was so impressed with the terms and tenor of this manifesto that she denied herself the opportunity of a shopping trip to Mallaig, and was indeed first on the site next morning, with a quarter of an hour to spare.

It was unfortunate, after all this, that the level greyness of the atmosphere precluded all camera work. Unfortunate for Hank's temper and the morale of the entire assembly that hour succeeded hour thereafter, and still no gleam of sun or colour transformed the toneless scene. A boatload of local crofters and bit-part actors, gloriously caparisoned, lay off-shore waiting, and the cliff-face was festooned with strategically-placed tartan-draped natives ready to receive them, Miss Marr prominent in an off-the-shoulder creation of mixed Buchanan and Macmillan. And gradually silence settled down save for the sibilant sigh of slow seas on the shingle, and the heartfelt and impassioned converse between Hank Delmonte and his Maker.

The feeling that it was all her fault grew on Alison Maclean, to become a burning conviction. Expiation most obviously was demanded. The only question seemed to be what form her sacrifice must take.

Even if it would only rain, and they could all go home and end this intolerable tension . . .

At one-thirty, with a groan, the Director gave the embittered word to knock-off for a picnic lunch. At two-five he was sleeping peacefully on his back, sombrero tipped over his nose, with just sufficient room for the cigar to remain in position beneath. And at two-ten the first pale blink of sunshine emerged from the serried banks of cloud.

It was an agonizing situation. To wake him, or not? Here was what they had been panting for—but wakened now he would be worse than any bear with neuralgia. If the sun came to nothing . . . ! And the cloud-ceiling remained substantial enough, still.

But by mutual though unspoken consent, and after much searching of sky and sleeper, it was decided to leave well alone meantime.

Unhappily, just as the next gleam of sun struggled through, Hank woke up with the glare in his eyes—and all hell broke loose.

The agitation and feverish activity was not entirely dissipated an hour later, when Joel Macdonald and another young man came crunching across the shingle towards them.

.   .   .   .   .

The impact was considerable—for he was a shatteringly good-looking, indeed beautiful, young man—and might even have held up the shooting had Hank Delmonte allowed it. But that *he* was not impressed was only too apparent.

" Say—you making pictures or rubber-necking? " he bawled. " And you," he snarled, turning on Joe and the newcomer, " get the hell outa my road! "

" Sure, Hank," Joe acceded, easily.

" Oh, I say! " his companion objected, in a delightfully modulated voice. " Not nice."

" Look, you bunch of goddam hams," the Director requested. " I told you, see. I told you guys, you gotta jump outa that blasted boat like you didn't care if you got your pants wet.

Will you jump, or hell—have I gotta come and push you in? Retake!"

Alison at least could afford to disobey, and take a look at the new arrival. Dressed in a superbly cut hacking-jacket of bottle-green tweed, with pale, almost white tight-legged cord trousers and a dove-grey silk shirt, open at the neck with the V filled with a choice blue polka-dotted silk scarf worn like a stock, he made a dashing figure. He had plentiful wavy golden hair that caressed his shapely head like a juliet-cap, his brow was high, his eyes very blue, and his sculptured features without blemish. Beside him, Joel Macdonald looked like some rangy mustang in company with the thoroughbred product of a maharajah's stables.

Mariota Marr's green eyes were not wholly clamped on the boat-landing, either. "Well, well!" she said, and a pink tongue-tip licked scarlet lips.

Alison, intercepting that glance, knew an obscure satisfaction.

The boatmen having achieved dry land once more, a little more wet-shod, Hank imploring all heaven to pity him, and them, jabbed a finger at Miss Marr. "You," he barked, "get down to meet them, like you thought they were the goods, see—like you thought this prince guy, this what's-it . . . yeah, Charlie, was there with his tongue hanging out. He's not, thank the Lord—but you don't know it, see."

"Yes, sweet. I got eyes—I can read . . ."

"Sure, you got legs too—we've seen them, some place. But can you run? Run like this clothes-horse guy was standing wide open for you? And don't fall over your damnation spinning-wheel—yeah, and say, close up your blouse some, sister—it's wasted at this range. Keep the cheese-cake for the close-ups, then we'll take all you've got and pretend we like it! Okay?"

The lady grimaced, the Clapper-boy clapped, the Focus-puller pulled, the Camera-grip gripped and the Director of Photography expectorated gloomily.

"Shoot!" Hank roared, and the cameras whirring, the stirring scene came approximately to life.

"Cut!" the megaphone rapped, and the groan that issued

from it thereafter was a heart-rending thing. "Tarnation—I told you, woman. You gotta run. It ain't no hip-parade, see. Run, like another dame was making the guy's hip-pocket first! Say—you'd better relax. Take it easy. Go think about it, some place, all by yourself. I guess this acting-business is too much of a strain for you!" Wearily he waved a beringed hand. "Come back in ten minutes, willya . . ."

"You fat slug, you! Gorblimey, for the price of two bloaters, I'd . . ." That was pure Cockney, and authentic.

Joel MacDonald's voice cut in, soothingly. "Hank—this is Victor Dufour. I brought him right along."

"I got eyes, too, unfortunately," the Director said.

The Dufour turned profile-on, in an expert gesture. "Extraordinary," he murmured.

"One hundred per cent Limey," Hank nodded dispiritedly. "I've seen the face before. Yeah—hundreds of times."

"I expect you have, indeed." That was no more than duly complacent.

"Yeah. Toothpaste adverts."

"Oh, I say . . ."

"Hank's bark is worse than his bite," Joe put in, earnestly.

"Sure. No bite—no teeth, see. So I ain't got all that much use for toothpaste, either! Nossir. You get me, Charlie?"

"I can't say I do, really. And my name's not Charlie, either."

"Oh, no?" That eloquent lower jaw thrust out. "Look—you're Charlie on this script, see. Only reason you got to be here is you're Charlie. So long as you're in Skye, you'll be Charlie—and like it, see!"

"Wrong again, my dear man," Victor Dufour assured, pained. "I'm no more Charlie than this is Skye."

"Eh . . . ?"

Joe's glance urgently sought Alison's.

"This is Rum. The Island of Rum. Not Skye."

"Gee—you nuts or sump'n?"

"I . . . I sorta explained to him that this is kinda part of Skye—the same group, Hank. . . ."

"Nonsense. It's Rum, a different island altogether," the

Englishman asserted. "I must say, I don't follow what all this is about?"

"Hell—and who asked you? You got a nerve!" Delmonte almost choked. "You reckon you're the goods, eh—a tough baby? You come here and start right into giving us the works—telling us where we are and where we ain't! This picture's being shot in Skye, see—and that's right here."

The other raised expressive shoulders. "If you people want to pretend this is somewhere other than it is, that's all right with me. I couldn't care less, really. But I've been in Skye —and this isn't it! This is a different island. Aren't there any locals, here? Ask them."

Alison cleared her throat, her eye rather desperately on Joel MacDonald for such poor guidance as he might give. "Of course . . . where we actually stand is Rum," she faltered. "It's . . . it's just the general area that you could call Skye. . . ."

"That's right. You could say we're in the Skye neighbourhood, just," Father Joseph came to her rescue.

"Just that," Dougie applauded, strongly. "Och, near enough."

"Skye is an island, and Rum is an island, madam," Victor Dufour maintained judicially. "I fail to see how you can call one the other."

"But there are hundreds of islands around Skye. . . ."

"Soay. Scalpay. Oronsay . . ." Dougie amplified.

"Perimeter." Father Joseph nodded. "That's the word— within the Skye perimeter."

"I wouldn't say that . . ."

"Hell—you said enough!" Hank Delmonte roared. "You sure said plenty. What is this, anyway—a sorority debate, or a motion-picture location? I don't give a spit in a brass cuspidor what the name of this dump is—but it was right here I was making a picture, God help me, when you poked your Limey nose in! Now—will you get the hell outa here, so we can do some work . . . !"

"All right. Keep your hair on. . . ."

"For the love of little blue angels . . . !"

"Look, Handsome—I guess it's time we were acquainted."

The lovely Mariota Marr had come up from behind, and took Mr. Dufour's arm sympathetically. "You don't need to pay too much attention to that big baboon—he thinks with his megaphone! Come along."

"Yeah—you run along with Momma, Charlie," the Director told him. "Or shall I call you Beautiful? I reckon *you'll* be safer with her than most are!"

Distinctly alarmed-seeming now, the newcomer ran sensitive fingers over the golden undulations of his hair, looking as though he would much prefer to remain safely attached to Joel Macdonald. But the pressure of the red-nailed hand on his arm was inexorable.

"Cameras!" Hank bellowed.

Alison edged up to Joel Macdonald. "Whew!" she murmured. "That was a near thing! What a horror!"

"I reckon Hank was pretty good, myself," the man suggested.

"Hank? Oh, yes—he was marvellous. What a relief! No, I meant the other creature. Did you have trouble with him coming over?"

"I'll say!"

"And d'you think it'll be all right, now—I mean, over this Rum-Skye business?"

"I dunno. I reckon it's a good thing that Hank found out this way—with this guy getting his back up and pushing him on to the defensive. But, whether it'll last . . . ? A lot's going to depend on when he tumbles to the population. Numbers, see—for these crowd scenes."

"Oh!" Alison groaned. "Well—we're discussing that to-night. Ten o'clock, in my room." She shook her head. "This development business is not so easy as it sounds."

He grinned at her, suddenly encouraging. "Chins up, the Macleans!" he urged. "We've hardly started yet."

"You think so?" Doubtfully she eyed him. "I hardly know whether to hope you're right or not!" She shrugged. "Ah, well—I'm off, anyway. I've had as much motion-picture as I can take for one day! I'm sure you'll cope with any further crises much better than I would, anyhow."

"Quitter!" the man hinted.

"Not at all. I'm going to Dibidil . . . to see Rory Mac-Neill!"

"Oh. That guy."

"Yes—that guy. He wants to see me urgently."

"Oh, yeah?"

"Yes." She nodded seriously. "About kilts, I believe."

.   .   .   .   .   .

The Executive meeting that night was one man short —Major MacNeill. The Hon. Secretary explained his absence.

"He is on the high seas, actually, in his motor-launch, heading for the Outer Hebrides, for Stornaway in Lewis," she told them. "He has been in touch with a friend of his there, Quartermaster of the Lewis Territorial battalion of his old regiment, the Seaforth Highlanders. He's managed to get a cleaning contract for two hundred and fifty of the battalion's kilts."

"A cleaning contract. . . ?"

"Yes. We couldn't think of any other way to lay hands on so many. Army kilts get cleaned every so often, apparently, and Rory's made an arrangement under what he calls Rum Home Industries, to collect the kilts, have them cleaned, and delivered in Lewis again in six weeks' time, at so much a garment. We'll have to send them to Fort William or some-where, eventually, to be done at a laundry or something, of course—but meantime, we'll have the use of two hundred and fifty perfectly good Mackenzie kilts that we couldn't possibly have bought in bulk, even if we could have paid for them."

"Well, I'm damned!" Joe marvelled. "Whose idea was this?"

"Well—we thought it up between us."

"Excellent," Father Joseph commended. "You know, I'm not so sure, either, that we'll have to be sending the things to a laundry. I'm thinking that we might have a go at cleaning them our own selves, here on Rum. We've got as good water and elbow-grease as they've got in Fort William. And we could do with the money."

"Damn, yes," Dougie agreed. "Just the thing for the women, of an evening."

Alison looked as though she was going to make some comment on that, when the priest interposed.

"Now, the only thing is—who is going to wear these kilts! Where do we get the crowds?"

"Yes. Yes, that's the rub," the girl acknowledged ruefully. "I must admit, I don't know the answer. Our Press publicity's been a complete frost."

"And only four more days in it," Dougie pointed out lugubriously.

"How much would proper advertising cost?" Father Joseph wondered. "To make a regular splash, just."

"Utterly hopeless. Newspaper advertising rates are wicked. It would cost the earth—hundreds, possibly thousands, to make any impression. Anyway, we've no time for that now. Oh, dear. What's the position with your people, Joe? Mr. Delmonte said nothing to me, this evening."

"We had a word or two, I'm afraid," the Texan admitted. "He doesn't care two hoots that he's on Rum and not Skye —but he's getting worried about his crowds. So am I, for that matter. We're just about ready to shoot them, now—and he doesn't see so many folks about. I've told him about this Rum Week, but he's not all that impressed, I guess. He wants to see the bodies pretty soon. Or else . . . !"

"Or else what, Joe?"

"Or else he'll pack up and go where the folks are. Only thing he can do."

"How *can* we get people to come here?" the girl demanded, banging small fist on knee.

Nobody answered her.

"There must be some way of arranging it," she went on. "Skye managed it."

"It took Skye a long time," Father Joseph pointed out.

"They've done a lot of organization," Joe agreed. "Long range stuff. Like this ship from the States."

"What ship?"

Joe felt in his pocket for a newspaper. "I was reading about it in one of these rags I got in Mallaig. It's a ship specially chartered by a bunch of Scotch-Americans to bring them over to Skye. Here it is. 'Yesterday, the good ship s.s. *Yonkers City* sailed from New York Harbour for the misty Isle of Skye, carrying four hundred American citizens of Scottish ancestry to take part in far-famed Skye Week which commences on Monday August 1st. A.P. Reporter visiting the ship before she sailed, interviewed Elmer P. Macwhirter, Grand Chief of the Illinois Clans Confederation, the leader of the pilgrimage. He said that it was the first visit to the Scotland of their forebears for practically everyone on board. They had all heard a lot about Skye, but none of them had seen its hallowed shores. This was going to be a great experience, they all felt sure.

"'The *Yonkers City*, specially chartered for the round trip, is due to arrive at Skye next Sunday night or Monday morning.'"

"The Saints of Mercy—a shipload of them!" Father Joseph gasped.

"Four hundred Yanks in a boat!" Dougie said. "Millionaires most like, every one. Och, just think of it!"

They looked at each other.

"If that ship was coming here instead of to Skye," the girl said, her voice trembling slightly, "all our troubles would be over."

The priest examined the bedroom ceiling. "So they would," he conceded.

"My Chove—that's right. Think of the dollars on that lot!"

The rasp of Joel's hand as he rubbed his bristly chin could be plainly heard. But he spoke no word.

"It's a terrible waste. To Skye." Father Joseph addressed the rain-blurred window.

"It's wicked, that's what it is," Alison asserted. "It makes you wonder at Providence."

"Och, well—maybe not just that," the Church contested. "But it's a real temptation."

"A temptation—that's what it is, whatever," Dougie agreed.

Joel Macdonald stared at the worn carpet with knitted brows, and said nothing.

The priest sighed. "A-well, a-well—what's to be will be, I suppose. Yes, yes."

Dougie shook his head. "Four hundred Americans just running to waste, just!"

"Enough to put Rum on its feet. Enough for all the crowd-scenes," Alison all but keened.

Joel's fist opened slowly, deliberately, till all fingers were fully outstretched. He seemed to be counting them. "It could be done," he said, and nodded.

Three breaths were indrawn, as one.

"How?"

"It could. . . ?"

"Yep. It would take some doing—but I reckon it could be worked. Look—this is an American ship, and it's coming direct to Skye. I guess Americans have mistaken Rum for Skye before this!"

"Yes. Yes. Indeed," the girl agreed eagerly. "But wouldn't there be a pilot or something?"

"Yeah. Probably. But I was reckoning *we* might provide the pilot, see!"

For a moment there was a lovely silence, as infinite possibilities began to dawn on receptive minds. Then everybody commenced to speak at once.

When Joe could make himself heard, he put it this way. "We'll leave the details, for now. But I guess it might be possible to bring that ship into your Loch Scresort—especially if it made these parts around nightfall. The skipper would have to be looked after—but say, we might provide a hospitality deputation to go out with the pilot, and be real darned hospitable! Skye's Committee of Welcome, see. I reckon the pilot would be left to sorta bring the ship in, alone!"

Alison clapped her hands. "Heavenly!" she cried. "And once we got them ashore, we'd give them such a time they wouldn't notice they weren't on Skye, for a few days, at any rate. It would be bound to come out sooner or later, of course —but we'd have time to make an impression. . . ."

"And have got the cream of the dollars off them, whatever," the practical Dougie added.

"And Hank Delmonte get his crowd-scenes. I can see them all wearing Rory's kilts, and loving it!"

"My goodness me, it's just magnificent," Father Joseph declared. "We'll give them twice the time they'd have on Skye. It's a poor place, when you come to think of it. A kindness we'll be doing them. They'll thank us for it the rest of their days."

"It'll take a deal of working out," Joe warned. "The details. We can't leave much to chance, on a thing like this."

Gaily Alison jumped to her feet. "You've got Wednesday, Thursday, Friday and Saturday to work it out, Joe," she trilled. "Yippeee!"

9

WEDNESDAY, THURSDAY, FRIDAY AND SATURDAY passed that week, on Rum, as seldom those days can have passed there before. Activity was feverish, planning incessant, and security an ever-present preoccupation. Unfortunately all coincided with an intensified cinematographic assault, Hank Delmonte seeming to be determined to show the unwilling Victor Dufour just how films should be made. Joel Macdonald by no means found time to hang heavily.

The problem of security—who should know what they were planning to do, and who shouldn't—was of first importance. The matter was considerably eased however, when, after certain judicious soundings, Joe decided to confide in Hank, at least partially—and found him entirely co-operative. Hank was a showman, of course, and saw the entire proposition through a showman's eyes. The ship-business appealed to him enormously, on its own merits; it was camera-stuff— he might even work a bit into the picture, out of it. The four hundred tourists he could do with, and no mistake—especially as they were Yanks and would be motion-picture-conscious;

they'd sure get a kick out of acting extras. It would save the Corporation a lot of time and expense, too, if they could finish the shooting here, without having to move elsewhere. What might be called the ethics of the matter concerned him no whit; success was the yardstick by which such affairs should be measured; he would withhold no helping hand if it looked like coming off.

Nothing could have been fairer than that. The rest of the film company merely were informed that a ship-load of American tourists was expected at the week-end, who were to be coaxed to stay on the island for a day or two, to provide crowd-material, if possible. Many of the Rumaich themselves were told no more, the Minister in particular not being burdened with unnecessary details.

These details were teased and sorted out, as the days progressed. The question of a pilot came first on the list, naturally. There were plenty of people on Rum capable of a degree of navigation, but it was small boat stuff, and none had experience of conning and handling a large ocean-going ship. The plan demanded an expert; no appearances would serve here—or they might well be having a wreck on their hands. They found the answer in Jock Laidlaw, the cheerful and less than straitlaced mate of their Glasgow coaster, the *Ailsa*, still lying off Kinloch. Jock, grizzled-haired, red-nosed, and sociable, asserted that he was an experienced deep-sea mariner, and claimed to have held a Master's Certificate. The past-tense of this scrap of paper was not dwelt upon, and the question of reward barely mentioned, as between gentlemen. But Jock was their man. Given a bit look at the *Ailsa's* charts, and a bit co-operation from the shore, in the way of lights, he'd pilot the bluidy *Queen Mary* into Loch Scresort any dark night. No trouble, at all.

The pilot-cutter presented no difficulties; the Dibidil launch would serve admirably. Rory MacNeill, when he arrived back from Stornaway on Wednesday night with his kilts, entered heartily into the thing. He would pilot the pilot.

The Welcome Deputation on the ship Alison took into her own two hands, and with Father Joseph organizing the shore reception, they might rest easy on that score.

A problem that exercised them considerably was how to know when the *Yonkers City* was in the offing, and where. There was a lot of sea off the Hebrides, and the ship might approach Skye from more than one angle and at any hour of the day or night. This puzzled the strategists to such an extent as to come between them and their much-needed sleep . . . until in desperation they put the matter to Jock Laidlaw, who laughed and assured them that it was perfectly simple, just bairns'-play. It was all done by short-wave radio. They would send out a signal to the *Yonkers City* from the *Ailsa's* wireless-cabin on Sunday afternoon, appointing a rendezvous—that was all. This seemed excessively simple and highly satisfactory—but what if Skye was sending out similar messages? Wouldn't they probably be providing a pilot for their visitors too? Jock admitted the possibility, but pointed out that Portree was the only deep-water harbour in Skye, and being tucked-in away up the far east coast of the island, the chances were that they would do their piloting much later—waiting until the ship was well down the Sound of Raasay. Rum ought to be well ahead, with any luck. But it was a chance that had to be taken, apparently.

The general Rum Week preparations were speeded up and intensified, now that there was the prospect of unlimited visitors. Never was there such a practising of piping, Highland dancing, singing, and reciting. Spinning-wheels that had not seen the light of day for generations were dragged out of cupboards, repaired and oiled. Handlooms were restrung and furbished up. Boats were repitched and repainted, the island's modest stills worked overtime, and a spate of whitewashing swept the place. The turnips were a nuisance, coming on for thinning at such a time—folk couldn't be film-extras, folk-lore exponents, home-industrialists, caterers and turnip-thinners too, all at the same time. Morag Ross added a class on the Second Sight to her evening lectures on the hotel-trade.

The kilts, of course, were a godsend. Major MacNeill had improved on the original contract, and brought three hundred and twenty of them, fine substantial pieces, and warm around the middle however chilly about the knees. Soon every man on the island was equipped with one, and though they did not go the length of wearing them, save for perhaps half an hour's practice in the day, the film people adopted them with enthusiasm and wore them continually, Hank Delmonte included. It was a pity that Rory MacNeill hadn't thought of bringing some knee-hosiery with them, perhaps on a darning contract. Short socks had not the same effect, at all. The knitting of stockings was just one more priority, when time could be found.

Was it any wonder that Sunday was upon them betimes?

After church, on Sunday afternoon, Alison and Joe had an appointment with Jock Laidlaw in the wireless-cabin of s.s. *Ailsa*. The coaster did not carry a separate operator, needless to say, but the mate could turn his hand to this as well as to the next thing. Headphones on, he sat at the operator's table and fiddled with the knobs of the instruments. "Should pick her up any minute," he assured. "Nae bother."

Whether the reception was at fault, the transmission, or it was just plain damned inefficiency on the part of *Yonkers City* as Laidlaw contended, response to their signals seemed to be very slow. The mate could not risk broadcasting details to all and sundry, of course, and had to confine himself to a pathetic and plaintive repetition of Calling *Yonkers City*, *Yonkers City*, *Yonkers City*, which began to pall after an hour or so. It grew very hot in that tiny metal cabin. The fumes of stale spirits arising from Jock Laidlaw almost could be seen.

But they persisted—since there was nothing else that they could do. And they had their reward. In the late afternoon they received a reply. *Yonkers City answering. Yonkers City. Over.*

"Just heed to them—just like that!" Jock complained. "And here's us just aboot coopered oorsel's. . . ."

"Send the message, man. . . ." Joe pointed to the sheet of notepaper.

"Fine that. They'll no' run awa' noo." He tapped out the signal. *This is Welcome Committee. Am sending out pilot. Give position Yonkers City.*

There was an interval.

"Awa' to tell the skipper," Jock interpreted. "Och, here he's."

Yonkers City. Thankee kindly. Position 95 miles due west Barra Head. Speed 15 knots.

Laidlaw made a pencil circle on the chart in front of him, and drew a line towards Barra Head, at the very tail of the long archipelago of the Outer Hebrides. "Here. Fifty from here. Ninety-five. One-forty-five. Seven hours sailing," he computed. "Off here by midnight."

"Fine," Joe said. "Attaboy. Tell him we'll rendezvous with him . . . let's see—about here. What's this point— Mills Rock? Say a coupla miles south of Mills Rock. How far's that from here? About fourteen miles. And fifteen knots is about twenty-two miles, isn't it? At eleven fifteen, then. Right?"

"The sooner we're aboard that ship, the better," Alison suggested. "The less likelihood of them collecting a message from Skye."

"Something in that," Joe agreed. "Make it another ten miles out, then—at ten-forty-five. You got that, Jock?"

"Uh-huh. Say twenty miles E.N.E. of Barra Head, ten S.W. of Mills Rock, at ten-forty-five. I'll send that." After a minute or two, Jock looked up. "He says, wouldn't it be better to wait for daylight, to come in?"

"Hell—no!" Joe jerked, beneath his breath, as though he might be overheard. "Say we'll bring him in safe. Tell him we got a reception fixed up for him. To-night."

"Anything you say." And, presently, "Okay. He'll be there."

Alison heaved a great sigh of relief. "Well—thank goodness for that! Now, we can get busy."

"We'll have to," Joe declared. "It's five-twenty, and we got plenty to do!"

.   .   .   .   .

At eight-thirty all was in train. The night was grey only, as yet, but a faint smirr of rain gave promise of darker clouds to come. The sea was jabbly but not rough. Major Rory had brought the Dibidil boat, a fairly powerful and roomy ex-ship's launch, round to Kinloch. He wore his kilt, plaid, bonnet and a single eagle's feather. In beside him trooped Alison, Joe, Jock Laidlaw, Dougie with his bagpipes, General Maclean resplendent in the gallant full-dress uniform of a colonel of Seaforth Highlanders bearing a basket of assorted bottles, and, of all people, Mariota Marr. She insisted on coming, despite Alison's plea that there wouldn't be room—an assertion which she very quickly disproved by snuggling down between Joel Macdonald and the speechless Major Rory, pulling part of the latter's plaid around her, and playing with one of the long hairy tassels of his sporran. The General had been a bit doubtful about the whole business at first, but Hank Delmonte's co-operation and approval converted him; he had achieved a great admiration for Hank.

They made a finely representative party for Father Joseph, Hank himself, the Minister at the last moment, and indeed most of Rum, to see off.

Down Loch Scresort they went. On either side, on the flanking cliffs that guarded its mouth, the film unit's electricians were busy transporting and setting up their generators, as lighthouses. Into the open sea they turned, south by west, the launch pitching and slapping into it, with every now and then a thin shower of spray—which had the effect of making Miss Marr nestle in still more closely between her protectors. Neither showed any sign in the least of minding, Alison noted; she sincerely hoped that they both would keep their minds on the serious business ahead. At least, the chill and the spray would tend to restrict any limb-displays.

With leaden, white-veined seas meeting them sullenly, the last of a poor sunset no more than a single dirty yellow bar low down ahead, and Eigg a shapeless shadow on their left merging into the dropping curtain of the night, they ploughed on. After a bright and brittle start, conversation flagged, save for an intermittent whispering and girlish giggling from the stern. In the interests of uplift and morale, it was Alison's suggestion that Dougie should give them the benefit of some pipe-music as they went along. And at least, it put whispering out of the question.

The launch made eight knots, and they had approximately twenty-two sea miles to go. There was time and to spare. The General, in all his finery, went rather obviously to sleep, never having been really musical.

A thin rain fell, darkness came down, and Dougie who really needed to strut about to do justice to his medium, fell back on dirges and laments. They crept out towards the lonely Mills Rock, isolated between the Outer and Inner Hebrides.

At quarter-to-ten Rory MacNeill made one of his brief announcements to say that they were off the unseen Mills Rock now. Another eight miles, and they'd be where they wanted to be. Throttling back the engine, they dawdled south-westwards across the empty sea.

At just before ten-twenty, Jock Laidlaw in the bows, pointed away, right of front. "There she is!" he said. "A wee thing previous, but near enough on course for a Yank! That's begging your pardon, Mister."

For a space none of them were able to see what he claimed to see. But presently a twinkling yellow light became apparent, and grew, and burgeoned into many lights—a fine sight.

"She *might* not be the *Yonkers City*, of course," Joe pointed out.

"The chances o' anither passenger vessel that size being in these waters at this time dinna add up to much," Jock asserted. "This is no' the Tail o' the Bank!"

In a little it became evident that the big ship was either hove-to or next to it, and there could be no possible doubt as to her identity. The launch had been showing her sailing-lights, but now Rory switched on a headlamp affair which sent out a good beam. Blinking this a few times, he opened the throttle and surged on towards the ship. They had the satisfaction of seeing her lights coalesce into one glow as she turned bows-on to them.

She seemed very big as they neared her, like a tall block of flats rearing out of the black plain of the sea, with every light blazing. Dougie was playing his lustiest now, his feet stamping the floorboards. The decklights above showed the rails to be black with watching people.

As the Major cut back his engine, Jock Laidlaw raised his voice. " *Yonkers City* ahoy? " he bawled.

" Sure thing, Scotland," came back to them. " You coming aboard? "

" Yes. Pilot and party coming aboard."

" Okay. Port side ladder's down."

Revving up again, both engine and bagpipes, the launch moved in along the vessel's port side, as a searchlight from aloft flashed down on a long collapsible ladder which two seamen were descending. As the white glare picked out the boat, there was a great cheer from the crowded decks above. Dougie blew and blew, to drown it.

At the little platform Alison pushed Dougie, Jock Laidlaw, and the General forward. " Go on. The piper, then the pilot, and then Daddy," she directed. " You look so official. And for heaven's sake, be careful what you say! "

" I'm telling no lies," the General warned with dignity, clutching his basket.

" Dinna you worry, Miss—it's in the bag," Laidlaw assured. " Come on, Piper—jump! "

" Now—all Father Joseph's saints be with us! " the girl prayed fervently, and followed on.

. . . . .

At the head of the ladder two men were waiting to receive them, backed by a great gathering of vociferous passengers. Dougie played right up to them, turned around, and only when he was finished the last bar let *The Skye Boat Song* die away. The man in uniform, who had been standing practically at attention during the rendering of these hallowed strains, relaxed, stepped forward, hand outstretched.

" I'm Cap'n Ed Lynski," he announced. " Mighty glad to make you folks' acquaintance."

Jock Laidlaw shook hands solemnly. " I'm just the pilot, Captain," he said. " This is General Maclean."

" That so? This is sure an honour, General. But, look— meet Mr. Elmer P. Macwhirter, from Detroit, Illinois."

He did not really need to urge the General to look—or any

of them. They all were looking, dumbfounded. For Mr. Macwhirter made a Colonel of Seaforths look very small beer indeed. Not only was he clad in a kilt and voluminous plaid of a brilliance seldom before seen on these shores, but he wore a tartan doublet as well, of a different hue, with silver buttons the size of crown-pieces, boldly-diced stockings of red and yellow, with white spats, an array of medals of some sort that was in itself a treat for the eye, and a notably high-crowned Glengarry bonnet, the loftiness of which, besides adding to the effect, undoubtedly was needed to support the quite splendid bunch of assorted feathers that burgeoned thereon. And behind this truly eye-catching figure was drawn up rank upon rank of serried tartan, silk, and feather, with, a little to the side, an entire pipe band in white tunics, drawn up at the ready.

"Lord . . . !" the General had begun, when Mr. Macwhirter, swinging round, signed to the band, which forthwith burst out into full blast. The extremely humdrum Rum deputation were turning to eye each other, crestfallen, when something about the beat of the music struck Alison as vaguely familiar.

"Goodness—it's *God Save The Queen*!" she gasped. Grabbing the tails of her father's kilt, she tugged, yelling, "Daddy—it's the *Queen*!"

"Eh . . . ? Nonsense, girl—not on the *pipes*. . . !"

"It is. It is."

"My God!" Groaning, the General straightened up as near to the attention as was practicable with a basket of bottles in his arms, while the unique interpretation proceeded, his expression rapt.

As the redoubtable melody and the last beat of the big drum quivered into silence, Mr. Macwhirter extended his hand. "Happy to know you, General," he assured, warmly. "Skye for ever!"

"Eh? Ah . . . 'Evening," General Maclean said, setting down his basket carefully.

"Sure. That's right. You've said it, General. Say—meet the little woman. Dolores Ann."

"Ah. H'rrr'mm. Ma'am."

126

"Oh, General!" the little woman crooned—and not so little, either.

"Yes. Ummm." He looked unhappily behind him.

Alison came forward to his rescue and was introduced after a fashion, and in turn introduced the others. Mariota Marr naturally made the greatest impression. They were all tickled to death to meet her—and of course, her Skye friends too.

An invitation by Mr. Macwhirter, to come and meet the boys—and come to that, the girls too—with consequent signs of withdrawal from Captain Lynski, was Joel Macdonald's cue.

"Say—the General's brought a selection of the real stuff. A genuine Misty Isle welcome, see," he pointed out. "We reckoned that would be the best way of meeting the boys—down below some place, maybe? You too, Captain."

"Yessir. You got something there, I guess," Mr. Macwhirter conceded heartily. "So has the General, eh? Okay, boys—let's go. Down in Number One Saloon." He took Mariota Marr's arm, to lead the way. "You coming, Cap?"

"Wal—I guess me and the pilot's gotten business on the bridge. But later, maybe."

"Take me up there, Captain, and you can leave the rest to me," Jock Laidlaw assured. "I'll take her right in."

"Sure, Cap—that's what he's here for," Joe amplified. "You got to get your real Highland welcome, too."

"Do come, Captain," Alison reinforced sweetly, her hand seeking his arm.

"Wal—you're mighty kind. Maybe later, see. I gotta get up above there, right now. . . ."

"Then I'm coming with you—to bring you down again in just two ticks!" Alison declared, and never was her essential ingenuous girlishness more delightfully evident. "That is, of course, Captain, if you'll *have* somebody like little me up on your bridge?" And she almost pronounced it bwidge, at that.

"By hokey, mam—it'll be an honour," the rugged mariner asserted, and patted her hand to reassure her. "C'mon." And with Laidlaw on one side of him and the girl on the other side, Captain Lynski led the way up to his bridge. The others, to musical accompaniment, made their way down below.

Despite her recent shameful seduction of the poor sailor-man, Alison Maclean was quite overcome by the great roofed and glass-fronted bridge, lit only by small panel-lights to illuminate the impressive array of instruments and navigational apparatus without dazzling eyes that must view the night without. Three or four very efficient-looking men stood and paced up and down therein. However, they were none of them so distressingly businesslike as to fail to take a very good look at the young woman, as well as to make appropriate noises. Captain Lynski introduced to her his Second and Fourth Officers, direct if not bold-eyed men—as they would need to be, peering into that darkness—the latter very young indeed. The helmsman, without actually being introduced, signified general approval of the visitor.

Jock Laidlaw, in seafaring cap—on which a replica of the red-and-white Trinity House pilotage flag had been capably stitched by Alison herself—pushed to the back of his grizzled head, did not seem overawed in the least. Straight to the Second Officer's side he rolled, cast his eye over the instruments, glanced at the chart-table, shot a question at the helmsman, and then nodded, presumably in general approval also.

"My cutter cast off, Mister?" he enquired authoritatively.

"Eh? Oh, sure," the Second Officer said. Alison had forgotten all about poor Rory MacNeill in the launch.

"Can we hae the engines, Captain?"

"Sure. Carry on, Pilot."

The Second Officer reached for the engine-room telegraph.

"Half-speed," Laidlaw directed. "Helm—three points north."

"Three points it is."

"Keep her at that."

Alison looked at Jock Laidlaw with a new respect.

"Pilot—how long d'you reckon before we make a landfall?" the skipper asked.

"At half-speed, an hour and a half. Deep water a' the way. Nae bother. Awa' below, and hae your nip, Captain. Everything's okay here."

"Yes, do, Captain. . . ."

"You aim to make this place—Portree, ain't it?—to-night, Pilot? In the dark?"

"Sure. But it's no' just Portree itself we come in at—Kinloch the bit's called. And they'll hae lights lit for us."

"Wal—seems like you got it all fixed. . . ."

"Yes. Do come down," the girl pleaded. "And you too, Mr. . . . er . . ." She smiled at the Second Officer. "You don't need him, do you, Mr. Laidlaw?"

"Take him awa'," Jock nodded, eyes on the night.

"He can come, can't he, Captain? Just for a little while?"

"Oh, I guess so. . . ."

Linking arms with both officers, Alison steered them towards the bridge-ladder, with the deep and satisfactory throb of great engines beating far below them.

Down in Number One Saloon, the party had got off to a flying but none the less promising start. A wall of tartan, bare shoulders, cigar-fumes and noise met the bridge party. Pipers were playing, competitively apparently, both singing and dancing were proceeding independently, and Mariota Marr was already up on a table-top giving her own stylized version of a Highland can-can. For so brief an interval the progress was next to uncanny. Though the bars at each end of the great saloon were doing a roaring trade, most vigour and spirit undoubtedly was emanating from the central table at which Miss Marr performed, and where General Maclean sat at the benevolent dispensing of proof whisky to selected and highly gratified recipients.

"Say—this looks sump'n like it!" Captain Lynski declared, and co-operated in the process of steering for the beacon of the General's scarlet tunic.

"Yippeee!" the Second Officer agreed.

Joel saw them coming, and hastened to bring them to the source of supply. Elmer Macwhirter, obviously much affected by the warmth and strength of the Hebridean welcome, beckoned with both hands.

"C'mon—git a load of this hooch, Cap. General's hooch. It sure will knock the bar . . . barnacles off your keel!"

Two brimming glasses were proffered with no room for soda or water—and sailors, of all people, could not have refused.

"Here's hair on your knees!" Captain Lynski said, and tossed off a manly draught. "I . . . by Gemini!" Gasping, he got it out, tears starting from his eyes as he just saved himself from choking. "Gee—that sure is hooch! Eh, Sam?"

But Sam, the Second Officer, was temporarily beyond words —though his expression was eloquent.

"Plenty more where that came from," Joe assured, standing by with the bottle.

"Gee . . . !" Captain Lynski whispered.

.   .   .   .   .

At what stage in the party the Captain, never forgetting his responsibilities, suggested a trip to the bridge to see how the poor goshdurned pilot was getting along, was the subject for discussion afterwards. But it was at a good-going stage, any-way—and indeed was a good-going suggestion, up to the highest traditions of the sea, that was taken up with acclaim. It was unanimously agreed to crocodile there—and though Captain Lynski, a dignified figure, frowned at the levity im-plied, he was no spoil-sport, and presently found himself lead-ing the way, with Mariota Marr's arms clasped round his middle, Mr. Macwhirter making a very poor third, and Alison and Joe coming in somewhere thereafter. Unfortunately the Second Officer was unable to accompany them mean-time, as were quite a proportion of the beneficiaries of proof-spirited welcome. The General excused himself on grounds of weight and girth. Dougie piped them to the approximate tune of *Coming through the Rye*. As he said to the General in passing, malt would have been more apt, just.

Throughout and about and around the *Yonkers City* the Captain found himself propelled, maintaining an admirable upright gait, and showing the flag, as it were. Chanting, they paid a visit to the engine-room, circumnavigated the tables of the dining-saloon, threaded the corridors of the passen-ger accommodation to the surprise of certain of the less enthusiastic pilgrims, explored the promenade-deck and the boat-deck, before finally coiling up and on to the bridge. The chant had changed imperceptibly to the high and the low roads to Scotland via Loch Lomond.

Jock Laidlaw, at the binnacle, observed the apparition without noticeable change of expression, but the young Fourth Officer goggled. As for the helmsman, he took one glance, a second, and then looked straight in front of him and stayed that way.

Seldom can a man have striven so dutifully to uphold the dignity of the Merchant Marine in the face of such odds as Captain Lynski. But his tail, and General Maclean's lethal whisky, were really too much for flesh-and-blood. Time and again he sought to make contact with the pilot, and to convey suitable support and guidance. But always something came in his way. Eventually Jock Laidlaw took pity on him, shouting that he and Mister Mate had everything under control, that the ship was on course, and that he'd come for instructions when they were required, sir. At which gratefully and gravely the Captain saluted, and was borne away, duty done.

Unfortunately, going down ladders is not so easy for crocodiles as is going up, and the descent from the bridge rather broke up the party. Mr. Macwhirter, especially, was a disappointingly weak link. Dougie clung faithfully to the headquarters group, of course, which select little company found its way presently to the Captain's cabin. Here, most necessarily, hospitality fell to be returned, and despite Joe's production of a spare bottle of the real stuff that he had thoughtfully brought along, the Captain insisted on opening a bottle of Jamaica Rum from his own locker. The effect of its contents, on top of the General's proof whisky, was interesting, especially for those who did not actually try the experiment. At the third toast, Captain Lynski sat down on his bunk, and fell abruptly and happily asleep. After a little tentative shaking, his guests arranged him more comfortably and then tiptoed out of the cabin, Joel and Dougie taking between them an anonymous gentleman who yodelled. Leaving him to practise his art in the first state-room that they came to, the trio made its way promptly up to the bridge again.

At its portals, they tapped on the glass. "May we come in, please?" Alison asked.

"Sure—step right inside," the Fourth Officer urged. "How's Cap Lynski?"

"Fine. Fine," Joe assured. "He's having a lie-down, right now, on his bunk. But he's available to take over when required, of course."

"Sure," the other agreed, soberly.

"How are we doing, Mr. Laidlaw?" Alison enquired, but listlessly.

"Everything in order, Miss." Silently he pointed a stubby forefinger at a point on the chart midway between Eigg and Rum. "We should be seeing the two lights in ten minutes, aboot."

"Good," the girl said. "Good." But she sighed as she said it.

"We'll be in in half an hour then, Pilot?" Joe asked.

"Just aboot it."

The young Fourth Officer looked just a little bit alarmed. "Say—no docking or anything to do, is there?"

"Na, na, laddie—there's an anchorage off-shore. Dinna fret yoursel'."

Relieved, the other nodded. "I was only wondering," he said.

Laidlaw strolled out of the bridge-house into the chill wet night air, the trio from Rum following him. "Well—you made a guid job o' the skipper?" he suggested, *sotto voce*.

"Sure. Though he fought against it to the end," Joe said. "I reckoned we were maybe going to be too late."

"I didn't like it," Alison declared, in a rush. "It wasn't really fair—a mean trick. I feel ashamed of myself." She half turned her back on them. "We deliberately . . . we deliberately debauched a good seaman—led the captain of a fine ship to fail in his duty!"

"M'mmm. I guess I know how you feel," Joe said, less than comfortably. "But it's not all that bad, I reckon. . . ."

"My goodness—wasn't that what we came for, whatever?" Dougie demanded.

"I suppose so. But I'm not very proud of it, now. There's

132

a decent man lying snoring on his bunk who should be up here on his bridge, bringing in his ship. . . ."

"Na, na—that's where you're wrong, lassie," Jock Laidlaw told her. "When the pilot takes over on the bridge, *he's* in charge of the ship. The skipper can go sleep on his bunk if he likes, so long as he leaves an officer wi' the pilot."

"Oh, well . . ."

"You're just tired, I guess," Joe explained.

Laidlaw went back to his place on the bridge, but the other three stayed where they were, staring out into the night. Presently Joel Macdonald touched the girl's sleeve.

"Cheer up, Maclean!" he whispered. "We're doing fine."

Her arm stiffened. "Is that so? Time will show. And, talking about time, isn't it about time that you went and looked after your girl friend?"

"Eh? Whassat?"

"Miss Marr. It's conceivable that she requires your aid!" She sounded as stiff as her arm felt.

He laughed. "Say—last time I saw Mariota, she was doing fine too," he said. "Just fine."

"Look—there's a light," Dougie cried. "That'll be the one at the point. Aye, and there's the other."

"I wonder where that young fellow in there reckons he is?" Joe murmured.

But the Fourth Officer seemed to have no suspicions. Which was not surprising, really. The pilot was in charge. They were in narrow Hebridean seas, off as difficult a seaboard as the world could show, heading for one island amongst a thousand, and proceeding on practically the same course as formerly. Why should he smell a rat?

Making a wide sweep, the *Yonkers City* entered the mouth of Loch Scresort, between the brilliant beacons of Hank Delmonte's arc-lights. Nor were these the only illuminations. Bonfires blazed at half a dozen points around the loch. And as they steamed slowly on, the crash and reverberations of a twenty-one gun salute rolled out, echoing and re-echoing from the hills, and an array of coloured lamps flashed on and off around the jetty. The North Atlantic Props Department was making its presence felt.

Unfortunately, though Joel and Dougie, and even the General, presently, hurried through the ship, seeking to draw attention to all this, neither it nor they could make much impression. Taken by and large, the *Yonkers City* had entered so fully into the spirit of the first barrel of their Highland welcome as to be unable to do justice or even to recognize the second barrel. It was most disappointing. Mr. Macwhirter, for instance, when awakened and informed, merely emitted a dutiful whoopee, and relapsed into beautific slumber.

As the engine-room telegraph tinkled and tinkled and eventually indicated Finished with Engines, the anchor-chain rattled out, and the *Yonkers City* swung majestically with the tide quarter of a mile off-shore, and the sound of cheer upon cheer drifted out from the fairy-lit land, Dougie it was who shouted through cupped hands from the rail.

"Och, away home with you! They're not heeding, out here, at all! It's a waste, just. Away home."

"Better make it to-morrow morning," Joe called in his turn, wearily. "D'you hear? Make it nine o'clock. No—make it ten."

"What's the matter? Something wrong?" Father Joseph's great voice boomed across the dark water.

"No. It's okay. Guess we've been too successful, that's all. They're all asleep. I say *asleep*."

"The hell with this for a party!" a megaphonic bellow reached them. "They got a nerve!"

"Yeah. Sure. Make it to-morrow. Ten o'clock. . . ."

Grumbling like the rumblings of elephants' bellies rose and fell and died away, from the loom of the shore. And presently lights went out, singly and in groups, and one by one the bonfires died down. By one o'clock Rum was in darkness and silence, and though the great ship was still ablaze with lights, hardly a sound issued from her to challenge the sigh of the waves and the patter of the rain as she swung slowly round with the Hebridean tide.

The Deputation of Welcome stretched out or curled up on the settees in Number One Saloon, the battleground of their victory—except for Mariota Marr, that is, and Jock Laidlaw.

The former's whereabouts were unknown, and the latter was adequately occupied making up for lost time, duty well done.

Rum Week was one hour old, by the clock.

IO

JOEL MACDONALD HAD BEEN WISE WHEN, ON SECOND thoughts, he had changed the hour of the postponed ceremonial landing from nine o'clock till ten—despite the fact that when Alison woke up at six-thirty, cramped, stiff, and lacking inspiration, it was a brilliant morning with Rum at its very finest, and all these visitors ought to be out seeing it while it lasted. But though she aroused her immediate companions—and with difficulty—the rest of the passenger-list remained oblivious to scenic beauty, as to all else. A profound inertia encompassed the *Yonkers City*.

The ship's services, however, all worked most efficiently. The plumbing was magnificent, the feeding superlative. After a hot bath in a palace of glass and chromium, and a sumptuous breakfast served by negro waiters in dazzling white, the Rum contingent at any rate felt considerably better.

As the sun crept higher, and Rum's cloud crept lower on Askival and her sisters, one by one the principals of the previous night's activities appeared on deck—almost without exception avoiding the dining-saloon like the plague. Mariota Marr arrived from nowhere in particular, bright and beautiful as the morning itself, but likewise with just the hint of cloud somewhere. Captain Lynski made a very brief and formal appearance, saluting everyone meticulously but with his glance tending to be distant and preoccupied with the thronging and unremitting responsibilities of the master mariner. Elmer Macwhirter and his little woman made a non-simultaneous entry and seemed to remain unaware of each other's presence. But that is not to say that they neglected their duties. Each gathered around them groups of pilgrims of their own sex, and blinking a little in the trying glare of slanting sunlight on sparkling water, exclaimed and rhapsodized over the scenery.

As well they might. They had come thousands of miles to see this sort of thing, and Rum at least was not disappointing them. Embosomed in the painted hills, the white ship lay at the head of the narrow two-miles-long blue loch, landlocked and hidden save for the east-facing trough behind her, up which the morning sun came flooding—and even that vista was blocked by the long rampart of the Sleat peninsula a dozen clear miles away. Below them, the tinted sea-bed of the Hebrides was coloured by a score of different weeds on silver sand. Around them the land rose, from white cockle-strands, green machar dotted with croft-houses, through bracken slopes and birch-clad braes to the already purpling heather, and beyond, to the great precipices and screes and corries of the bald summits and soaring peaks. And everywhere, in sunlight or glooming shadow, water gleamed or foamed or glittered, and out of every fold and hollow the white mist-wraiths of morning coiled and lifted.

"That's pretty good, I guess," Elmer Macwhirter acknowledged. "You certainly brought us right into it. That's what we've been waiting to see. Get an eyeful of that, folks."

"Yessir. That's Bonnie Scotland, all right."

"One hundred per cent the real M'Coy," it was agreed. "Say—take a look at that mist. The Misty Isle, see."

"Those lovely mountains will be the Cuillins, I guess?" a knowledgeable lady suggested.

"Well—I suppose they're all part of the same geological formation," Alison Maclean it was who answered, swiftly. "But the Cuillins proper are quite a bit further over."

"H'rrr'mmmph," her father said.

"Say—if they're better than these they're pretty good."

"Oh, they're not. That's all just propaganda. Sales-talk, you know. . . ."

"My—just fancy that!"

136

"And say—this isn't Portree, is it? This handful of houses?"

"No. No—Portree's quite a bit further over, too. This is Kinloch. It's the best centre for, for all sorts of things—much better than Portree. So we thought we'd make your headquarters here—for a day or two at least. It's a good anchorage for the ship, too. . . ."

"I'll say it is."

"And we'll be able to tour the island by bus from here, I guess? I'm just longing to see that castle—you know, with the Fairy Flag."

"Bus. . . !" Alison swallowed. "I'm afraid . . . I don't know about buses. . . !"

"Sure. That was what this guy that wrote, said—Macdonald," Mr. Macwhirter substantiated. "Macdonald—that was his name, wasn't it? He said a fleet of buses would take us round, see."

"Oh. Well, I don't . . ."

"My name's Macdonald," Joe came gallantly to her rescue. "And, say—we've fixed up something better for you than buses, see. Buses aren't Highland enough for you, we reckoned, and the roads aren't any too good for buses around here, anyhow. Shake you up. So we've got ponies for you—Highland garrons. The real thing. Travel the Highland way, see," And he darted an urgent glance from the girl to Dougie, and back.

"Just that," Dougie conceded. "There's nothing at all like the garrons for seeing the country. A right comfort, just. And devil the ticket in it."

"Ponies. . . !" Elmer Macwhirter said. "You did say ponies. . . ?"

"Hosses? You mean, sorta young hosses. . . ?"

"Sure. Garrons. They're not all that young. But they're small—and quiet, see."

"Quiet—my Chove, if they was any quieter they'd be on their tiptoes, whatever," Dougie amplified, loyally.

"Look," Mr. Macwhirter said earnestly, "I can't say I've done a lot of horse-riding recently—not a lot, see. And I guess some of the other boys . . ."

137

A skirl of girlish laughter came from the ladies' group. "Oh, Elmer—I'm sure going to enjoy seeing you on a horse!" his wife cried. "I'm going to be tickled pink."

"Mike's gonna look cute, too," another spouse shrilled. "Say—I wouldn't have missed this for anything!"

"Can't you just see them, Sue? I recollect Henry, one time, at a dude-ranch. . . ."

"Look—I didn't hear anything about buses for the women, either!" one unchivalrous husband pointed out, heatedly.

"Och, there's the motor-bikes," Dougie informed. "Plenty motor-bikes."

"Eh. . . ?"

Fortunately perhaps, just then the sound of pipe-music drew all eyes shorewards. A crowd had assembled around the jetty, the same banner that had welcomed the film company to the Misty Isle held high, three pipers pacing, fully a hundred people, and practically every male dressed in a Seaforth kilt. A brave sight for ten-thirty of a Rum morning.

Alison sighed her relief. "They're waiting to receive you," she said, unnecessarily. "I think we ought to be going ashore."

"Is it an Official Welcome?" Elmer Macwhirter demanded.

"Well—yes, I suppose you could call it that."

"Then I guess we got to go and change. We can't greet them like this," the Grand Chief of the Illinois Clans Confederation decided. He, like his colleagues, was dressed this morning merely in a light summer suiting of alpaca.

"Say—there's no need for that," Joe asserted. "You're swell as you are."

The General, who obviously was feeling distinctly uncomfortable himself in all his crumpled finery at this hour of day, agreed heartily.

But Elmer Macwhirter was adamant, as indeed were most of his fellows within ear-shot. They weren't going to insult Skye and Scotland by appearing for an official occasion in outlandish clothes. Those guys were all dressed in the kilt to receive them, weren't they? Give them half an hour. . . .

Joe was turning away, shrugging, when Alison touched his sleeve.

"Just as well," she whispered. "It'll give Dougie time to slip ashore and get some garrons rounded up. We'll have to go through with that, now."

"Yeah. That's so. Sorry. Guess I couldn't think of anything else than ponies, at short notice."

"No. I know. I was grateful, too . . . but now we've got to live up to it. Dougie—how many garrons can you get together? Within an hour or two, I mean?"

"Och, let's see—twenty, maybe. Och, more than that. Thirty."

"For four hundred! Never mind—they'll have to do. Get them, Dougie, and bring them to Kinloch just as quickly as you can. And tell Father Joseph we'll be half an hour yet. There's Jamie MacVarish—give him a shout, and he'll take you ashore. Good luck!"

.   .   .   .   .

All the *Yonkers City's* lifeboats, reinforced by half a dozen assorted craft from the shore, effected the main landing—and undoubtedly nothing like it had been seen in the Isles since the clan-warfare days, if then. The pipe-band—Detroit's pride— went first, in a boat by itself, and succeeded in maintaining a truly remarkable barrage of sound despite trying conditions and lack of piping space, quite drowning the puny efforts of the artistes on shore. Elmer Macwhirter's boat came next, like a state-barge, containing besides his own resplendent party the remainder of the Rum contingent—with the exception of Jock Laidlaw who had not yet put in an appearance. Behind, in flotilla formation, came the great and goodly company, whooping and yippeeing in really heartening fashion.

By the time that Macwhirter's boat could disgorge its passengers on to the jetty, the band was lined-up in two ranks, and rendering Skye's anthem. As the new arrivals entered this avenue, Father Joseph and his supporters could be espied at the other end, open-mouthed and dumbfounded—and it took a lot to dumbfound that representative of Holy Church. A little way aside, Hank Delmonte stood, a fresh cigar clamped in a mouth that certainly was not open, his expression inscrut-

139

able. Morag Ross held him by the arm, and beat time to the music with a wooden porridge-spoon that she happened to have with her.

Alison made the introductions, stumbling a little over the Grand Chief business and some of the lesser titles. But it is to be doubted if much of it all sank in. Appearance spoke louder than words—and undoubtedly eyes were busy, all round.

Mariota Marr took a hand, introducing the motion-picture world's Number One Director, Hank Delmonte—and thereby transforming the situation. That was a name that would make any good American sit up. It passed from mouth to mouth back through the disembarking ranks and over the water itself. Thereafter, there was a great deal of shaking of hands—Hank's, in the main—and a truce to formality.

Father Joseph could not get his carefully prepared speech in, anywhere.

Four hundred holiday-making United States citizens determinedly off-the-lead, even when of Scottish extraction, can be a distinct handful. Father Joseph was forced to appeal to Alison, and Alison to Joe, and Joe went and borrowed a drum-stick from its leopard-skinned custodian, and beat vigorously on the big drum.

That achieved its effect. Into the residuary vibrations, Joe shouted. "This is supposed to be an official reception, and the Reverend Father here's got something to say."

Climbing up on to a fish-box, the priest, in kilt, black coat, and dog-collar, cleared his throat. "My very pleasant duty it is, to welcome you all to our island," he began, and everybody cheered. "You've come a long way to be here, and we for our part have been very anxious that you should reach here safe and sound. These are tricky seas, and many a ship's been lost hereabouts before this. But, praises be, you've been delivered safely into our hands, and here you are.

"Now, I expect General Maclean, the Chairman of the Committee, and the rest of the deputation we sent to meet you on the great waters, will have been after saying all that really requires to be said by way of welcome. . . ."

Prolonged cheers.

"For the rest, the island you've come to visit will express its welcome in its own way, as time goes on—a welcome I'm thinking you'll never forget. Every house has an open door for you, every islander is your host. Our ambition is to make you feel more at home here than ever you did back in your own country. All that it falls to me to do now, ladies and gentlemen, is to sketch in the programme we've prepared for you. As you'll be well aware, this is by way of being a special sort of week with us, a week when, as well as laying ourselves out to entertain you, we try to compress a sort of—h'm—of reflection of our island year's activities, our way of life. You'll all have heard plenty about Skye Week. I hope what you see and experience here won't be any sort of a disappointment, whatever. There'll be ceilidhs, dances, Highland Games, shinty matches, a regatta, pony-racing . . ." (Feminine cheering.) ". . . demonstrations of our island industries, folklore and local history lectures—och, and a deal more besides. And there's sea, loch, and river fishing, for all who'd like to try. Och, yes—and there's the film-making. Mr. Delmonte will be glad, I'm sure, to let you have a bit glimpse at that. Altogether, I don't think you'll weary here, for a day or two. But if you do, just come and tell us, and we'll see what we can do about it."

"Attaboy!"

"The Skye's the limit!"

"Yippeee!"

"Exactly. Now, here's the immediate programme. Four hundred's a bit many to be taking around in a bunch, see you—so split yourselves up. Into eight parties of fifty, say. And we'll take you round, and show you what's to be seen. Each party will be under a guide or two, and will be fed at different centres. It's all organized, and you've just got to divide yourselves up. I think that's about all, ladies and gentlemen."

In the resounding applause, Alison shook the priest's elbow. "Keep talking," she urged. "The Minister's looking as though he wants to say something. And anyway, Dougie won't be here with the garrons for ages yet!"

"Och, mercy to goodness—I can't just go on speaking," the

other objected. "It's thirsty work—and tricky too, I tell you
You could put a foot wrong just any moment . . ."

"Say—I wanna word with these guys," Hank Delmonte wa
at their side.

Father Joseph yielded him the fish-box with pleasure.

"Look," he said, "you folks did that landing pretty good
But not good enough, see. Not good enough for Hank Del
monte. No, sirree. You missed your chances, see—lots
chances. You gotta do these things like you meant them
You gotta give all you got. I could make a scene outa tha
landing, done good. But it's gotta be done good, see—n
piking. Now, if you folks'll get right back to your shi
and do it again, see—do it good—I'll get the camera
working."

"Goodness!" Alison gasped, as Father Joseph turned t
stare at her.

A murmur rose also from the listening ranks, rose loudly

"That's mighty nice of you, Mr. Delmonte," Elmer Mac
whirter declared cordially.

A second gasp from Alison Maclean.

"Gee—we're to be in a picture!"

"Oh, goody! Just think of that!"

"Say—he's a swell guy. . . ."

"Yeah—but what do we have to do, Mr. Delmonte?"

"You just do as I tell you, see, and you'll be okay. That'
all I ask. Now—get along back to the ship. And I don'
want you all coming ashore at this pier, see—lining up like
you were waiting to get into a morgue. Some of you
jump into the water, see—like you were in a hurry to get here
Put some pep into it. Sure—some of you dames, too. Hitch
'em up. Splash around some—they'll dry out, on a line
quick enough. And you get so goddam wet on this island any
how, you'll never notice a thing like that!" He chewed a
mobile cigar while the ladies' delighted screams rang out
"Now—the band gotta keep playing as it lands, see. Neve
mind about the sound—we can fix that later. But it's gotta
look like it was giving us the whole works. Yeah—drums too
A pity you ain't got a drum-majorette, with legs—no, no
you, Stupid! Never mind. . . . Okay—get going."

The official reception broke up, with a surge back to the boats. A trifle crestfallen, the Rum Development Association gravitated into a number of groups and huddles—out of which it was cleared promptly and authoritatively by the Director of Photography and the Master Prop, with their minions.

Sitting on a grassy bank, elbows on knees, chin cupped in hands, Alison spoke as Joel Macdonald hurried past. "I must say, this is all a little different from what I'd visualized," she mentioned.

"Never mind. They're loving it. So long as they're happy . . ."

When Dougie the Post arrived, herding the best part of two-score long-tailed mane-tossing garrons, an hour later, the first two waves of the landing parties had been repulsed by Hank Delmonte's rasping tongue, but were returning gallantly to the attack, undefeated and in the best of spirits, indeed with colours flying if a little wet.

A somewhat bewildered Dougie was greeted by a broadside of protest against his big-footed clattering rodeo. Couldn't he keep his outfit off the location. . . ?

"What in hell are the broncs for, anyway?" Delmonte wanted to know.

Alison explained. "They're to mount the tourists on—the visitors. Or some of them. To get them around. We've little other form of transport. . . ."

"Say—these gonna ride these?" and the Director's eloquent finger stabbed in a half-circle.

"Well . . . that's the idea, anyway. I don't know if . . ."

"Holy Mike—that oughta be worth shooting! We'll do them, in the afternoon—if the rain keeps off. Stick around some place, with the nags, you—but not too close, see."

"Oh, well . . ." Alison said, sighing.

.   .   .   .   .

Though lunch was awaiting the visitors in various parts of the island, the meal eventually was held in the familiar surroundings of the *Yonkers City's* palatial dining-saloons. And an excellent and satisfying repast it turned out to be—even though much of it stuck in Alison's throat. As she pointed out to Joel Macdonald, all this wasn't earning a single dollar for Rum.

They were going to have the landing-scene done just once more. Hank Delmonte was wondering whether Captain Lynski had still sufficient steam up to shift his ship a bit—the picture would look a whole heap better with the ship in a slightly different position—and Father Joseph was warning that there wasn't all that room in the anchorage with the *Ailsa* lying there already and the mail-steamer due in that afternoon, when Alison was struck all of a heap. The mail-steamer —of course! She had forgotten all about it. Agitated, she hastened to drag the priest and Joe aside.

"Look," she pointed out. "The *Lochgarve*. When it calls this afternoon, it'll see this American ship hidden here —and our secret will be out! By night, everybody in Mallaig will have heard there's a liner at Rum, and by to-morrow all Skye will know where its boatload of Americans are!"

"Whe-e-e-ew!"

"Mercy on us—I never did think a thing about the mail-steamer!" Father Joseph admitted.

"What are we to do?"

"The boat'll have to be kept from coming into the loch," Joe said.

"To be sure. And Jamie MacVarish could be sailing out to the mouth of it, there, to meet them. That's it."

"What good would that do?" the young woman demanded. "They could still see in—right up to the head of the loch. And they'd only be more suspicious. This great white ship would stand out a mile, as they crossed the mouth of the loch."

"Ummmm."

"If only the mist would come down now, when it's wanted! Oh, how on earth can you hide a ship this size?"

"Smoke," Joe told her. "I guess that's the way the Navy does it."

"Smoke? *Smoke!* Of course!" Alison cried. "That's

the answer. A curtain of smoke across the mouth of the loch."

"Yes, yes, my dear—but how?" Father Joseph wanted to know. "We'd need an awful deal of smoke . . ."

"That's right," Joe agreed. "I don't see . . ."

"Why—moorburn, of course!" the girl told them. "Heather. In March and April the island's often just about blotted out under smoke, when we burn it for the pasture and the grouse. And it smokes for days. We'll set fire to the heather on the south side of the loch, and the south-west wind that never fails us will blow the smoke right across the mouth of it. Then Jamie can go out with his boat to meet them, and tell them it would be dangerous for them to steer through it."

"Lovely!" Father Joseph beamed. "Beautiful!"

"Would you get enough smoke to hide the loch? Thick enough?" Joe wondered.

"You don't know how moor burns, or you wouldn't ask," he was assured. "We'd better tell Rory—it's his land! And we haven't much time. It's after two now, and the steamer's due in at three-forty-five. We'd better get ashore."

"What about the visitors?"

"They're getting along pretty well without us!" That was just a little tart. As was the question she threw at Joel Macdonald. "*You'll* be too busy film-making to come long, I expect?"

"C'mon."

And so a large party of islanders, all somewhat at a loose end owing to the failure of the arranged programme, was hastily mobilized and hurried along the south shore of Loch Scresort, escorted by the entire juvenile population of Rum. Dougie, abandoning the bulk of his horseflesh, rode on ahead with Major Rory to plan out the actual areas to be burned, having respect to the strength and direction of the wind, the state of the heather, and the grouse prospects.

Moorburn is something of a science, if it is to be controlled and guided. First of all, parties largely composed of children were sent down-wind through the selected areas to beat out livestock, sheep, cattle, and wild things—a noisy and cheerful proceeding. Then key fires were lit to leeward of each area to be burned, and from these the incendiaries lit bog-pine torches. In line abreast they spread out to ignite their tracts, still from the lee side not from the windward as Joel had anticipated; he had visualized the breeze blowing the flames before it—but apparently the reverse applied and the fire ate back into the wind. Flanking the torch-wielders were beating parties armed with juniper-boughs and old sacks, to keep the fires within prescribed limits.

At first the heather appeared to be reluctant to burn, but presently the flames shot up and caught hold with a heartening crackling and splutter. No vast quantities of smoke seemed to be generated, and Joe was beginning to shake his head over this, when the first great yellow-brown billows rolled up *behind* the flames. The heather itself seemed to burn cleanly; it was the sub-strata of blaeberries and moss and roots and incipient peat that made the smoke. In due course the entire braeside was spouting acrid sombre clouds that surged and lifted and fused into one great canopy, and then was swept away satisfactorily downhill on the westerly breeze, on to the surface of the loch.

All this took some time, of course. Watches were consulted with increasing frequency. It was three-twenty before Alison and her coadjutors were satisfied with the smoke. Then, all must hurry round the fires and uphill to the summit of the ridge, to watch for the ship.

She was in sight when they reached the crest, four or five miles off. From up here it was apparent that the smoke did indeed mask the whole trough of the loch; more than that, it filled it. And far beyond that, on the north shore it spread and drifted. And even as they watched, out from under the pall of it, seaward, emerged the water-beetle that was Jamie MacVarish's boat, in good time, to wait, rising and falling on the broad bosom of the sea.

The *Lochgarve* wasn't going to escape Jamie. They could see him standing up, waving, from their hilltop.

"My Chove—if he goes and upsets his boatie and drowns himself, my mails will be lost on me, entirely!" Dougie complained.

146

But the gallery was denied the excitement of watching this possible development, for another excitement altogether. An elderly crofter who had elected to remain below, came panting up to them, with the word that the fire had taken a loan of them, whatever. A draught of air from a sort of corrie in the braeface had caught it and sent it off in a new direction, it had jumped yon bit green and moss, and now was away down the burn straight for Angus Og's bit croft. . . .

Angus Og let out a wail, and dashed off downhill. The entire company streamed after him.

One time, there had been crofts all along that broad hill-side, but depopulation had taken its toll, here as elsewhere, and now there was only Angus Og's left. The heather had crept over the others, as is its way, and the sole survivor was left in a green enclave amongst the purple and brown. And now, the very burn that watered it was traitorously leading fire down on it.

The silent Rory MacNeill took charge, without debate. There would be no stopping the blaze coming down the funnel of the burn. The only course would be to create some sort of fire-break below, where the burn-channel opened out into the wedge of cultivation. Heather and bracken came right down to the edge of Angus Og's patch of oats, already beginning to yellow towards harvest. Those oats would burn—and represented the winter feed without which the crofter's beasts would not survive. They had to be saved.

Running down past the flaming gully, the Major set his people on to lighting a new line of fires, in the face of the oncoming conflagration—small fires that they could control, to counter the large fire that they could not. The trouble was that now they were working in the dense rolling clouds of smoke that not only set them coughing and their eyes streaming, but obscured their vision almost entirely. And it was stifling hot. They could hear the roar of the big fire behind them above the feeble crackle of their new line, though they could not see it now. They worked with handkerchiefs, scarves, any sort of cloth, dipped in the burn and tied over their noses and mouths.

Feverishly they laboured, lest the devouring blaze should reach their infuriatingly slowly growing burned area while it was insufficiently wide to stop it. The lighters worked from the windward now, with a strong party in front to keep their new fire from going too far towards the grain. And it was a fierce wind that blew on them now, funnelled down the burn-channel and enhanced by the hot onrush of expanding air from the conflagration. When the first line of the fire-break was well alight, Rory ordered a second line to be lit, and then a third, right up to the oats. Coughing, gasping, eyes swollen, faces blackened, the company fought and wrought in that swirling choking confusion.

When they were hard up against the standing stalks of the corn, on a hundred-yard front, they had to turn and wait. They could do no more. How wide and how well burned their precautionary charred area was, no one could tell for sure, because of the smoke. Rory estimated it at thirty yards. Would it be sufficient?

A murky orange glow began to stain the dun obscurity of the smoke. It grew stronger, brighter. Scores of pairs of aching red-rimmed eyes peered through narrowed lids at it. Would it leap on, swallow up their smouldering break—or would there be insufficient fuel left to maintain its headlong career? For perhaps three hectic menacing minutes nobody knew the answer. And then it became apparent that the glow was no longer growing, was even declining. The roar was less loud. Isolated shoots and fingers of fire darted forward and sideways, but the main wall of flame was held. Once out of the air-shaft of the burn-tunnel, the force was less concentrated, the fire spread and dispersed itself. Poor as it was, the fire-break was enough to check it. The croft was saved.

But the weary, sore-eyed, and begrimed company could not rest, yet. All round its now far-flung perimeter, the fire had to be beaten, stamped and belaboured into harmlessness—a less urgent and difficult task, since, save in the burn's area, it was eating back *against* the breeze, and with the smoke blowing away therefrom. Still, it was slow, hot, and tiring work. Before the last of the waves of that red tide had

148

ebbed, and only isolated upsurges and spurts of flames survived out in the black wilderness where glowing feelers wriggled, it was an exhausted and bedraggled party that assembled to wash itself as best it might in that deplorable burn.

Joel looked as though he had been sweeping chimneys the hard way, Rory MacNeill had lost quite a proportion of his handsome moustaches, and the General's fine full-dress uniform never would be the same again. Even Alison was considerably less than her usual pleasantly effective self—though it was amazing how much more she was able to do with a little burn-water and a pocket-comb than were the others.

"Well," Joe said, rubbing at the remains of his eyebrows. "I guess we made your smoke."

That was neither contested nor amplified.

Father Joseph wiped white furrows on his cherubic countenance. "As well Mr. Delmonte wasn't with us, I'm thinking," he observed. "I wouldn't like to be spending the evening doing retakes of this."

It was after six o'clock before the battered company got back to Kinloch—to find the place deserted, save for Morag Ross who sat on Father Joseph's fish-box knitting. They had all gone back to the ship for their supper, she announced. Mr. Delmonte was very annoyed about the pony-riding—they'd wasted his afternoon on him. Now they'd have to shoot that in the morning, he said. And there was an invitation for them all to go out to the ship that evening as guests at a concert the Americans were going to give, with a dance to wind up.

Alison all but burst into tears. It was all wrong, she declared heatedly—everything was upside-down. It was themselves that were supposed to be doing the entertaining, not these people. All the food they had prepared, all the things they had organized, all the plans they'd made, and the trouble they'd gone to . . . ! And not a dollar, not a cent had they collected! A whole day past of Rum Week—and Rum no ha'penny the better! She for one wasn't going to their wretched concert—she was going home to bed. And

149

all Americans—all Americans without exception—could go to . . . to Skye, for all she cared!

The men eyed each other, the way men do on such occasions. "Well, well," Joe said. "You're sorta tired, I guess."

"A cup of tea—that'll make a new woman out of you," Father Joseph asserted, patting her shoulder.

"An aspirin and a couple of fingers in a glass," the General suggested. "Never fails."

"Ah . . . umm," said Rory MacNeill.

"I'm not! It wouldn't! You know nothing about it! And don't stand there grunting at me!" the young woman cried, at each of them, consecutively and convulsively. "Dougie—take me home."

And then the rain began.

On the Nine O'clock News that night, it was announced that some slight concern was being felt in some quarters over the continued non-appearance of the United States cruising liner *Yonkers City*, 12,000 tons, last seen by H.M. destroyer *Dunmow* some 220 miles W.S.W. of St. Kilda early on Saturday morning. The ship was on a cruise to Skye in Scotland, in connection with the well-known Skye Week now proceeding. She had been expected to anchor off Portree on Sunday night or Monday morning, but no sign had been seen or heard of her in the Hebrides. There had been no rough weather or fog reported, which might have delayed her, or forced the vessel to take shelter in some unfrequented harbour or anchorage of the island. While there was no reason for anxiety over the safety of the ship, which was a modern vessel equipped with every scientific device, coastguards and coastal shipping were requested to keep a look-out for her.

II

ALL NIGHT IT RAINED, AND CONTINUED ON TUESDAY
morning with a level and ominous persistence. Even the most
optimistically inclined meteorologically—which for once did
not include Alison Maclean—could voice little conviction that
sunshine was just around the corner. The wind had shifted
to a couple of points north of west, and the pessimists talked
about three days of it. Alison could have screamed.

The Eight O'clock News reported that there had been no
word of the missing American steamship, and that the Royal
Navy and the R.A.F. had been ordered to institute a search.
Aircraft from Coastal Command's Ardblair Station would
quarter the Hebridean area.

This news was received on Rum with mixed feelings—
though, perhaps fortunately, it was not received very exten-
sively, for owing to lack of electricity on the island and the
difficulty of getting batteries charged, there was insufficient
radio activity to make it really worthwhile for anyone to pay
for a licence. The General picked it up, however, as did
Father Joseph, and the latter, hastening across to Kilmory
House, convinced Alison that it was time to call another
meeting of the Rum Development Association's Executive Committee. Rested, but only a little less depressed
than on the previous evening, the Hon. Secretary gloomily
agreed.

They assembled for a sort of early elevenses in the library
of the Rum Palace—to which Hank Delmonte and his
colleagues had not yet returned from their concert and dance
on board the hospitable *Yonkers City*. Only Victor Dufour,
who did not like tartan parties, remained on the premises, and
he was still in bed, where alone he could find the escape that
he increasingly sought, from all Americans, Scotchmen, and

tiring people generally. The General, exercising his undoubted *ex officio* privilege as Chairman of the Association, sat in at the meeting. In fact, he did more—he led the discussion. He felt that it was just about time that they stopped all this nonsense, he said. He should have put his foot down before this. It was one thing taking a crack at those morons in Skye, but now that the Navy and the Air Force were coming into it, it was different. They'd have the police involved next—and once the police got a foothold on Rum, Heaven knew what a bother they might be, poking their inquisitive noses into matters that were no business of theirs—like the odd whisky-still, motor-vehicle licences, or even these wireless-sets! It would be the height of folly to have any of the breed descending upon their island, under any pretext.

Thoughtfully, Dougie admitted that there was something in that.

Father Joseph observed that, och, that was right enough, but they mustn't be too hasty. They'd gone to a lot of trouble that it would be a great pity just to waste altogether, at this stage. Joel pointed out, from his experience in the air photography service, that if it was the planes that they were worrying about, this rain and low cloud would successfully blind any aircraft foolish enough to come snooping about Rum. As long as it lasted, they wouldn't find any liner.

But as long as it lasted, *they* wouldn't be able to get these American tourists involved in Rum Week and the spending of dollars, Alison contended. And that was the whole point in them being there—not to play at being film-actors. They had never thought of being able to retain the ship for more than three days, or maybe four—the secret was bound to come out, one way or another—and here was the second day, and nothing achieved. It was heartbreaking. . . .

Och, it wasn't so bad as all that, the priest averred encouragingly. They could still go on with most of the programme. What was a drop of rain, at all . . . ?

To them—nothing! But to Americans, it seemed to be a disaster, the girl declared. They wouldn't budge out from under cover, as far as she could see, so long as it fell. They'd never get them ashore.

This might be something of an exaggeration, Joel was suggesting mildly, when the General interrupted to assert that whether it was or wasn't, was neither here nor there. The point was, it was time that they got rid of that ship. They should pack it off to Skye, right away.

Father Joseph wouldn't disagree with the General, of course, but he thought that they owed it to their own folk, and to these Americans too, to do a little better than that by them. What would the poor creatures find to be doing on Skye? If they couldn't get any of them ashore in the rain, could they not at least lay on some of their ploys out on the ship? They could have at least home-industries demonstrations, folklore and history lectures, ceilidhs and so on—the indoor things—out there. They might even hold a sheep-shearing competition aboard. If Mahomet wouldn't come to the mountain . . .

Hear, hear, Dougie applauded. He doubted if they'd get the garrons on to the ship, though. . . .

Admittedly they couldn't keep the vessel there indefinitely, the priest went on. They'd have to reckon on it being away tomorrow or the next day, anyway—the earlier if the weather cleared. But let them be making the most of it while it *was* here.

Joel, sitting back, guessed that it wasn't a whole lot to do with him. But he'd reckoned that they'd have more guts than to throw in their hand at this stage. Those folks on the ship were okay. They were prepared to be tickled to death here, and it was up to themselves to see that they *were* tickled to death, come rain, Navy, Air Force or what-have-you. They should get out and aboard the ship right away, and do their stuff. And had they forgotten Hank Delmonte? That guy wasn't going to let his crowd-scenes sail away till he'd finished with them, he'd be bound. What did they think? They'd have these tourists with them till the weather was fine enough to resume shooting—or he didn't know his Hank! So what?

Somewhat startled at this conception of the situation, the Executive Committee exchanged glances. All but Alison Maclean. She was staring straight ahead of her out of the rain-blurred window, and something of the old shine was beginning

153

to return to her blue eyes. Noting it, Joel Macdonald grinned and lifted his lanky figure to its feet.

" Well, I guess this is where we ring the gong for the second round! " he said.

.   .   .   .

So the early afternoon saw the quite surprising spectacle of a wholesale descent upon the liner of large numbers of islanders ferrying out the most unlikely cargoes in the teeming rain. There were spinning-wheels, and hand-looms, bolts of tweed, an iron dye-pot, black-boards, ancient weapons, lobster-pots, cured hides, fish-nets, baskets, utensils and implements of every kind, and the best part of a flock of sheep. It says a great deal for Captain Ed Lynski that he not only permitted all this to come aboard without spoken protest but even allowed his crew to assist in the operation. It was not long before his spotless vessel resembled the Highland and Agricultural Society's annual show.

There was no doubting the impact made on the visitors. They were tickled, unquestionably, pink if not to death. They were loud in their interest, their questions, and their praise. Demonstration of the Celtic way of life proceeded apace.

The difficulty was, of course, to translate demonstration into exploitation—especially with the traditional Highland good manners as an added handicap. In certain minor items there was no great problem. A crofter weaving on a hand-loom could sell homespun tweed entirely naturally. A man carving stags-horn trinkets or a woman knitting socks and jumpers did not require to deny that similar goods were readily available, at a suitable price. There was nothing to prevent Morag Ross getting willing scientific researchers into a corner and demon-strating second-sight, at a scientifically appropriate fee per time. But these were mere flea-bites, making no real impres-sion on the close-packed wads of dollar-bills that undoubtedly stuffed those transatlantic pockets and handbags. Alison racked her brains for a dignified and effective method of bridging the unfortunate gap. There must *be* a way.

154

Her trouble was that she herself was lecturing on Rum history, and that required all her application, being almost entirely creative work and a real tax on the imaginative faculties.

The strange thing was, the problem really solved itself in the end. For a wet afternoon that one went like lightning, and before Alison had finished her fifth batch of historical students, she became aware that preparations were afoot to entertain the entire Rum company to an evening meal on board. This had to be nipped in the bud promptly, needless to say—for if they were to accept this sort of hospitality on the ship, then it would be incumbent upon them to feed all the Americans for nothing when they came ashore—thus quite demolishing their carefully cherished catering-trade. So Alison had to round up all her people, and insist on them going ashore forthwith—at the same time assuring their pressing hosts that they would be back in the evening for the ceilidh that they were going to present; they would need to change, and fetch instruments and so on with them. . . .

It was only then, as the disembarkation began, that it became apparent that though the islanders were going ashore, albeit reluctantly, the curious and diversified cargo that they had brought with them was not, none of it—except the sheep. Without exception every item and implement, all apparatus and equipment, every curio and accoutrement, was staying aboard—sold as souvenirs. Spinning-wheels and looms, claymores, targes and *sgian dubhs*, lobster-pots and fish-nets—all had been snapped up. Even the big iron dye-pot and the spade for digging peats had gone. The sheep alone had survived the onslaught of the world's most assiduous buyers, and even their fleeces had disappeared.

Bewildered, as they proceeded homewards, the girl listened to the tales, the sagas of trade and commerce, and unbelievingly handled the crisp green-backs. Sheaves of them. Nobody knew quite what to do with all this paper—since even British money did but little circulating on an island largely self-supporting. In theory, dollars sounded wonderful, but in practice they lacked any immediate utility. In the end, Alison was given them all to keep. Astonishingly, when added up, they totalled almost eighteen hundred dollars—not far off seven hundred and fifty pounds. It seemed unbelievable . . . but there was the money, in her hand. And there was a lot more where that came from; four hundred avid souvenir collectors are not readily satisfied, once the fever grips them. It was an extremely thoughtful-eyed and preoccupied people who wound their ways home through birchwood and heather to croft and cottage that evening.

The ceilidh was a modified success . . . but undoubtedly it would have been more so had the performers and company generally had their minds fully on the programme. There was too much whispering in corners, too much knowledgeable nudging, nose-tapping, surreptitious hand-shaking, and even crackling of notes, for true artistry to flourish. Also, the bars were a decided distraction. Still, the thing went very well on the whole, and the items contributed by the visitors themselves created a great impression—particularly the *pièce de résistance* presented by some of the ladies, of a sixteensome reel translated into a Middle West idiom and danced in cute tartan panties and bras. This triumph left Rum literally speechless. Outnumbered four to one, the islanders tended to relinquish the initiative as the evening wore on, and they learned quite a lot about ceilidhs in consequence. Indeed, at well past midnight, they learned how to sing Auld Lang Syne, with sundry unique and appropriate gestures, and even were provided with a selection of authoritative translations and interpretations of the libretto. It was an unforgettable night.

Bemused as they were apt to be, the islanders were able to hand over to Alison Maclean almost another eight hundred dollars before parting.

. . . . .

Wednesday morning was as wet as Tuesday, and the News gloomily informed the sort of people who enjoy dire disaster added to the other distresses of breakfast-time that the American ship was still missing, and the possibility that she had met with mishap, while not probable, could not be dismissed altogether. Unfortunately, the weather over the north-west of Scotland was poor, with visibility very limited, and aircraft were much handicapped—though an improvement was forecast. The Navy and R.A.F. were continuing with their search.

Alison was uncertain as to programme. The weather looked hopeless—though the wireless said that it might clear. But how seldom had weather-forecasts any relation to weather on Rum? Hank Delmonte was stamping about in awe-inspiring wrath. This goddam rain was costing untold wealth. A couple of hours' shooting time, and he'd have his crowd-scenes complete. Just a couple of hours—that was all he asked. Anybody not in a position to give him those two miserable hours had better keep out of his way.

Alison decided to go out to the *Yonkers City* for a conference. She got as far as the jetty at Kinloch. There the tide of mackintoshed, burberryed and sou'-westered pilgrims met her like a flood. Rain or no rain, they were coming ashore.

Surprised, the girl sought for Mr. Macwhirter. But Elmer wasn't there. Elmer must still be on board. What *was* this, then? Where were they going? Just any place—any place, see. A stroll. A walk. Stretching their legs. . . .

Then they must get this organized, Alison cried. They had any amount of things on the island to show them yet—a shinty match, a regatta, pony-racing, Highland Games, competitions. They hadn't scratched the surface of Rum yet . . . she meant, of course, of this rum little island!

There was much nodding and smiling. She sure ought to contact Elmer about all that. Elmer would fix it. They were just having a stroll, see. . . .

It was quite apparent that the stroll was the thing, and organized entertainment was not what they had come ashore for. In fact, only those close under her eye were doing the standing and smiling—the rest were drifting away, dispersing, determinedly strolling. Alison was loth to let them go—but she perceived no way of holding them, unaided.

More were coming ashore, and as the girl turned to see if Elmer Macwhirter was amongst them, those to whom she had been talking took the opportunity to escape. The Grand Chief was not present yet, but one of the newcomers, a voluble lady, was more forthright than the rest. They were just going to take a look round, to see if they could pick up some little memento of their visit, a souvenir, see. Some of the folks on board had gotten some mighty cute things yesterday. Something to take back home to show Junior. . . .

So that was it! That was the magnet that prevailed over the rain! Alison shrugged, and stood back. Apparently there were more ways of killing a cat than choking it with cream. Far be it from her to stem the spate. If this was what they wanted. . . . Still, she sighed even as she shrugged. After all their fine preparations . . .

She went and sat on a hillock in the rain, and watched the *Yonkers City* launches ferrying the people across in a steady stream. It looked as though the urge to buy, and buy one better than one's neighbour, had swept the ship.

And so, like a swarm of entirely amiable but efficient and competitive locusts the pilgrims swept over and despoiled the island, spreading out along every track and pathway, engulfing every croft and cottage. That they were not completely rebuffed became early evident, as gradually a smaller tide began to flow the other way, as triumphant passengers headed shipwards again, laden, islanders assisting them to carry away their own familiar plenishings and household goods, old folks, children and garrons pressed into service. The fever to sell can be as virulent and contagious as that to buy. The semi-auto-spoliation of Rum had begun.

It took time, of course—all that soaking day. For one thing, distances were great, transport difficult, and rivalry keen—after all, there were up to four hundred buyers to forty-odd houses, ten apiece. Also, the Highlander is a mannerly, conversational, and essentially civilized individual, loth indeed to allow any subject to be defiled and contaminated and commercialized by any unsuitable reference to money, and not even a creepie-stool or a pair of stag's antlers could change hands without first exhausting all due discussion on the weather, the state of the crops, foreign policy, and the flat rate for fish. If this had the effect of delaying deals, it also undoubtedly increased keenness to possess and heightened the bidding.

When it was obvious that the affair had become a major operation, the Executive Committee perforce accepted the situation philosophically, and started to organize transport. Dougie was extremely useful here, running a sort of pony-express with strings of pack-garrons. These and flying-squads of bearers kept the traffic moving and kept goods from piling up. Depots were established at Kilmory, Guirdil, Papadil and Dibidil where heavy and bulky articles, duly marked with the new owners' names, could await transportation by pony team. It was found convenient to use the erstwhile Folk Museums for this purpose—these having been more or less cleared in the first wave, of course, like alluvial diamond-fields. From these centres, carrier parties wound across the heather, bearing the gathered and collected chattels, keepsakes and white elephants of generations, from butter-churns to battle-axes, and cromachs to cradles. Few were the objects considered too difficult, bulky, or unprepossessing to tranship to the States, for private satisfaction, public display, or in the cause of science and education. There was even a proposal to purchase, dismember, and number for eventual re-erection, an entire croft-house, but this promising project came to nothing unfortunately, owing to problems connected with transport and the lack of dry-stone builders in Detroit.

There was no ceilidh or entertainment that night. All concerned, islanders and passengers alike, were much too tired, with walking, talking, bargaining and porterage. Also, there was considerable head-steaming, foot-steeping, and other anti-catarrhal measures aboard the *Yonkers City*; it had rained all day, without a break—though it was apparent to the knowledgeable that beyond Rum the sun was now shining. Hank Delmonte's cameras had not turned once, and the film people slunk about, striving to keep out of sight and sound of their Director—except for Mariota Marr, of course, who seemed to like trouble. The General's wireless-set declared that despite better weather conditions the tourist ship had not been traced, and that it was understood that the matter was now being discussed at Cabinet level.

Altogether, it was no night for ceilidhing.

A brief meeting of the Executive was held in Morag Ross's Beehive Inn—to be out of the way of the irate Delmonte, and brief because of the lateness of the hour, Alison having spent the entire evening counting dollar bills. The business was dispatched with commendable celerity. It was unanimously agreed that the *Yonkers City* should be packed off to Skye just as soon after daybreak next morning, Thursday, as Hank Delmonte's well-known and imperative requirements permitted. Things were coming to a head, if the Cabinet was now involved; Victor Dufour was suspected of having informed certain of the visitors that they were on the wrong island; and moreover, the mail-steamer called again at 9 a.m. on Thursday, and another fire would be just too much—even if the soaking heather would burn. Mallaig would be bound to know by noon, and everybody else thereafter. Anyway, forty-three thousand dollars was probably as much as they could expect to collect off one ship-load . . . and Skye was welcome to the rest. Only, life looked as though it would be somewhat Spartan for the population of Rum for the next generation or two.

Even Joel Macdonald gasped at the disclosure of the total takings. Forty-three thousand bucks—that was all of sixteen, no, seventeen thousand pounds, wasn't it?

Alison supposed that it was, really. It seemed a lot of money. It meant that their visitors had spent about a hundred dollars a head. And she hadn't the faintest idea what they were going to do with it all. But at any rate, they had justified the existence of the Rum Development Association . . . she supposed.

On that pensive note, the meeting adjourned.

12

ALISON HAD THE IMPRESSION THAT SHE HAD barely set her head to the pillow, when she was awakened. Dougie was at her window, tapping.

"Miss Ailie! Miss Ailie!" he said in a penetrating whisper. "Och, will you wake up, for goodness sake?"

"Eh . . . ? What's that? What's the matter . . . ?"

"I've just had Torquil Mackinnon at me. He says there's a couple of Skye boats landed near Guirdil!"

"Skye . . . ? Goodness me. *Now*, you mean . . . in the dark?"

"Yes. An hour or so back, maybe. He came right over. . . ."

"And what are they up to? What are they doing—these Skye people?"

"Och, the good Pete knows, at all. But no good, I'll be bound."

"But . . . do we have to do anything about it? Just now, I mean?" Bed felt extremely comfortable.

"My Chove—those borachs wouldn't be after landing here, at a bit like that, in the middle of the night, would they, and leaving their boats in a lonesome bay, if they weren't up to mischief?"

"Oh, well . . . I suppose not. All right. I'll join you in a minute. Look—have you done anything about Joe—Mr. Macdonald?"

"No—not yet. I came right here."

"Well, I think you should get him. And Hughie Bain, maybe. How many of them are there—the Skyemen?"

"Torquil didn't just say . . ."

"All right. I'll bring two or three garrons down to the road. . . ."

By the time that Alison, clad in jodhpurs and sweater, with three saddled ponies, reached the road-end, Joel was standing in sombre silence beside Torquil Mackinnon, a middle-aged crofter of Altbeg near Guirdil, collar turned up and hands deep in pockets. It had stopped raining, and stars were gleaming, but the night wind was chill. His greeting was limited to a grunt.

Mackinnon's story was told, with all the Highlandman's appreciation of detail and atmosphere, as they waited for Dougie and Hughie Bain. He had been just for going to his bed when he had remembered some old lobster-pots that he had dumped in a bit cave at the little bay of Camus na Croe a year or two back. He'd been after selling two-three lobster-pots to the Americans that afternoon, and he just minded of these ones that they might go the same way. A pity to be wasting them, and old lobster-pots not wanted just every day. So, taking his son, young Alicky, with him, he thought he'd go right along and get them, in case the Americans were for off early, and he hadn't the time in the morning. The cave was about half a mile just from his croft, and they were nearly there when they heard voices. It was a queer time and place to be hearing the like, so they went quietly. And there was a bunch of men tying up two motor fishing-boats, and away inland with them. He couldn't say just how many—it was dark. A dozen, maybe. He had had a look at the boats, and they had Skye registrations on them. Not just liking the sound of that, he'd sent Alicky after them, to be keeping an eye on them, and then he'd hurried back home and got his other boy, Wee Kenny, out of his bed to go keep in touch sort of, with his brother. Then he'd come straight on here, on his motor-bike.

Dougie and Hughie Bain had now come up, and a brief council was held. What these Skyemen were up to was problematical, but they were probably a strong reconnaissance party. And undoubtedly, they could not be allowed to roam about Rum at will. If they once got over to the east side of the island, they could scarcely avoid seeing the brilliantly lit-up *Yonkers City*. That must be prevented. But it was no use making plans at this stage, with no indication of the intruders' intentions available. The obvious course was to get after them as quickly as possible, and formulate plans later.

Dougie got out his motor-bike, to accompany Torquil Mackinnon back at speed, to rout out one or two more crofters from the Guirdil area, while Alison, Joe and Hughie rode the garrons. It was one of Kilmory's trafficky nights.

The thud and splatter of their going made up for the lack of conversation. Up the dark and streaming track to Bobadil, and right-handed, down the Shellesder River, the riders pounded, with the bicycles, lightless, far ahead in the gloom. Only one remark Joel Macdonald made, as they clattered down the westwards-facing glen beneath the canopy of the stars.

"I guess nobody ever dies in their beds, on Rum," he observed grimly. "The old-timers' West's got nothing on this island!"

Where the track forked, just above Guirdil on its bay, two dark figures awaited them, the Maclean brothers Donald and Sammy, whose croft lay nearest at hand. Dougie had roused them. One of them had brought a shot-gun with him—which Alison at least couldn't help feeling was excessive in the circumstances. Joe and Hughie drew up behind them on their ponies, and they took the right-hand fork.

Altbeg, the Mackinnon's croft, lay almost a mile north of Guirdil, up over a small headland and down again. With the land towering black on their right and the sighing sea glimmering wanly on their left, they urged their sturdy mounts over the cliff-path. Dougie was waiting for them at Altbeg, with another Maclean known as The Whale. Torquil Mackinnon had gone on ahead to try to contact his boys. He had a bit of an electric-torch with him, and maybe he'd be able to signal back to them.

Alison suggested that since the Skyemen had set off inland, it would be a waste of time for them to go right along the coast to this bay, Camus na Croe—especially as the ground rose almost into cliffs behind it, and much more gently from here. This was accepted.

Leaving the ponies and the bicycle at Altbeg, the six men and the girl set off inland and upwards; they would do better on foot, now.

This north-westerly corner of Rum consisted of a five or six-hundred-foot plateau of peat and old heather, lochan-dotted and water-logged, known as Monadh Dubh, or the Black Moor, a poor place at any time but especially so at night and after wet weather. Strangers would be lost easily in that waste of hags and hummocks and pot-holes—nor readily found.

Once on high ground, they took a north-easterly course. The Whale saw the light first, away due north of them, a tiny yellow eye winking in the purple night. Towards it they made, an unpleasant scramble along the broken edge of the escarpment. Nevertheless the light was not so far distant as they had thought. They found Torquil Mackinnon waiting beside a great outcrop, with his younger son Wee Kenny. Kenny was hiccuping with smothered excitement.

"They're away east, on the line of Loch Scarishal," Torquil reported. The largest pool in that puddly wilderness went by that imposing name. "Alicky's on their tails."

"I don't like that," the young woman said. "East is the one direction we can't afford to let them go."

"A terrible long (hic) time you were coming," Kenny reproached. "Och, they'll just be lost on us now. When I was after (hic) leaving Alicky . . ."

"Quiet, you," his father mentioned. "Alicky says there's a dozen of them, about, and one with a right English toff's voice to him."

"The Colonel-man . . . !"

"Colonel Lomax-Lincoln!"

That was Dougie and Alison in a chant.

"We'll make for this end of the loch," Torquil suggested. "Away you on, Kenny—we'll see you at the head of Scarishal."

And like a ferret the youngster darted off into the shadows.

"Poor Kenny," the girl exclaimed, with misplaced sympathy. "He must be worn out. And how on earth can he be expected to find them, in this?"

"Him!" his parent said. "Yon one is as worn out as a wriggling eel, whatever. And for finding them, he'll smell them, just—aren't they from Skye?"

They plowtered on over that benighted waste, and if their

progress inevitably was slow and erratic, at least they could console themselves with the assurance that almost certainly they would be making better time of it than would their quarry, who would not know the terrain. It was familiar ground to all of them, with the exception of Joe; indeed it was a favourite spot for the General's hind-shooting in November and December, and for other folks' shooting at less specific times. They took the poor best of the routes across, then—and made heavy going of it.

Soaked about the lower parts and liberally bespattered with peat mud, they came to the dreary head of the lost water of Scarishal, at nearly two-thirty on Alison's watch. The redoubtable Wee Kenny was not in evidence when they arrived, but within five minutes he materialized out of the gloom. He had seen Alicky again, he reported breathlessly—over a bit, half a mile maybe, at the head of the Bobadil Burn. Away down the burn the borachs had gone, and not that far ahead.

Alison groaned. That looked as though they were heading straight for Kinloch. That burn would lead them down into the green amphitheatre of Bobadil that was the geographical heart of Rum, the hub of all its glens. And a continuation of the same line that these people had followed hitherto would bring them straight into the glen of the Kinloch River. "We've got to stop them getting within sight of that liner's lights, somehow," she explained.

"Head them off?" Joe suggested. He was less than voluble, this night.

That was not so simple, either—for the most direct line was the very line that the Skyemen seemed to be taking. Still, by cutting over and downhill, southwards, they would reach the main cross-island track again, near the head of Glen Shellesder, and that would offer much quicker going than to follow the burn. If their guess was wrong, of course, as to their quarry's objective, then they stood to lose them altogether. . . .

They had to take a chance on it. Alison, Joe, Dougie and The Whale decided to try to make an encircling movement, via the track, while the others continued to follow on the heels of the strangers.

They parted company without more ado.

A series of particularly obnoxious peat-pools and lochans held up the flanking party wickedly on its dash for Glen Shellesder—nor did the rock-falls, streaming aprons of surface water, and tangled brackens of the ultimate descent aid their passage. Panting and dishevelled, they set off up the track down which they had so recently ridden. They could have done with those garrons now.

On the hill, Alison had been no sort of drag on anyone, but here on the level her legs, adequate indeed in every other respect, lacked the stride of those of her companions, and she was forced into a jog-trot to keep up. But no complaint passed her lips—which could protest to good effect, on occasion. Undoubtedly the men noted the fact—though Joe, at least, had little breath for comment.

Two miles of this, past the lonely croft of Bobadil itself, and the road-end to Kilmory, and they were into the glen of the Kinloch River. They had glimpsed no sign of movement save from flouncing sheep and disturbed shadowy deer—but of course the line of the burn that the others seemed to be following ran parallel to their own. There were two tracks down the three-mile glen to Kinloch—the main one, that could be termed the road, on the south side of the river, the lesser on slightly higher ground on the north bank. They had to make a choice, and selected the north one; it was closer to the line that it was presumed the Skyemen were taking, and certainly could be expected to be the least frequented—though whether that would weigh with them at three o'clock in the morning was doubtful. The chances were that that would be their route if Colonel Lomax-Lincoln was leading them.

Again, it was a problem to know how far down the pathway to go. They hoped that the strangers were not still ahead of them, but they could not be sure—though certainly a struck match revealed no footprints in the mud. And about a mile and a half down, the glen took a bend, beyond which it would be possible to see Loch Scresort and the illuminated liner. It was decided that Dougie should hurry on a bit, to make sure that there was nobody in front, and the others should wait by the path-side in the cover of a clump of scrub birch.

Alison it was who posed the question, after a blessed minute or two for recovery of breath. "What are we going to do if and when these people turn up?" she wondered.

"Well, now," The Whale said, and scratched his head.

"I reckon we'll have to talk to them," Joe suggested, with a certain lack of conviction. "Keep them engaged till the others come up."

"And still be outnumbered two to one!"

"Och, they're just Skiachs, lassie."

"That's the spirit, Whale," Joe was beginning to brighten up, at last.

"Just the same, I don't think we ought to use physical violence," the girl demurred. "Especially with a dozen of them. . . !"

"What's a dozen Macleods and Macdonalds and the like. . . ? Och, my goodness—I beg your pardon, Mr. Macdonald! I do so. It's just these ones they do be having in Skye. . . ."

Alison chuckled. "Spoken like a good Maclean!"

Joe enunciated deliberately. "Of the Macleans around here right now, there's one that's nothing more than an asthmatic wind-bag that needs only a pin to burst, and the other that I aim to lay across my knee, first time we get a little privacy, and belt soundly where a belting will do a Maclean most good, see. I been promising myself that for some time."

"Oh. . . !" the young woman said.

"Yeah."

"It's a very fine night that's in it," The Whale observed courteously. "Just that."

Which was true enough.

An appreciative and suitable silence developed. Twice Alison opened her mouth to speak, and twice changed her mind. The mournful calling of the curlews, the sough of the river, and the whisper of wind over heather, voiced the sentiments of the night.

But not for long.

"Here's Dougie coming back," the girl said. And at the same moment, Joe held up his hand.

"Here they come, I guess," he whispered.

Straining their ears, they listened. Undoubtedly, there was

167

somebody hurrying along towards them from the east—that could only be Dougie. But equally certainly there was movement in front, less hurried. And voices. Closer at hand too, if anything.

"Oh, dear," Alison gasped. "Dougie's going to run right into them."

"No," Joe snapped. "That mustn't happen. Lose any chance of a bluff. We got to stop them, first. Look—reckon I'd better shout. . . ."

"There they are!" She pointed. Round a bend in the track before them, a moving knot of figures had come into shadowy view.

"Yeah. Got to take a chance. . . ." Suddenly the Texan was on his feet. "Hey, boys!" he yelled. "There they are, Right in front. There's only a dozen of them. Come on!"

And into the echoes of his words, Dougie's voice rang out, behind them, loyally. "Coming! Coming!"

The Whale lifted up a rich bass, and produced a composite roar, like a stag in a rut, very heartening.

"At them, boys!" Joe added to the chorus. "Some of you, round behind them!"

That was enough for the invaders, for the moment. A few muffled grunts and exclamations from in front, a scuffling and thudding of boots, and the whole party were off the track, into the heather, and scrambling up the hillside to the north. Indubitably they imagined that black clump of scrub birch to be a mass of angry Rumaich.

"After them!" Joe bawled. "Quick—don't let them get away." And he beat a tattoo on the pathway with his shoes, his colleagues following a good example.

Seldom could four people have projected such a volume of sound into the Rum night.

.   .   .   .   .

That was a peculiar chase that developed—with the pursuit no more anxious to close the gap than were the pursued. Too close an approach would only reveal the discrepancy in numbers. On the other hand, the illusion of a chase must be maintained, in order to head these people away from such parts as would give them a view of the *Yonkers City*. That meant that they must be edged away from all this east side of the tableland on to which they were now climbing—Mullach Mor, the twin plateau to Monadh Dubh where they had been earlier. Alison would have been happier had they bolted southwards into the high hills—but that would have meant them having to cross the Kinloch River. And so, shouting and calling to each other, and well spread out, to leave no doubts as to the potency of the pursuit, they followed—but not too quickly—on the heels of the Skyemen, working ever over to the right, to the east, so that as steadily the quarry was forced north and west.

Slowly they worked uphill and on to the morasses of the high moorland, and their hullabaloo faded notably for want of breath. Still, they made enough noise for Torquil Mackinnon's party to find them readily enough—and the added lung-power was a considerable relief. The young Mackinnons especially found this sort of thing to their taste, and the night resounded to their apparently inexhaustible ululations and eldrich screechings. Brushing and stumbling through high and wiry old heather up to their thighs, slithering across peat-hags, splashing into burnlets, the chase ploughed on.

But it all took time. It was rather like beating for grouse—or better, like herding sheep, which, without the benefit of dogs, is always a slow business. It was the protractedness of it all that began increasingly to concern the girl, and set her peering at her watch. It was quarter-past four, and already the stars were paling. It would be dawn soon, and sunrise about five-thirty. It was going to be clear weather, too, of all things, with no cloud to assist them. And once it was light, the painful inadequacy of their numbers would be apparent—six men, two boys, and a woman.

She spoke to Joe, nearest to her in the wavering line, a little hoarsely, inevitably. "I don't like this. It'll be light enough for them to see how few of us there are, in less than an hour. Light enough to see to work round us too. Sunrise soon after—and it's going to be sunny, too!"

"Uh-huh. I guess you're right. But what can we do?"

"If we can get that ship away, before these people have time to make any real trouble, it's not so bad. But that means doing without your Hank's two hours on his crowd scenes."

"He'll not stand for that, trouble or none!"

"No. I daresay. But, look—you know what Rum weather's like, now. Early morning sun means nothing. It may be pouring before ten. I suggest that Mr. Delmonte has those passengers out of their bunks bright and early—just as soon as he can after sunrise—and gets his cameras turning while the sun lasts. They'd do it for him—they'd do anything for Hollywood's uncrowned king! And then the ship could get away at once afterwards. Meanwhile, we'll try to keep these wretched folk out of the way, as long as possible. . . ."

"I guess you got something there," Joe admitted. "Yep—that's about it. That means, somebody better get 'way back to Hank, right now. Better be myself, too, I guess." He rubbed his chin. "Though I can't say I'm going to enjoy interviewing that guy in his bed at dawn!"

"You're the only one who *could*," the girl pointed out. "And it's in his own interests, as well as ours. And when you've got him moving, maybe you could collect a few more of our own people to help keep these types up here out of mischief?"

"Well . . . I suppose so. It's a pity communications are so darn difficult on this island of yours. It's going to take time, as it is. How long'll it take me to get to Kilmory, from here?"

"A good hour, I'd say. It'll be three miles, at least, as the crow flies."

"And I'm no crow, see," the man pointed out. "Well, give me a line to go on, will you, and I'll see if I can make it."

"Yes. Well, keep on the line we're on just now—a bit more to the left, perhaps. . . ."

So Joel Macdonald left them, and took his lonely way into the deeper fastnesses of the moor, and the weary shepherding of the invaders took its exhausting course. Any excitement and satisfaction had died out of the night's proceedings, and only tedium remained—and sore throats.

Grey dawn found them spread out across the watershed, and gradually revealed the Skyemen as bunched together on slightly rising ground ahead. Alison passed the word along, presently, to halt—to let themselves be seen now and again but not to move forward meantime.

This development, when observed, seemed to puzzle the opposition, who, after a little hesitation, went to ground also. Thus, at about six hundred yards range, the two parties sat and eyed each other, while the light grew on the land, one side seeking to appear larger than life, the other smaller.

Alison did not mind how long this went on—the longer the better, as far as she was concerned. It was now a question of getting time to pass, time for Joe to do his stuff, for the film cameras to get working, for reinforcements to be aroused and sent up, minutes and hours of time. From where they were now, the intruders could not see Kinloch. Let them stay there, then. . . .

So they did, for perhaps half an hour. But as the shell-pink glow that heralded the sunrise began to suffuse the eastern sky, the visitors grew restive. Probably they felt that all this was getting them nowhere. At any rate, presently they were up again, and making for the skyline, with many a backward glance. Alison set her people to jumping up, bobbing down, scuttling along bent double and appearing somewhere else, but making little advance until the strangers had disappeared over the heather ridge. Then forward.

This leap-frogging performance became the pattern, and the sun rose on its repetition as the exercise moved northwards. But more and more it became patent that the Skyemen were becoming less urgent in their flight, less worried about the people behind, less inclined to be pushed northwards—which was not to be wondered at, with the hunters most obviously in no hurry to come to grips. How long could this ridiculous proceeding go on?

It was with a sinking heart that, topping one of the interminable heather ridges of that undulating wilderness, Alison perceived that the quarry was beginning to veer round eastwards once more. As they watched, there was no doubt about it—there was a distinct and deliberate trend into the rising sun. That could mean only that these people were starting to call their bluff. It was only half-past six, and they were no more than three miles north-west of Kinloch. The situation looked less than hopeful.

The best that they could do was to get down behind this ridge again, and hurry eastwards themselves, to take up a new line to discourage advances in that direction.

This manœuvre was only very partially successful. The strangers, on viewing them in the new position, were forced a point or two back into the north, but that was all; they maintained their eastwards inclination determinedly. And a repeat of the procedure, still further over, produced no improvement. The hunted were not really frightened of the hunters, any more. And they were drawing dangerously close together; no more than three hundred yards or so separated the parties now. A showdown could not be much longer delayed. Alison was at her wits' end.

What would have been the outcome of this long-drawn contest in fieldcraft, only can be guessed, for geography suddenly took a still more potent hand—and on the wrong side. The main massif of Mullach Mor sank gradually eastwards, but threw out an isolated buttress, a small hill called Meall a Ghoirtean. Between this hill and the main plateau, a burn rose out of a lochan, and had cut a deep cleft for itself on its southern course into Loch Scresort. And in their circling movement, the Skyemen had worked round until they were in a line behind that gap and that lochan, with the ravine of the burn opening a peep-hole, an avenue of vision, for them right down to the glistening waters of the loch. And dead centre, plumb in the sights as it were, the white liner lay agleam in the slanting flood of the morning sun.

That it was seen, and recognized, was only too evident from the shouts and gesticulations of the strangers.

The game was up.

13

SOMETHING LIKE DESPAIR LAID HOLD OF ALISON
Maclean. She even had to blink back the sudden welling of
tears into her eyes. An almost sleepless night and an empty
stomach may have had something to do with it. But, after
all her efforts . . .

It was the eyes of all her colleagues, however, turned automatically to her for guidance in this sorry pass, that braced
her.

"Well—that's coopered it, just!" Dougie declared lugubriously. "We've had it, whatever."

"Not at all." Surprised almost to hear her own words,
Alison gave back strongly. "Nothing of the sort. We just
have to change our tactics, that's all. They know about the
ship, now. We . . . we've just got to make out that we *wanted*
them to know, all along!"

"Eh . . . ?"

"I mean . . . look." She was working this thing out in her
own weary mind. "We've got to make the best of it, now. We
must pretend that we've been trying to catch up with them
all the time, to tell them about the ship. Or, better—we can
pretend that we look on them as a deputation from Skye,
come to take over. Yes, that's it. We're out to welcome them,
really, for coming to take over our responsibility for this ship-
load of tourists. We've been sheltering them, you see . . .
in the bad weather. Now, we're glad to be able to hand over,
to our friends from Skye!"

"Mercy on us!" Dougie requested. "And us after chasing
them and shouting at them like . . ."

"Yes—but we've just been trying to catch up with them,
to get them to stop and talk. Don't you see? It's them that
have kept running away. It's our only chance now, anyway."

Doubtfully the men looked at each other.

"Can you think of anything better, then?" she demanded. Scratched and wagged heads were all the response that she obtained to that.

"All right." She jumped up on to a hummock, in fullest view, and raising an arm, waved it and shouted. "I say! I say, there—don't keep running away from us! We want to speak to you. It's important."

That she captured the attention that she desired, goes without saying. Every glance was on her, every eye wide. Colonel Lomax-Lincoln, clearly to be distinguished now in knicker-bocker checks, actually produced a monocle to aid his vision, that shone bravely in the morning sun. But response was quite a different matter. Blankly, they all gazed at her.

"It's all right," she cried. "Really. We just want to talk."

No reply, of any sort.

"Look—wait there. We're coming over . . ."

And as with one accord, the Skyemen did the reverse. Turning about, they bolted—for the lochan, for the gap, due north-eastwards.

"Oh, *damn*!" the girl swore, and stamped a foot into the bargain. "What absolute idiots! Come on."

So the chase began again. It was easier, apparently, to reverse one's plans than to get one's opposition to realize the fact.

As they began to pound, almost desperately now, in pursuit, Dougie exclaimed. "Round this way! Bog there is, at the head of the lochan. We'll cut them off."

That was good advice, and following it they soon began to draw ahead. The others saw it too, however, and swung away, so that the two parties presently were glaring at each other from either side of the lochan, with the Rumaich on the firmer ground and making the better time. Perceiving this, the Skyemen obviously abandoned their intention of making straight down the ravine, and turned to head directly up the side of the hill, Meall a Ghoirtean.

"Oh—did you ever see such complete fools!" the young woman gasped. "Come back! Come back, you ridiculous asses!" she yelled, in unladylike fashion. "We won't eat you! You're nothing but great cowards!"

Which was a little unfair undoubtedly, on the gallant Colonel and his band, who almost certainly were brave as lions, where mere unthinking valour was called for. It seemed probable that, in this highly uncertain and fluid tactical situation, the Colonel had decided that a wise commander's course was to avoid pitched battles and close quarters until the enemy's extremely impalpable intentions, numbers and dispositions were better established.

At any rate, that appeared to be the programme, carried out with a fair degree of expertness. It entailed constant circling to the east and a considerable expenditure of time and energy; but the gap was maintained, physically and mentally, all round that hill and its eastern and southern flanks.

But though it delayed, this scalloping progress could not avert the inevitable conclusion—the geography of the island saw to that. At quarter-past eight of a brilliant August morning, the Skyemen worked out of that upland wilderness, to look directly down to the head of Loch Scresort, there to pause only for seconds before plunging on and down towards the stirring scene below, their determined welcomers a bare four hundred yards behind.

And a stirring scene it was. Scores, hundreds, of imaginatively apparelled Highlanders were milling about on the open space above the jetty at Kinloch, their colours outrivalling those of that vivid landscape, while the cameras turned and shifted and refocused, and megaphonic directions competed with spasmodic pipe-music to fill that hollow of the eternal hills with rousing sound. To and from the great white ship anchored near by, launches shuttled, busy as water-beetles. And feeling its way cautiously up the narrow waters of the loch, came the long and wicked grey shape of one of H.M. destroyers.

* * * * *

All this, and especially the latter item, Alison Maclean took in at a glance, as she poised, in turn, on the brink of that final slope. And if her heart sank, she was past the stages where its sinking had any effect on her actions. With something between a groan and a cheer, she waved on her heavy-footed party, down to the ultimate onset.

It was a race, that last descent, and a spirited one, considering the weariness of all participants—and less uneven than the four hundred yards gap might have suggested, for the Skye competitors were a little further east than were their Rum rivals, and had to slant back slightly towards the winning-post of the crowd around the jetty; moreover, the locals knew the ground. Thudding down, stumbling, sliding, tripping, the two groups drew closer and closer together. And whatever the megaphone directed, everybody in that packed arena stopped to turn and watch.

In the end, it was practically a dead heat. Converging from slightly different angles, the leaders of the now strung-out contestants came panting up to the crowd, Dougie slightly ahead on the one side, with Alison a good second—and, it is to be feared, Colonel Lomax-Lincoln less well-placed on the other. Right and left the vividly caparisoned throng drew aside to let them through, raising a considerable cheer and with shouted encouragements to all concerned. In the centre, beside the still-turning cameras, stood Elmer Macwhirter, Hank Delmonte, Mariota Marr, Captain Lynski, and Father Joseph.

The foremost Skyeman, a crofter type, slithered to a halt beside this imposing group, and naturally, had nothing to say. Dougie, drawing up alongside him, nodded portentously and grinned widely, but likewise did not commit himself to words. Alison, however, coming up, seized the Skyeman's hand, and pump-handled it vigorously. She retained hold of it, too, smiling determinedly up into his astonished face. But though her lips moved, no sound issued therefrom, save puffs and pants.

A loud clapping arose from all around.

"Och, well—very nice too," Father Joseph said acutely. "Just that. It's a fine morning for it, and that's a fact."

"Say—this the start of your Highland Games, or something?" Elmer Macwhirter wondered.

The girl wasted no precious breath on him. Twisting round

176

to face whence she had come, she pulled her captive round with her. And drawing a long, deep, quivering breath, she laid a hand on her shapely chest to seek to still its tumultuous heaving, and somehow spoke, as the rest of the visitors came lumbering up.

"Welcome . . . to Rum!" she gasped. "Good to . . . see you. Represent . . . ing Skye." She sought to swallow her unruly tonsils. "Been trying . . . to speak with you . . . for hours. Meet Mr. Elmer . . . Macwhirter, Grand Chief, Detroit. Captain Lynski, *Yonkers . . . City*. Mr. Hank Delmonte . . ."

Colonel Lomax-Lincoln was spluttering. Words as yet were beyond him too; he could only fix and unfix his monocle, and make protesting noises.

Elmer Macwhirter thrust out his hand. "Mighty glad to know you, sir . . . gentlemen," he said, heartily. "We sure appreciated that race you put on for us. A right nice gesture, that."

"Excellent," Father Joseph substantiated. "Fine style. Good leg action."

"These gentlemen are from Skye, Mr. Macwhirter. Come to escort you . . . to Portree."

"Eh? Whassat? Where . . . ?"

"Skye. Skye proper, that is. Oh, of course, this is all part of the Skye district . . . but we can't claim to be what you might call metropolitan Skye, here at Kinloch. Not like Portree. Can we, Father?"

"No, no. Not a bit of it. That would be presumptuous, my goodness."

"But . . . but, say . . . ?"

"Look here!" the Colonel got out. "What's all this . . . ?"

"It's all perfectly simple," the girl assured, her respiration getting back into its stride. "This is Mr.—er—Smith. Isn't it? And his friends. They're a deputation from the main island of Skye, come looking for the ship, the *Yonkers City*. To escort it to Portree. Isn't that so, Mr. *Smith*?" And her smile was sweetness and light—though very firmly directed at the Colonel.

"No! I mean . . . well, in a way, I suppose." That gentleman coughed, and looked a little uncomfortably at his supporters, all of whose eyes seemed to be dazzled by the brilliance of the tartan display around them. "We've certainly come to find this ship. We—ah—suspected . . ."

"Exactly. And we're very glad you've come, too. We've been looking after our American friends to the best of our ability, during the bad weather, while they've been sheltering with us. But our resources are only limited, naturally. Still, I don't think they've wearied while they've been with us. Have you, Mr. Macwhirter?"

"I'll say we haven't, young lady. You sure have done us proud. And you, of course, Mr. Delmonte. And, h'm, Miss Marr . . ."

"It was a pleasure. It's always a pleasure," that other lady murmured. "Any time." Her eyes were on a muscular member of the Skye deputation, speculatively.

"M'mmm. Quite," Mr. Macwhirter said. "But, say—I'm not too clear in my mind about this Skye and Portree business, see. We going to Portree, now. . . ?"

"That's right. Isn't it, Mr. Smith? Just as soon as Captain Lynski here can get steam up . . . though probably he keeps a little, up his sleeve as it were, all the time? You must go while the clear weather lasts. You want good weather to go in to Portree."

"Portree is a better harbour than this," the Colonel asserted stiffly. "You would have been much better there, all along. In fact, I don't see . . ."

"Now, now, Mr. Smith—I won't hear a word against our good friends here," Elmer Macwhirter declared. "They've been mighty kind—kindness itself. Ain't that so, folks?"

A swelling murmur of agreement rose from all within earshot.

"That may be so, Mr. . . . ah . . . But that doesn't alter the fact that you should never have been here, at all. This is not Skye."

"Not Skye. . . ?"

"Of course not. This is Rum—a very different island, believe me."

" But . . ."

" Isn't that just what I've been trying to tell you people, all along? " an elegant voice mentioned languidly from the background. Victor Dufour obviously felt that at last he had come across a civilized and educated man in the Colonel. " If you'd only listened to me, in the first place . . ."

" Quiet, you! " Hank Delmonte snarled. " If we gotta listen to you saying your lines, that's enough, see. Too much. On location, you paid to speak when I tell you to speak. Other times, you're Dumb Charlie. See? "

" Oh, I say . . . ! " Adonis looked around him, pained, for support. He would have received it, too, from at least a proportion of the ladies, if not their menfolk, had it not been Hank Delmonte that fell to be opposed. As it was, the only solidarity came from Lomax-Lincoln.

" What this gentleman . . ." He rather stressed that word. ". . . says is perfectly reasonable. It's all a mistake, you being here . . ."

" Hell—who says it's a mistake, hey? " That was like a whip cracking, cigar or none, as Delmonte swung on the last speaker. " You? "

Somewhat startled at the tone and power and sheer venom of that, the Colonel dropped his eyeglass. " Well—it's a fact. We've had our arrangements made. . . ."

" Oh, yeah? *Your* arrangements? Other folk got arrangements too, see."

" I'm afraid ours are the official ones, sir. They take priority. . . ."

" Goddam! " Hank said deliberately, and as deliberately looked round the entire company, his pugnacious jaw at its most prominent. Silent for a moment he stood, and all that gathering silent with him. Then, " Reckon I don't like this little squirt. Reckon he's a nut," he said, " Hey? "

And at what was practically a royal command, the assembly raised a suitable growl. It had been obeying orders from that voice for some time, and loving it.

If the Colonel's valour ever had been called in question, it was vindicated now. He took an involuntary half-pace backwards, but promptly recovered his ground again. "Are you seeking to be offensive, sir?" he demanded.

Strangely enough, it was Alison Maclean who plunged in to his aid, the essential peacemaker. "No, no—of course not," she cried. "Mr. Delmonte is just pointing out that his arrangements have their importance, too. It's all a question of timing, really. At this end, we've done our bit—stepped in in an emergency, as it were. Now, it's your turn, Mr. Smith—Portree's, and the main island of Skye's turn."

"*Main* island, young woman? I fail to understand you...."

"Oh, you know very well that there *is* a main island, though Skye comprises scores of lesser ones...." Rather desperately, the girl cast her glance about for help and inspiration in this difficult situation, unto the everlasting hills and unto the great waters, both. And neither failed her. Up on the hillside down which they had so recently plunged, another and larger company was now streaming down to them, with Joel Macdonald unmistakable, indeed well in front. Alison's heart lifted to the sight of him. In that moment, she knew unmistakably wherein lay her future and her destiny—whatever muddled and sketchy thoughts on the subject she may have entertained on the matter previously. And glancing lochwards, there was the warship, nosing its way round the tall bulk of the liner, which had hidden it hitherto from observation from this angle.

Her voice rang out with renewed confidence. "And here comes the Navy, to lead you into Portree, in style. Now you won't be long."

All eyes turned towards the loch, and quite an outcry arose at sight of the destroyer—not all of them carefree and joyous. Father Joseph, especially, gobbled like a turkey-cock.

"Good for the Navy—always on the job!" the girl called, in a gallant effort to reassure him, and others.

Into the buzz of excited comment, the metallic voice of a loud-hailer sounded. Captain Lynski looked interested, shouting for quiet. He claimed that it was calling his ship. But nothing could be distinguished, and at that moment somebody noticed the party in headlong descent of the hill, and now all but upon them. Promptly, the centre of attraction changed over, and everyone was cheering on the runners, Hank Delmonte shouting at his camera crews not to miss this.

Joel reached them a good thirty yards ahead of a somewhat motley field, General Maclean lying well back. The Texan came in in the chronic state of breathlessness—for which Alison at least was thankful; there were sundry things that it was expedient that he should hear before he started making remarks.

"Hullo, hullo!" she greeted him, gaily. "We're having lots of fun, aren't we!" And as he began to gesticulate wordlessly towards the loch and the destroyer, "Yes—the Navy's here, too. Isn't it splendid? Just on time. They'll convey our friends into Portree in style. And we've got Mr. Smith, and his deputation from the main island of Skye, with us too. They'll be able to take over from us, officially. I think it's all *most* satisfactory. Don't you?" She had never been awfully proficient at winking, that young woman, and her grimaces now were next to alarming.

Joe stared. His mouth was open anyway, of course.

"This guy been shooting out his neck," Hank Delmonte amplified, jerking a square thumb at the Colonel.

"No, no—I'm sure it's all a misunderstanding," Alison interposed. "Isn't it, Mr. Smith?" At least *she* seemed sure of her course through the somewhat involved sequence of events, which was more than could be said for many around her.

The somewhat distrait individual thus appealed to, shook his head, and after a glance at his bewildered Skye colleagues, cleared his throat. "I'm afraid that I . . . ah . . ." he began courageously, when he was interrupted.

"B'George . . . Slinky Lincoln, by all that's wonderful!" That was General Maclean, thudding up, red as a lobster.

Alison gasped. "Oh. Oh, no, Daddy. This is a Mr. Smith. From, from somewhere in Skye. Isn't it, Mr. Smith. . . ?"

"H'rr'mmm."

"Nonsense, girl! That's Slinky Lincoln. Know him anywhere, with that, that . . . Knew him in Egypt. One of these gunner fellows."

"G . . . ah . . . umm," the Colonel said.

The young woman swallowed. Charting these unpredictable waters required a very open mind and certain rapidity of decision. "Then you're not Mr. Smith at all?" she accused, more in sorrow and gentle reproach than in anger. "You were just deceiving us, sir—masquerading under a false name when you were staying with the Minister! Was that why you left us, so suddenly?"

"Dearie me. Tut-tut," said Father Joseph, shaking his head. "Bad, bad."

"Not at all," the Colonel protested, but with less than his usual assurance. "My name *is* Lincoln. I happened to be using a—a pseudonym when I was here previously, when I was . . . ahem. Incognito, as it were. I am Colonel Lomax-Lincoln of Tornadamh, Isle of Skye, and a member of the County Council." A little reassured obviously by the sonorous sound of all that, he turned. "As for you, sir, though your face is vaguely familiar, I'm afraid that your identity escapes me. I was on the Staff, of course . . ."

The General drew a long breath. "Quite," he said. "You would be! But I wasn't in Ismailia under a pseudonym, nor yet incognito, for all that! I was Commander, 19th Mountain Division . . . and what the devil we were doing there, I never found out! Maclean, the name."

"Oh! Ah . . . General! Of course . . . you must forgive me. My eyesight—not what it was, y'know. Tropics, and all that. . . ." The Colonel fumbled with his monocle, almost put it to his eye to stare, and then thought better of it. "This is a—a pleasure, sir. It's a remarkably fine morning, isn't it?"

Alison's sigh of relief almost choked her.

A bark from Hank Delmonte turned all eyes towards the shore. "Shoot!" he cried. "I can use those gobs."

A grey pinnace from the destroyer was approaching the jetty, its immaculate paint and neat rows of upright white-capped A.B.s tending rather to emphasize the tumbledown state of the landing-stage. Alison ran a pink tongue over her lips.

"Don't you think a cheer would be in order?" she suggested, tentatively.

"Why, sure," Elmer Macwhirter agreed. "Fine."

"Damn, yes," Joel Macdonald cried, his voice patently recovered. "C'mon, folks. Ya-a-a-ah!"

And so a tremendous if hybrid shout of acclaim rang out, compounded variously of rah-rahs, yippees, hip-hip-hoorays, and feminine squeals—an inspiring sound. The two officers sitting in the stern of the pinnace exchanged glances, as well they might.

Alison proposed the pipes, as a follow-up—an idea that was received with enthusiasm. After an urgent assertion by the General that *Britannia Rules the Waves* would not render well on the bagpipes, the well-tried strains of *The Skye Boat Song* lifted into the morning air, and to that accompaniment the naval officers landed and came marching up, spick, span and determinedly poker-faced. Both were of the lean, square-jawed Senior Service type, and young enough to commend themselves to the ladies.

Raising outstretched fingers to peaked caps, in answer to the frank and generous female tributes, the unsmiling pair stalked on. They did not let their eyes stray to the busy pipers and drummers, but they did cast a wary glance or two at the great whirring cameras with their crazy crowns of film. Without any noticeable hesitation they made straight for Colonel Lomax-Lincoln, who, with his monocle, sporting-checks and look of general disapproval, seemed sufficiently representative of the English ruling-classes as to stand out as an oasis of sanity and authority in this riot of tartan and honky-tonk. The one with the gold braid on his cap saluted, very briefly.

"Morning, sir. Commander Onslow, H.M.S. *Dunmow*."

"Indeed. Quite. Good day, Commander. I'm Lomax-Lincoln, Skye. Colonel, and County Council, and all that, y'know."

"Ah. Decent weather."

"Yes. Been wet."

"Looks more settled."

"Definitely."

"Barometer rising," the junior officer, with the two gold rings of a lieutenant, informed.

"Ah."

183

"Say—if you guys got the weather fixed, would you mind stepping back a piece? And facing the other way—up the hill, see. Yeah. And the heavy brass this side. . . ."

"Oh, later, Mr. Delmonte—later," Alison broke in, hurriedly. "We must welcome these officers to the island properly, first. We're delighted to see you, gentlemen—aren't we? Always glad to see the Navy, of course. But, naturally, this is rather a special occasion. You have come to look after the *Yonkers City*, haven't you? To see that she gets into Portree safely. That's grand. We've been giving our American friends such shelter and hospitality as we could, here, during the bad weather." She hardly took time for breath. "But now that it's cleared, you'll be able to convoy them. Colonel Lincoln's come to welcome them, too. Now—this is Captain Lynski, of the *Yonkers City*—with whom I'm sure you'll get along famously. And Mr. Elmer P. Macwhirter, of Detroit, Grand Chief of . . . of . . . Mr. Hank Delmonte, the famous film-director. . . ." Etcetera. The young woman spared those sailors nothing. Every person whose name and style she knew, she introduced, until they blinked and wilted. Silent Service or none, perforce they remained speechless. As a softening-up process, it served very well.

"Ma'am," the Commander got out, at length, "I'm happy to find everything so—er—satisfactory. But I've been looking for this American ship for days—the Air Force, too. Admiralty orders. We've gone to a lot of trouble." He turned to Captain Lynski. "You might at least have given us a signal."

"How come, Commander? Have I gotta keep the British Navy informed where I sail my ship?"

"No. No—of course not. But in view of all the trouble . . ."

"Say—what trouble? Been no trouble here—so far! And who asked you guys to come snooping around my ship? D'you reckon I ain't capable of looking after her, heh? This is a United States ship, see, and . . ."

"Quite. Certainly. Of course. Don't misunderstand me, Captain . . ."

"Oh, but he *does*!" Alison intervened, earnestly. "You
184

all misunderstand each other! So silly. It's all so simple, really. The Commander is only concerned that you should be suitably welcomed to these waters, Captain, as befits—er—ambassadors of our great transatlantic ally! He has missed you somehow, with the bad weather—the same weather that has kept you with us, here. Isn't that so, Commander? Though we've loved having you, of course. We wouldn't have missed it for worlds. You've all been terribly nice. And now Colonel Lincoln and the Commander have come to take you on to Portree. . . . It only remains for us, here at Kinloch, to say good-bye and wish you Godspeed. . . ." Her voice broke, effectively.

Strong men cleared their throats, much moved—though who was in most doubt about what was going on, Commander Onslow, Captain Lynski, Colonel Lomax-Lincoln, or Elmer P. Macwhirter, was debatable. Further explanations, however, mercifully were cut short by the loud and imperious blasting of a siren from seawards, that jerked all heads in the direction of the loch. And there was the mail-steamer *Lochgarve* hove-to between *Ailsa* and the *Yonkers City*, and looking as impatient as a mail-ship can.

"Mercy to goodness, my Chove!" Dougie cried. "The Post—and us failed it! Jamie—Jamie MacVarish! Your boat, man—or yon Postmaster-General will have the skin off me!" And he led the way down to the shore at a run.

"Lord—this place gets more like Tilbury Docks every day!" the General complained.

"Look—I got a picture to make," Hank Delmonte mentioned, with awful patience. "And the sun's out, see. If you guys with the gold braid would quit stalling and gimme some co-operation, we might get some place before the rain comes on. I guess I could use you two. . . ."

"No. No—quite out of the question, sir, I'm afraid. Not to be considered for a moment," the Commander declared, startled.

"Say—you telling *me* what to consider, huh?"

"Not at all. Of course not. At least . . . we just don't want to be photographed. The Admiralty wouldn't like it, I'm sure."

"Who's asking your Admiralty? Admirals never like nothing, see. Now, look . . ."

"Please. It's quite impossible. Er . . . I think we'd better get back on board, Number One." Commander Onslow turned his back deliberately on Hank and his cameras, and promptly the Lieutenant followed suit. "Captain—er—Lincoln, is it? Ah . . . Lynski. I think we might have a word together, about our course to Portree? I'm anxious to see you there just as quickly as possible."

"Okay. Suits me, Skipper."

"Perhaps you would come aboard. . . ?"

"We'll all get back aboard, I guess." That was Elmer Macwhirter decisively. Obviously the Grand Chief's authority required to be reasserted, and all these Service people kept in their places. "Feels like breakfast-time to me. Say . . ." He raised his voice. "Ladies and Gentlemen—I reckon none of us will have had our breakfasts this morning, 'cept maybe the Navy. That sure could account for the ruffled tempers, eh? With Cap Lynski's permission, I invite you all out to the ship as my guests for breakfast. Everyone—the whole boiling. And that goes for the Navy, too," he added, graciously but firmly. "No refusals, please. A sorta farewell feast. Okay?"

"Hooray!"

"Yippee!"

"Good show."

"You are a lamb, Mr. Macwhirter," Alison said. And undoubtedly she meant it.

. . . . .

That was a memorable breakfast, looked at from any angle. All-embracing, Elmer Macwhirter decided that it ought to be, and all-embracing it was. Every islander that was not either bed-ridden or cot-bound was there, the Skye deputation, the entire company of the coaster *Ailsa*, a representative naval contingent—even the skipper and certain of the mail-steamer's personnel somehow were embraced. Embraced, most decidedly, was the word. The *Yonkers City* was that sort of ship.

From Father Joseph's rousing Grace, there was no doubt about the success of that farewell feast. After all, at least ninety per cent of the feasters were of one mind that it should be a fitting climax to a noteworthy interlude—and there were some expert climax-mongers present. Before they were through the grapefruit and prunes, Dougie was despatched post-haste back to Kilmory House for certain residual supplies of the real stuff. A Rum Brose, far outdoing the Athole variety, was due to be added to that already catholic breakfast menu.

The speechmaking began fairly early on, spontaneously as it were and without waiting for any chairmanly promptings or toasts. And despite the hour of the morning, an astonishing degree of eloquence developed. Much that had not been entirely apparent hitherto, even to the speakers themselves, now became clear, pellucid. Conclusions were reached that had escaped most of them before. Points were appreciated that previously had failed to register. Such was the effect of replenished stomachs and a modicum of conviviality. Even the Royal Navy, though true to its traditions and not bursting into oratory, melted considerably. By the time that Dougie got back, things were going pretty well. Thereafter, they went still better.

By mid-forenoon, with the party still warming up, and no sign of any of the shipping setting sail, Alison began to get a little bit perturbed—despite the fact that she had had some really beautiful speeches made in her honour, had her health drunk on innumerable occasions, had been the centre-piece twice for "She's a Jolly Good Fellow", and even had been the beneficiary of one or two tentative suggestions indicative of personal masculine approval. It was a pity—but the trouble was, with every minute's delay she began to foresee further complications. And she felt that she had had almost enough complications to be going on with. She foresaw more questions being asked in authoritative quarters, unnecessary hazards looming up, as the mail-steamer failed to come within hours of its schedule at Mallaig, as H.M. destroyer joined the list of missing ships, as the hue and cry for Colonel Lomax-Lincoln and party arose in Skye, as more busybodies were drafted into the search for the errant Americans. It was high time that the whole lot of them were away, she felt, felt with conviction. She had had enough trouble getting these people here in the first place—now she couldn't get rid of them. It was like everything else—the film-making, the Rum Week entertainments, the reception of this silly ship, even the heather-burning—everything. It all went wrong—got out of hand. It was easy enough to *raise* the devil . . . but laying him again was a vastly different matter. On Rum, at any rate.

Alison, of course, was tired. Her bed called to her.

She detached herself from her current admirer, and went in search of Joel Macdonald—that is the kind of breakfast it had become. She appealed to him, a little pathetically, to do something, anything, to get this party broken up, to get the whole lot of them sailing away. Joe nodded, but apparently was listening to her with only the one ear. The other was cocked in an altogether different direction.

"You hear what I reckon I hear?" he interrupted her. "A plane—and a big one!"

"Oh, no! No!" the young woman groaned. "Don't say that."

"There's such a helluva noise here. . . ! But that's the way it sounded."

"That . . . that would be the last straw!" she declared. "Come on—let's go up and see."

By the time that they had gained the main deck, there was no doubt about it. The heavy drone of powerful aero-engines filled the air. Joe's glance, after a swift circuit of the sky, came down to earth again. There, taxi-ing majestically up-loch towards them was one of the great flying-boats of Coastal Command.

"Oh, I can't bear it!" Alison exclaimed. "This is too much. More enquiries. More explanations. More people to be placated and cajoled! Men with great bushy moustaches. . . ."

Her plaint was interrupted by the authoritative voice of the destroyer's loud-hailer. Thereafter, a Yeoman of Signals, stationed on the liner's bridge, went hurrying below.

The effect of all this was extraordinary. That well-doing breakfast party was broken up with a speed and finality that seemed scarcely credible. The Royal Navy was having no Junior Service R.A.F. types cutting in on its show. The *Yonkers City* might almost have been H.M.S. *Dunmow's* prize. The Navy men were up and about in less time than it takes to tell, brisk commands snapped left and right, immediate sailing the order of the day. The destroyer's Number One was seconded to the liner's bridge, Commander Onslow hastened back on board his own ship, all land-based personnel were ordered promptly ashore, and a battery of baleful glares were trained on the interloping aircraft.

Strangely enough, now that he heard real orders, and found himself in a genuine naval atmosphere, Captain Ed Lynski co-operated readily and efficiently. The *Yonkers City*, from a floating pleasure-palace became a business-like sea-going unit. The islanders were whisked off and ashore before they could even make any adequate farewells, the *Ailsa's* company and the people from the mail-steamer scuttled back to their ships, and it was as much as the Rum Development Executive Committee could do to ensure that Colonel Lomax-Lincoln and one or two of his colleagues were retained on board, for onward transmission to Skye. Hank Delmonte was the last man down into the last shore bound boat, breathing deeply, his parchment-hued and expressionless face tinted with a delicate rose. From the *Yonkers City* that is; Mariota Marr was put ashore independently, in a pinnace, from H.M.S. *Dunmow*.

Meanwhile warship and flying-boat were formally signalling to each other, at approximately fifty yards range, with the unfailing courtesy and unyielding mutual suspicion of inter-Service relationships.

And so, while yet they completed the mastication of the last of their fine farewell breakfast, on the shore, on the jetty, in the island's boats, the Rumaich leapt to the high "Woop! Woop! Woop!" of the destroyer's siren, followed by the hoarse blasting of the mail-steamer, both joined by the sustained and powerful bassoon of the liner, as a great threshing of screws, backing, and manœuvring commenced. The roar of the aircraft's engines took up the tale, till all that great cleft in the hills throbbed and quivered and eddied with sound, and the screaming protests of the startled gulls were lost, as were the comments of men.

The long grey shape of the warship leading, the white liner turning augustly into second place, and the tubby *Lochgarve* cheerfully bringing up the rear, the convoy moved off, with the flying-boat ploughing along behind like a neglected duckling.

It was a sight to remember. With typical feminine inconsistency, Alison felt a lump grow in her throat as she watched and listened.

The destroyer and the mail-boat made only the initial flourish with their sirens, naturally enough; not so the *Yonkers City*. Steadily, all the way down Loch Scresort, that good ship blared her throaty farewell to Rum. Some of the watchers declared that they could just make out snatches of pipe-music, above the din. Indeed, Dougie with the ear of the trained musician, even suggested that the band was playing " We're No' Awa tae Bide Awa ".

" Well—there goes Rum Week's guests," Joel Macdonald said. " In fact, there goes Rum Week itself, I guess."

" Och—but less near-on fifty thousand dollars, whatever," Dougie observed cheerfully.

" Tut-tut," Father Joseph deplored. " A terrible outlook that, money just! " He shook his head. " Och, it's a shame for those Americans. A right dull time they're going to be having in Skye. What'll they find to do, at all? "

" I hope you got all you wanted, Mr. Delmonte? " Alison mentioned. " For there goes your crowd-scenes, too."

" Sure. Sure," the great man said. And for the first time, on Rum at any rate, he was observed to smile. " I got plenty. I got quit of our Charlie, too! " The single metallic snort was undoubtedly his own version of a chuckle. " Yeah—there goes our Charlie, too! I locked him in one of those toilets down below. Hell—if he's all that keen on this Skye, I guess it's time he went there! "

" Goodness. . . ! "

"You did—oh, Hank!" Mariota Marr's peal of silvery laughter lifted above the now mellowing chords of the siren. "Goodie! Say—I hope it was one marked Dames you locked him in!"

14

FOR ALISON MACLEAN, AT LEAST, WEARINESS, lassitude, and a sense of anti-climax strong upon her, the remainder of that already eventful-enough day held but the one imperative—sleep. Her couch beckoned her, and brooked no refusal. But before she bowed to its summons, she arranged for a full meeting of the Rum Development Association at Kilmory House that evening, at seven-thirty. Some sort of reckoning seemed to be called for.

Other folk were welcome to their own methods of filling in the day.

But when, with the usual par-boiled feeling common to active folk who take to their beds at untimely hours, she had toyed over a sketchy evening meal, some seven hours later, and gone through to prepare for the meeting, it was to discover a rather different attitude to the day's activities of other people growing upon her. Morag Ross informed her that Joel Macdonald and Mariota Marr had gone off alone in one of the film company's cars, after an early lunch, ostensibly to climb Askival. They had said that they would be back for tea. And when the cloud came down on the hills, and the wanderers did not return, Hank Delmonte had become surprisingly upset, all things considered, and now he himself was missing and another car with him.

Alison, of a sudden, was furious. Idiots, she fumed, and worse than that! This was the sort of thing that had to happen if she so much as shut her eyes for an hour or so. What on earth did that woman want to go climbing Askival for? And Joe taking her? And alone! The whole thing was just wicked. There was no other word for it. It was so barefaced and humiliating. A very natural and feminine reaction, undoubtedly—if perhaps a shade lacking in sympathy for wandered climbers.

Morag Ross nodded comfortingly. There was a little small bit of a cave up below the top cliffs of Askival, where cloud-bound folk could lie fine and snug. There was not a thing to worry about. Morag was an exponent of the Second Sight, of course.

There was no question in Alison's mind as to what had to be done. The meeting must look after itself meantime—as all Rum meetings were eminently capable of doing. Dougie and his motor-bike would take her, just as far and high as any wheeled vehicle could go. Thereafter, knowledge of the ground, a good sense of direction, and a strong feeling for the fitness of things, would have to serve.

At the door, as they were on their way out, they came on Major MacNeill arriving for the meeting from Dibidil on his own motor-cycle. Rory's substantial and unquestioning adherence commended itself to the girl, at this juncture, strongly. They took him along.

By Bobadil and the track over the high southerly pass to Glen Harris, they roared, past the lost loch that gloomed darkly, and on to a footpath that swung away left-handed to climb up on to the long face of Barkeval. Here they found the two film-unit cars parked almost side by side, their evidence mute but unmistakable. Who would have thought Hank Delmonte the man to act thus?

Their footpath took them, bucketing and slithering, round the broad western flank of Barkeval, and into the deep corrie that separated this lesser hill from the clustered giants of Rum, only two hundred feet or so beneath the cloud-level now. Occasionally, three footprints showed on the mud of the path —two men's and one woman's.

Even up on to the Allival shoulder they took those bicycles, coughing and snorting, by sheep and deer tracks, bumping over stone, noisily circling soft patches, brushing through high heather, engines almost red-hot, Alison nearly as often off as on. And just before they entered the lowering blanket of cloud that draped the tops, a voice hailed them, long and loud, from over on an adjoining spur of the hill. Sitting on an outcrop amongst the tinted blaeberries, was Joel Macdonald. And he appeared to be alone.

Dismounted, and waiting beside the bicycles as Joe came striding unhurriedly across the heather towards them, Alison felt a little less sure of herself than she had expected to feel. This was hardly what might have been anticipated. She had no difficulty in maintaining a stern, not to say accusatory mien, nevertheless. "Well?" she said, as the man came up.

"I reckoned you'd turn up," he greeted her. "In fact, I was sorta waiting for you. Old Morag would give you the works?"

"Morag told me that you had taken Miss Marr away up Askival, alone—for reasons best known to yourself! And that when the cloud came down and you didn't return as arranged, Mr. Delmonte came seeking you. And he hasn't returned either. So . . ."

"Sure. That's just about the lay-out," Joe acceded. "They're holed up in a cave up there, on your Askival. Me, I'm getting help, see. Mariota's feet are not so good. I reckon Hank's kinda shaken, too."

"But . . . goodness me—what on earth possessed you? To do anything so utterly crazy? You must have known that woman was quite incapable of climbing Askival . . . ?"

"Oh, I wouldn't say that," Joe disclaimed mildly. "She made it, okay. It was just the kinda shoes she had sorta gave out on her . . ."

"And need you wonder! I've seen the sort of shoes she wears! And Mr. Delmonte—one look at him, and anyone could see he's no mountaineer."

"He came on his own," the other pointed out.

"Well, anyway, I think it's a disgraceful and irresponsible business, altogether. . . ."

Rory MacNeill made a vaguely affirmative noise.

"Okay. Okay! That's what you think. But don't you reckon, instead of chewing the rag here, we'd be better to get up to these two aloft there?"

That, at least, was accepted, and Rory MacNeill took Joe on the back of his bicycle.

But thereafter, quite shortly, the going became too difficult even for these practised rough-riders—to say nothing of their passengers—and just where Allival runs into its more impressive twin Askival, they were forced to leave the cycles, approximately on the fifteen-hundred-foot contour, and well into cloud. As they climbed on and up, through the seething woolly mist, Joe favoured them with a very partial and notably casual account of what he declared had happened, Alison preserving a detached expression indicative of criticism if not unbelief.

Apparently, the cloud catching them up on the top of Askival, Joe had found this cave, well enough known as Donald Dubh's Cave, and installed themselves therein to await the lifting of the mist. When time passed and there was no bettering of conditions, he had advised Mariota, in view of the state of her feet and shoes, to stay where she was while he had a scout around to find the easiest way down through the cliffs and crags. He did not reveal that young woman's reaction to this suggestion. Anyway, he had left her there, and curiously enough, and after some little casting around, he had chanced to come on Hank Delmonte just below cloud-level, coming up to look for them. Morag Ross had directed him thither, it seemed. He had led Hank back up to the cave —Joe did not dwell, either, on what had passed between them on that climb—and there, leaving him with Mariota, for Hank was not in too good shape physically himself, he had set off once more downhill, for help. And here he was.

The three islanders exchanged significant glances as this somewhat patchy recital progressed. Their looks seemed to infer that seldom had any of them heard a more fishy story. It was only unfortunate that traditional Highland good manners prevented them from saying so in so many words.

Fishy or not, the story took a while to tell, owing to the steepness of the climb and the nature of the terrain; narration could be intermittent only, and the narrator markedly desultory in his delivery. There was more opportunity for rumination than for questioning, however unprofitable.

Though they climbed in cloud, their direction was plain; so long as they kept going upwards, they must come eventually to the peak of Askival. Up a long seam in the beetling summit precipices they crawled, panting, to reach at length an area of tumbled rock-falls under the ultimate crags. And amongst the crannies and crevices formed therein, one larger than the others gaped blackly.

Joe held up his hand. "Give me ten seconds," he requested. And though it was a whisper, it was an order too. Without waiting to assure himself of its acceptance, he moved forward over the stones, and silently. A projecting slab of rock jutted on this side of the cave's jagged entrance. Round it the man peered. Then, drawing back, he raised his finger and beckoned.

Mystified, the trio came over to him, and, consciously or not, following his example, they came quietly, to look round into the cave.

Mariota Marr sat with her back to the rock slabbing, a vision in ivory, old gold, and peat-broth. Hank Delmonte lay on the uneven stony floor, on his back, jacket off and feet bare, his head and shoulders pillowed on the woman's lap, gazing up into her eyes, while she leant over him, crooning to him and playing with a lock of his scanty hair. And Mariota was smiling gently as she crooned.

"My Chove, goodness me, mercy on us!" Dougie murmured.

Mariota looked up, and saw them. Her smile, so different from her usual brilliant and provocative achievement, did not fade nor alter. "Uh-huh," she mentioned, almost on the same note as her crooning, an eminently satisfied, all but maternal sound.

Hank struggled up, approximately into a sitting posture, his peculiar features distinctly bemused. "Ah," he said. "Eh. I'ph'mmm. Yeah. Say—meet the lady that's gonna be my wife!"

.   .   .   .   .   .

In the somewhat confused and mildly embarrassing situation that developed, Joel took genial but firm charge, as by right. He got the love-birds disentangled, in some measure back to earth and talking sense. He assisted and clarified the halting congratulations of the newcomers. He suggested that as it was eight-thirty, and the light beginning to go, they might be wise to be moving.

And when it came to the bit, Mariota's feet and Hank's general condition did not seem to be so bad. Or perhaps their exalted emotional state counteracted any mere physical trials. At any rate, they set out without any complaints, even if they hobbled somewhat. And when Rory MacNeill attempted to give Miss Marr a helping hand, he was brushed aside in a proprietary fashion by Hank himself.

Going down steep rock is never so simple as climbing up. But for all that, the company descended those fearsome cliffs without casualty—other than to Mariota's new-found modesty, and the final disintegration of her shoes. Thereafter, down all the deer and sheep tracks she went pick-a-back, mounted in turn on one or other of the male backs—and had not altered so direly as to fail to show every sign of enjoying the experience.

At the bicycles, it was Alison who issued the orders, however. Dougie would take Miss Marr on his pillion, Rory would lift Mr. Delmonte, as far as the cars, and she and Joe would walk. No—there was no need for anybody to come back for them with the bikes. They'd be perfectly all right on their feet. The cyclists had just better go on to Kilmory, and keep the meeting in hand for another hour.

Major MacNeill looked as though he might have liked to contest this programme if he could have found the words. But no help or encouragement was given him, and jehus and passengers were shooed off peremptorily. They departed in a welter of noise, smoke, peat-mud, and cautionary advice.

"And now, Joel Kruger Macdonald," the girl said, as peremptorily. "I want an explanation, please—and one that I'm able to believe, for preference!"

The man considered her out of the corner of his eye. "Hell

—I don't see what *I* got to explain," he protested, but without a lot of assurance.

"Go on," Alison said, levelly.

"I'd have reckoned the situation explained itself. . . ."

"Look." The young woman pointed away down the great heather flanks of the hills. "We've got all the way down there to go. It'll take us the best part of an hour to reach the car. Take your time. Pick your words, if you like. But there's no escape for you, this time. I want the whole story."

Joe sighed. But he had sighed much more heavily than that on Rum ere this—and might well again. And so, as they wound their way down through the heather braes, wine-red now that they were below the canopy of cloud and in all the blaze of the sunset, the man talked, haltingly at times, and requiring to be prompted on occasion. And prompted he was.

For quite some time he had been growing ever more convinced that Mariota Marr and Hank Delmonte were made for each other, and moreover, deeply involved emotionally. No two people could slang and berate and hurt each other deliberately and consistently as did these two, without very strong feelings of some sort to account for it. But they were difficult, extravagant types both, hard-cased and buttoned-up. And Hank was the more difficult. Hank was tough, but only on the surface. Hank, he was convinced, was frightened for Mariota, a timid man where his own emotions were concerned, unsure of himself in the face of so much physical excellence, too proud to risk any rejection. And Mariota sought to provoke him, by every means at her disposal—and she had plenty—till it all became a habit, an obligation, and a bitterness.

But they were friends of his, both of them, and Joe had come to set himself the task of bringing them together, if at all possible. Since Hank did not seem to let himself be moved by her indiscriminate amorous catholicity, he himself had sought to make the older man jealous by his own sustained attentions. But without success. Mariota had seen through him, of course; but co-operated readily enough—if without much optimism. He had hoped that here on Rum they might be brought together, if anywhere—for in the normal conditions of life in the film colony, the thing seemed hopeless. But it had not worked out as he had hoped. They seemed to be no nearer each other than when they came. And then, this morning, after the tourists had sailed, Hank had declared that they would sail themselves the next day, that there was nothing more for his cameras here. Joe had decided that if there was anything to be done—and he had various vague ideas on his mind for a while—it would have to be done at once.

So, he had prevailed on Mariota to come climbing with him, seeing the cloud beginning to form on Askival, with the deliberate intention of getting her lost and stranded up here. He had left word with old Morag as to the impression she was to give Hank Delmonte, when they did not return for tea, that Mariota was in trouble and possible danger—she was a great old girl, was Morag Ross, and had her wits about her, however scatter-brained she seemed. And Hank had reacted as he had hoped, at last. He had come away hot-foot, alarmed and angry, following the line Morag had advised. Joe had sought to organize his leaving of Mariota in the cave so that he would be able to meet the other man, and escort him back to her—and though he had had longer to wait than he had anticipated, it had worked out. And the most blistering, unpleasant and denunciatory half-hour of his whole career, that thirty-minutes' climb back to the cave had been. His ears were ringing, yet! His idea was, that if he could get these two alone in a wild and unfamiliar situation, with all the customary barriers, distractions, and pretences down, they might find each other, and themselves. Well, it seemed like he had been right, didn't it?

However halting and determinedly casual the retailing, this recital did not fail to affect Alison Maclean strongly—though much as the main theme intrigued her, two comparative side issues tended to dominate her mind.

" So . . . you are going away to-morrow? " she said, slow voiced.

A little surprised apparently, at this reaction, he glanced at her. " Well—the outfit was. Hank was. But, now—well he might wait a day or two, I guess."

"And you?"

"I reckon I might stay on, a little while. Tie up one or two loose ends, and so on, see."

"M'mmm."

They walked on down that stony track in the lap of the mountains, now side by side, now one in front, now the other, and the sun at its fiery sinking into the limitless ocean made a glory about them, transforming the plain of the sea into burnished copper, staining all the heather slopes with deepest crimson slashed with violet shadows, and even reflecting down on them in a rosy glow from the billowing ceiling of cloud suspended above their heads. The grouse kabek-kabeked from molten hillsides, the curlews trilled their sorrow for the dying day, and the man and the woman knew the inadequacy of words, the danger and the folly of them, and listened instead to the voice of the night.

It was Alison's long quivering sigh that broke their hush. "I am glad . . . about those two," she said. "I had thought . . . I was afraid . . ."

"Yes?" he encouraged.

She shook her head, with a sort of helplessness. "Well— I'm glad, anyway."

"Yeah."

A narrowing of the track set them into single file again. And at her back, presently, the man spoke.

"I'm just an ordinary sorta guy," he mentioned, tentatively. "Not in the Clan Chief and Generals social brackets, see. Just a . . . well, an ordinary guy."

A pink tongue tipped her upper lip. "Joel K. Macdonald, Associate Director, North Atlantic Motion-Picture Corporation," she said, to the listening hills. "Film industry executive. Big shot of the celluloid world."

"Sure," he agreed briefly. "That's just what I mean."

"Yes . . . ?" It was her turn to encourage.

But he seemed to have reached the end of his confessional urge. Though she waited, no sequel developed—even if twice she heard him kick at inoffensive stones on the path, apparently with some vigour.

She was forced to sigh again—but she did not turn round.

"Myself, I am merely a country girl," she avowed in her turn, small-voiced. "An . . . island bumpkin. Not used to the bright lights and the big cities. I wouldn't even make a . . . Continuity-girl!"

She heard him swallow.

"A country cousin, from a—a barren and backward island! Wasn't that what the Colonel-man called it?"

"Look—if you're a country cousin, then I'm a Dutch Uncle!" the man declared, forcefully at last. "And if Rum's a backward island, then, my godfather, I wouldn't want to see a forward one! Say—I'd give plenty to say that Rum was *my* island, my home, see—and you could keep your big cities and bright lights. I'd bed down here, if I got the least bit of encouragement. . . ."

"Bed down . . . ?"

"Sure. Settle down. Make my quarters here. You could do a lot with Rum, I guess—go far. . . ."

"Oh, I see. I thought, for a moment, bed down might be one of your vivid mid-Western figures of speech. A . . . proposal of marriage, even, or something . . . !"

He all but choked. "By hokey, woman—and so it is!" he got out. "What d'you reckon I been trying to say, this half-hour back? I told you—if you'd only give me the least bit of encouragement. . . !"

"Mercy on us—I've had to say the words for you, haven't I?" That sounded a little breathless, too.

He pulled her round on that path, at last, and anything but gently, and they looked at each other, their faces all flushed and their eyes alight with more than the glow of the sunset. "Gee, honey," he whispered, "I love you!"

She nodded, blinking those starry eyes. "Oh, Joe—I was scared to death you'd never make it. Like Hank. . . ."

"Damn Hank! I tell you, Alse Maclean . . . oh, gee, honey— I love you!"

She gulped, but produced the beginnings of a smile. "You . . . you've said that already. . . ."

"I know. I know. Say—I've directed a coupla score of guys how to do this properly. But, but . . ." He stopped.

"Say—what a helluva lot of talk!" And his arms opened wide.

She flung herself into them. "Oh, Joe, my dear, my dear . . . !"

"Gee, honey . . ." he began, and left it at that.

So well may we.

15

THE MEETING OF THE RUM DEVELOPMENT ASSOCIA-tion had been assembled for the best part of three hours before its Honorary Secretary put in an appearance—and even then she seemed to be in a somewhat bemused and abstracted frame of mind. Her fellow Executive member was little better, with his fixed grin and manifest uncertainty as to what to do with his hands. Morag Ross looked up from her fiddle-playing, eyed them both heedfully over her instrument, and then gave a little bird-like nod to Father Joseph, who nodded in return and beamed broadly. He went on nodding, and soon the nodding was general, and the beaming too, as the membership nudged itself, and considered, lips pursed, and came to the same conclusion as the experts. Only Rory MacNeill failed to nod or beam. A poor man who was rendering *Clanranald's Lament* to Morag Ross's accompaniment displayed modest satisfaction at what he took to be a more than usually favourable reception of his art. He gave them the last four verses over again, in consequence.

The General, from the Chair, having duly thanked the performers, pointed out that the Secretary was now with them, and no doubt would be prepared to give them some reason for having called the meeting. Could they have the Minutes, please? And if he had not been a General, he might have been said to leer.

Alison was beginning to frown, wondering why must her father always be so keen on Minutes, when such thoughts were overborne by the loud and continuous clapping. Surprised at this ovation, she shook her head.

"I'm sorry," she said. "I'm afraid I just haven't had time to write up any Minutes of the last—that is, the first meeting. I have been busy. . . ."

Cheers.

Eyebrows raised, she glanced round her. Refreshment undoubtedly had helped to while away the hours of waiting, as well as music. "But that doesn't mean that I've nothing to report."

"No, no. Who would think a thing like that?" Father Joseph encouraged.

Hughie Bain hooted with laughter.

"Order," the Chairman mentioned.

"A lot has happened in the meantime," the girl went on. "But you all know all about it, and don't need me to tell you."

Appreciative laughter, and smacking of thighs.

Warily considering them, Alison decided that this was the sort of night on which no great deal of business was likely to be done. Better to get it over as quickly as possible. She wasn't in much of a mood for public meetings, anyway. "It's late," she declared, "and I think the best thing we can do to-night is just to consider the results of our Rum Week efforts, the financial situation, and try to decide very roughly on—on where we go from here."

"To the Kirk, just," Dougie suggested, amidst delighted applause.

"Order," the General repeated, smirking.

Thoughtfully the young woman eyed the interrupter, and then turned her regard on Morag Ross, who now knitted industriously. Morag nodded back to her graciously. "The position is, at a final count, that our Association's activities during the last few days have brought us in almost forty-eight thousand dollars. That's a lot of money—not very far off twenty thousand pounds, I'm told. It seems astonishing, but there it is. That's including the money we've been paid by the film people, for our services, of course. The question is, now—what to do with it?"

An appalled silence settled upon the crowded library. At last she had them shaken. No single suggestion was forthcoming.

"Well—it's your money," the young woman put it to them. "What d'you want to do with it?"

Father Joseph scratched his head. "Och, we could invest it in those Defence Bonds, maybe."

"A fat lot of good that would do us!"

Rory MacNeill cleared his throat strongly, helpfully—but disappointingly failed to produce anything more constructive.

"Well, if you've no ideas on the subject, Mr. Joel Macdonald here has one or two suggestions. I think they may interest you. Mr. Macdonald?"

Joe rose amidst renewed and relieved plaudits. "The way I figure it is this," he said. "That dough belongs to you all, see—every man, woman, and child on this island. So you want to use it for the benefit of all—not just one or two. Invest it, for the benefit of Rum, see—but not in Bonds and suchlike. Now—what's Rum most in need of? Improved transport, eh—better communications with the outside world? Okay—with a quarter of that money you could buy an old L.S.T. One of these ex-Army landing-craft. There's scores of them laid up in the Clyde. They're seagoing craft, roomy, and can land on any beach—they don't need piers and jetties. With one of those, you could be independent of the mail-steamer. You could carry your own passengers, ship your own produce, and pick up your own stores from Mallaig. In fact, I reckon you could do the same for other islands, hereabouts. Establish a business, see. Say—you could serve all the south and west of Skye, places where the steamer never calls—make money out of them, over there!"

"My Chove—we could so!" Dougie cried. "Then we could starve them, just—have them eating out of our hands!"

"Hooray!"

"Och, where's your Christian charity?" Father Joseph wondered. "Where would be the benefit of starving them, at all?"

"We could form a Rum Sea Transport Company, as a branch of this Association," Alison put in.

"And who would run this venture?" the General asked.

"Well, you'd need a qualified skipper, I guess—but I reckon Jock Laidlaw, the *Ailsa's* mate, would take the job on without a whole lotta coaxing. For the time being, anyhow. Get it started. You'd need to set aside maybe another twenty-five per cent of your dough, as working capital and so on."

"That leaves us still with, och, twenty thousand dollars," Dougie pointed out cheerfully.

"Yeah." Joe rubbed his chin. "Now, don't get me wrong on this. I'm not aiming to cash-in on your dollars. In fact, I got two or three of my own I could add to the kitty, see, if it came to the bit. But I know something about the motion-picture industry, and I guess you could do something about it, here. Motion pictures have discovered the Highlands, see —but so far they're not doing them anything like justice. They're looking at the Highlands from the outside, and not getting the half of it. And this picture we been shooting here won't be any better—you can lay odds on that. Hank's talking about taking the outfit down to the Channel Islands, now —to get some sun, see—cutting out any reference to Bonnie Prince Charlie—he never did cotton on to that guy Dufour— and tying it up with a story about diamond-smuggling he's gotten hold of. . . ."

He waited till the uproar subsided somewhat. "Yeah— that's the motion-picture industry! Now, I figure that a small independent outfit, established up here on the spot, making genuine honest-to-God Highland features, would do pretty well. No ballyhoo, nothing ambitious, see. Just straightforward stuff—at least, to start with. The market's made for it. You folks got all that it takes. Hank'd help us with the distribution, sure. And I know the right people. I reckon it would go, and no sweat."

"Rum Films, Limited!" Alison cried.

"I think that would be very nice," Morag Ross decided, fingers busy. "Hear, hear!"

"Just the job, whatever!"

The Chairman stroked his chin. "This would—ah—seem to imply that you intend to—ah—remain with us here on Rum, Mr. Macdonald?"

The indrawn breath of the meeting was very audible.

Joe's adam's-apple jerked. "Well, sir—I guess that's right," he admitted. "Meantime, anyhow. That is, if you'll have me. Mind you, you sure bought this! If you'd let me go when I wanted to go . . ."

He got no further. The entire membership of the Rum Development Association was on its feet—and that included the Secretary, who stood up beside him, and put her hand into his, there before them all. She said no words, now—no words could have been heard anyway, and no words were needed. Morag Ross had done the vital speaking before ever they had entered the room.

The boldest Macdonald ever to have attempted to land on Rum—and the first ever to have achieved a toe-hold on its devoted shores—grinned down at her, grinned at them all. "Yeah," he said, and squeezed the hand in his. "Uh-huh. Sure."

Into the press of congratulation and acclaim, Major Rory MacNeill of Dibidil pushed his way. Sadly he looked at Alison Maclean, and thrust out his hand to wring Joe's silently. Then he turned away, sighing, a loser in the gallant tradition of the Seaforth Highlanders.

"You're not going Rory?" Alison cried, above the din. "Must you—*dear* Rory?"

Turning, that true gentleman found words, for once, for his sorrow. "Yes," he said simply, "I have three hundred kilts to wash."

THE END